MENDING ME

THE NAT. 20 SERIES
BOOK 1

REBECCA WRIGHTS

Mending Me • intended for readers 18+

Book Cover by Melissa Doughty of Mel.B Designs

Edits by Kristen Hamilton of Kristen's Red Pen

Proofreading by Kristen Hamilton of Kristen's Red Pen

Sensitivity reading by Marlene Contreras and Katherine Brito

CONTENTS

CONTENT WARNINGS:

Dear reader,

Before you read this story, please note that the following potentially sensitive subjects are included within the pages of this book:

- Domestic violence
- On page physical and sexual assualt; rape (described in flashbacks and nondescript)
- Physical violence from a parent
- Loss of a parent due to drunk driving (off page)
- Bondage
- PTSD/trauma

Please keep these warnings in mind before reading this story.

XO, Rebecca Wrights

DICKTIONARY

Mending Me in an open door romance novel with several on page sex scenes. This book is intended for mature audiences only.

If you wish to bypass the intimate scens of this book, please skip the following chapters. Please know that if you skip these chapters, you may lose some of the plot of the book.

Chapters to skip: 13, 16, 23, 24, 28, 32, 38

And for the girls who love the spice, go ahead and flag these chapters now. You know you want to.

AUTHORS NOTE:

Before reading Mending Me, please keep in mind that the characters within this book represent an interraccial couple. Hank Martínez is Mexican-American with parents who immigrated to the United States prior to his birth. As the author of their love story, I had the amazing opportunity to work with several Mexican-American readers and other readers from the Latine community to support me in making sure I represented this diverse culture as accurately as I can. Representing Hank and his culture was approached with the utmost care and respect.

Please note there is Spanish spoken on-page. The language has been read by several native Spanish speakers of both Mexican-American heritage and other Spanish speaking backgrounds. Please understand that the Spanish language has several different dialects and is a very nuanced language based on the background of the speaker. I have done my best to ensure I have gotten the language correct based on Hank's personal background and based on sensitivity reader feedback.

Translations have been included to help non-Spanish speakers understand what is being said. Simply tap the linked footnote on your Kindle, scroll to the end of the chapter, or read the printed footnote at the bottom of the page if you're reading a printed copy. I have done my best to make these translations as accessible and accurate as possible.

Thank you so much for picking up this book and I hope you love it.

XO,

Rebecca Wrights

To those who have been broken or bruised in the past, please know that you won't be broken or bruised forever. One day you'll find someone who loves all your damaged pieces and helps you mend.

1

BAILEY

If you've ever wondered what the biggest sign of a man without self-control or discipline is, it's a man who slams his weights around in the gym.

This is also a pretty good sign of a man with a tiny penis.

Some people think it's a man who can't keep his hands to himself or a man who spends all of his money at strip clubs over the weekend. But to me, it's a man who throws his weights down or lets the plates slap into one another once he finishes his set.

If you're strong enough to hold 100-pound dumbbells in your hands while you chest-fly, you're strong enough to carefully set them down on the ground when you finish your set. Period.

I was in the middle of my lift when I heard it. The ear-splitting sound of plates crashing into one another over and over again. Sitting up from the bench, my eyes scanned the gym to find the offender. My music was playing loudly through my over-ear headphones and I could still hear the plates crashing into one another. I pulled one side of my headphones back just in time for another crash of weights to cut through the morning gym air. Why are the idiots who do this always the same type of person? Is the role of gym lunk-head type casted at birth?

The man—no, *the bro*—at fault for the blood curdling sound at 5:45 a.m. was just like all the other men who were normally at fault for this kind of public gym faux pas. Black tank top and gym shorts with a three-inch inseam, muscles that were grossly engorged due to an overconsumption of protein powder and potentially banned substances, and a tiny head that more than likely matched his tiny penis. Sitting across the weight section of the gym, I watched as he reached up, grabbed the bar at the top of the machine with both hands and pulled it down, lifting at least 125 pounds worth of plates. With every pull, an animalistic grunt came from his mouth and I couldn't help but grimace.

I hated gym bros. You're in a communal space at the ass crack of dawn. The least you could do was pretend to be considerate. SMACK! I'm going to fucking lose it. How many years would I get if I bashed in a stranger's skull with a twenty-pound dumbbell? SMACK! It would probably depend on if he died or not. He would totally die if I swung a dumbbell into his head like a baseball bat. SMACK! I just need to turn my music up and go back to my workout. SMACK!

Pulling myself from my thoughts, I slipped my headphones back on both ears and gently laid back down on the bench. It was Tuesday, which meant it was chest and arms day. I personally hated Tuesday workouts but had good reason for wanting to get stronger in my upper body, so I showed up and put in the work anyway.

My friends thought I was crazy for coming to the gym so

early in the morning, but I loved it. It was quiet and never super crowded, and with the exception of today's gym bro, the people who came during this time of day were generally kind. One of my favorite things to do while here was people watch. Oh, and read. I always had a book with me when I came to the gym so I could read in between sets. I like to flip between listening to music and cracking my book open and getting lost in its pages. The mornings were generally the only time I had to read, so I tried to get in as many pages as possible when I could

Having finished another set, I sat up again and crossed my legs on the bench. Leaning over, I picked up my book which was another spicy romance novel I had swiped off my roommate's bookshelf when she wasn't looking. Ophelia had close to a hundred books on her shelves so I knew it wouldn't be missed. I pulled out the bookmark and played with its ribbon between my fingers. My eyes drifted through the lines, taking in every word as I let the book absorb me completely.

That was the magic of books. They could completely transport you into an entirely different universe with little to no effort. They acted like a guide to another realm where you could get completely lost in love or adventure or heartache. Books would carry you away from reality and let you stay as long as you liked. Books were a place to escape, to get away, to become someone new.

Someone without scars or bruises or broken pieces.

Someone you couldn't be in real life.

Someone you wished you could be, living a life you wish you could live.

Once I hit the end of the page, I nestled the bookmark back into the spine and tossed it onto the floor. I stood up, stretched my arms across my chest, and then turned to reset my rack for my next set. As I turned, something in the mirror caught my eye and I worked to focus on it.

Not an *it*.

But a *him*.

Different from the gym bro who had no self-control or discipline from before, this him was on the opposite side of the weight room setting up his rack with varying plate sizes and dumbbells. I tried to not be obvious with my staring, but no matter how hard I tried, I couldn't pull my eyes away from him. I'd never seen him here before, which was interesting because the 5:00 a.m. crowd was nothing if not consistent.

Dark hair that had a slight curl to it. Caramel skin that I knew kept its hue no matter what time of year it was. And strong arms that stretched the short-sleeved shirt that was wrapped around them. He was wearing dark gray shorts that showed off his muscular legs and a black T-shirt. A tattoo covered the bottom half of his left arm and snaked its way up and under his shirt.

I would pay good money to see that up close and personal, I thought to myself as I continued to observe him from afar.

The thing that struck me the most about new guy were his boots. They weren't just any boots, they were combat boots.

New guy was a soldier.

A soldier who wore his boots to the gym.

Curious.

2

HANK

When I landed back in Charleston yesterday, the first thing I did was Google the closest gym to my apartment. Working out was like cheap therapy and God knew I needed it. I also probably needed actual therapy but that's not something I'm willing to get into right now. I had just finished my last tour and was set to start my new job next week. Without access to the base and the gym that sits behind the gated entrance, I knew I was going to have to find a place to get in my daily lift.

It was weird to think that I was "retiring" from the military. I was only twenty-nine for Christ's sake. But I'd served for almost eleven years and it was time to move on. Enlisting right out of high school was something I never regretted. It got me out of a shitty home life, out from under my alcoholic father's fist, and helped me gain some insight on the world. Plus, it didn't really count as retiring because to retire from the military you have to serve for over twenty years, and I hadn't done that. After my last tour though, I was ready to head home and try civilian life for once.

When I called my buddy to see if he had any need for an

ex-Army man to work at his security firm in Charleston, he told me to hurry up and get my ass home. So that's what I did. I told my commander that I was ready to move on, filled out all the paperwork, and that was that. I finished out my active duty requirements and got on the first flight back to the Lowcountry.

My alarm didn't even need to go off this morning before my eyes were open and I was ready to start the day. My body was still on military time and had me up promptly at 0430. Thankfully for me, I found a gym not even ten minutes from my apartment that opened at five. I got dressed, snagged a water from the fridge, and headed out the door. Since it was close enough, I jogged over from my place in order to get in some cardio before starting my workout. When I walked through the door, I was surprised by how many people were here so early in the morning. Most of the people in my life groaned when I told them about my early-morning wake up calls, but this place had at least twenty people in it already and the doors had just been unlocked.

I scoped the place out, taking in all the machines, racks, and places to workout. It wasn't the biggest gym I had ever been to, but it wasn't small either. There were plenty of cardio machines and free weights for people to use, and a solid amount of free standing weight racks too. Since I'd already ran and stretched before coming in, I walked towards one of the open racks to set up for my lift.

As I passed the stairmasters, I saw a girl who looked like she was my age sitting at one of the free racks near the front of the gym. Her legs were crossed in front of her and she had her head low. When I got closer, I realized she had a book in her hands and looked like she was fully entranced by whatever she was reading. My head spun to watch her all the way from the opposite side of the weight room.

Who reads when they're at the gym?

Eventually, she lifted her head and closed her book. I tried to avert my eyes so she didn't catch me staring at her. The last thing I wanted was to be pegged as the gym creep. As she completed her set, I started to notice more about her.

Dios mío, ella es bonita.[1]

She had blonde hair that she had pulled back into a high ponytail that sat right on top of her head. Based on the length, I guessed that when it was down, it would hit her just below her shoulders. She was fit and had strong legs that I knew could probably leg press close to 300 pounds. She was wearing a black, short-sleeved cropped shirt that hit a few inches above the tight, black biker shorts she was wearing. A few inches of her stomach was exposed between the gap of her shirt and shorts. On her feet were a pair of white Nike Blazers, the black swoosh noticeable from across the gym.

Those are probably way more suitable for lifting than my boots I thought, looking down at my dusty, worn in combat boots. I thought about changing before leaving my apartment but I had always worked out in them before and I wasn't going to change that now. Just because I was no longer in the military didn't mean I wasn't an Army man.

Army men wore their boots. Always.

Realizing I had spent way too much time watching reading girl from across the gym, I finally finished setting up my rack to start my lift. I couldn't help but cast my eyes over to her every now and then to see if she had her nose in her book. More often than not, she did.

A girl who goes to the gym at 0500 and reads in between sets.

---

1. Gosh she's pretty.

Interesting.

3

HANK

"**W**ell I'll be damned. Don't you look hot as fuck." I shook Kolbi's hand as he extended it towards me. "For a guy who lived in ratty jeans and oversized T-shirts growing up, I almost didn't recognize you. Dear god man, how much did that suit cost you?"

"More than I would like to admit, brother," he laughed and pulled me in for a hug. I'm not usually one for hugs but Kolbi comes from a big family where hugging was just as normal as waving hello to someone. "We missed having you here in the Lowcountry. Conrad and Malcolm are already planning their characters for our next campaign when it starts again."

He was one of my three best friends. Malcolm and Conrad were the others and we had all grown up together here in Charleston, South Carolina. I had been the only one to get the hell out of dodge, enlisting in the Army as soon as we walked across the stage at graduation and not coming home until I landed last week. The three of them had decided to stay and start their own lives here, working and staying close to home while I was gone.

I followed my friend and new boss down a fully marbled hallway and into an elevator. He pressed a button and we talked as the elevator took us to the top floor.

"You've really made a name for yourself," I commented, finally seeing what my friend had built for himself. After graduating from college, something I never did, Kolbi started a security firm for businesses and homes around the city and grew it to be the largest security firm in the area. Based on his suit, I knew he made more in a year than I did during my entire stint in the military.

"Yeah, well, after years of hard work and building connections around the city, it's all paid off."

We walked down another long hallway and passed people sitting at desks and large tables. The office was an open concept with some people standing at their desks and other people sitting on couches. Everyone was dressed casually which I found interesting, seeing as how my best friend was in a full suit. Some people looked up at me as we walked past and waved. Once we reached the end of the hall, he pushed open a large glass door that led into what I assumed was his office.

"Holy shit, Kolb." My mouth hung open as I took in the view. Every wall of his office was floor to ceiling windows looking out into the harbor. Downtown sat right on the Ashley River which then led out into the ocean. From his office, you could see all of downtown and miles down both ends of the coast.

"Like I said, it's all paid off." He handed me a soda and sat down at his desk. "So, I was thinking I could have you head up my high security division."

Finally pulling my eyes away from the water, I sat down

in one of the plush chairs that sat across his glass desk. Who the hell decorated this place? Definitely not Kolbi— the guy grew up riding skateboards and sleeping on an old couch.

"Sure, man. I'd be fine with anything really." The military had been all I'd done with my life and now that I was out, I didn't really know what to do with myself. Having not gone to college, I didn't have a degree to help me get any kind of job with a retirement plan or health insurance. Sure, I had benefits from my time in the service, but I couldn't rely on that for the rest of my life.

"It's mostly a management role but the people you would be overseeing are great and really good at what they do. This division oversees high security needs such as events, high-profile weddings, and they cover security whenever celebrities or politicians come into town. And of course, the rich and wealthy of Charleston."

"Like the people they name bridges and schools after," I joked, half laughing.

"Exactly like the people they name bridges and schools after," he confirmed without a hint of humor in his voice.

"Sounds easy enough. I'm game for whatever, I'm just thankful you're hooking me up with this Kolb."

"I would do anything for you, brother. We're all really happy you're back. We didn't expect you to be gone for over ten years when you enlisted after high school. Shit, some of us didn't think you would make it past bootcamp." He chuckled.

"Yeah, I don't think I expected to be gone this long either but, it got me out of my house and forced me to grow up in places I needed to grow up. I'm happy to be back."

We talked about everything included in my role—what my requirements and working hours were, and he filled me in on who I would be working with. When he told me how much he would be paying me, I choked on my drink.

"Is that *actually* what it pays or is that what you're paying me because I'm your friend?" I questioned. I didn't want special treatment and if that wasn't what he was going to pay someone from off the street, I didn't want it.

"Yes," was all he said to answer my question before continuing, "Now, you'll need to go to the floor below this one and talk to Margie in HR. She will have all your paperwork, badges, and keys for you. Once you fill it out and she files everything, you will have your sign-on bonus in your account. That should help you get settled and set up with everything you need now that you're home. Do you need a place to stay?"

"Uh, no. I have an apartment north of the city."

"*Where* north of the city?" He dragged out his words slowly and furrowed his brows.

"Kolbi stop. It's in a safe area and I like it. I don't need you giving me any more handouts. The job is enough." I stood up from my seat and extended my hand towards him. He mirrored my movement and took my hand to shake.

"Alright, well if you decide you don't want to stay in some shithole anymore, you let me know. I have a few places around town I keep as safe houses if you need a place to crash."

"I'll be fine, thank you." I dropped his hand and started walking towards the door to head to HR when he called out to me.

"Oh, and just a word to the wise, Margie is really sweet and good at what she does, but she will try and get in your pants. She might be old, but she's not shy. Keep your guard up."

I turned slowly to look at him and gave him a puzzled

look. "You hired a horny old lady to work in your *Human Resources* department?"

"I didn't know she was horny when I hired her. She was really nice during her interview, even brought homemade grits for me. It wasn't until after she was hired that she invited me to a hotel room to meet her for drinks after work." He was laughing now. "I promise, she's harmless. Just always tell her no, no matter how many times she asks."

He raised his hand and waved to me before sitting back down at his desk. I pushed the glass doors open again and walked back toward the elevator, bracing myself for my meeting with a horny, elderly woman. Only Kolbi would hire someone because they brought homemade grits to their interview.

———

TWO HOURS and multiple sexual advances later, I was free from Margie and officially an employee. My official next day would be tomorrow and I was expected to be at the office by 0830. After leaving my meeting, the first thing I knew I would need to do is figure out how I was going to get in and out of the city. I had left home at eighteen and never had my own car, so when I came back last week, I didn't have one waiting for me. It hadn't been a big deal since the gym and the grocery store were within walking distance of my apartment, but now that I had a job, I was going to need a way to get around. I would just take the bus to work like I did today until I figured it out.

Exiting the office and walking out onto the sidewalk, I was hit with the sounds and smells of downtown Charleston.

Growing up here, I always enjoyed walking around the

city and watching the tourists take it all in. Charleston wasn't huge, but it had a big city, small town vibe to it that was charming enough to make it a popular tourist destination. The weather was warm already and the humidity was sinking into my skin with precision. I could feel the beads of sweat spring up on the back of my neck as I stood just outside the office. Not wanting to idle too long on the sidewalk, I turned left and headed towards the water where I knew the ocean breeze would help to break the heat.

As I walked towards the pier, I passed couples and families enjoying the city and sights. Charleston is old, really old, and that added to its charm. Horse-drawn carriages pulled groups of people down the street as guides educated the passengers on the history of the city. I couldn't help but laugh at the stream of cars that had gotten stuck behind a carriage and now had to wait until it moved over to pass.

A few blocks down, I ducked into a coffee shop to grab a coffee and something to eat. I sat outside at a small metal table and watched as people took photos, laughed with their friends, and walked down the slate sidewalks. I watched as a couple got what I assumed were their engagement photos taken by a photographer holding an oversized camera. The girl was wearing a white dress and laughed as her fiancé dipped her back in the middle of the street, the photographer snapping photos as he did. When he pulled her up, he kissed her on the neck and she smiled for the camera. A lump grew in my gut as I watched them. I was nearly thirty years old and I hadn't been in a relationship since high school. Sure, I'd been kinda busy serving my country and all, but still, it had been a while.

My mind flashed to the image of the girl from the gym who read in between sets. I wondered if she had someone in her life. Suddenly, I was picturing her in a white dress in the middle of the street and me being the one who dipped her back for a photo. *Get a grip man, you don't even know her name.* I blinked the image out of my head and stood from the table to throw away the remnants of my lunch.

After a ten-minute walk, I hit the pier and pushed out a deep breath once the ocean breeze hit my face. The more the sun rose, the warmer it got and the more sweat started to roll down my back. It was early June and I knew that the heat and humidity would only get worse from here. My eyes watched as cargo ships rolled in and out of the harbor and smaller shrimp boats pulled in their morning haul. I loved coming down to this spot of town because of the big open grass area that looked out on the water. Kids were playing in the fountains and young men and boys were passing out sweetgrass roses to people passing by. They made me think of Kolbi.

I started to look for a bench to sit on and think about what I was going to do the rest of the day. I knew I should get on the bus to head home, get groceries, and figure out how I was going to get to work tomorrow, but it was too nice to leave the city just yet. My phone buzzed in my pocket and I pulled it out to see a notification from my bank. Pulling it to my face, my eyes grow as I read the number that was just deposited into my account. A text from Kolbi came in close behind.

> KOLBI:
>
> Your sign-on bonus should be in your account. Happy to have you home, brother.

I suddenly knew what I was doing the rest of the day and what I would be taking to work tomorrow.

4

BAILEY

My hand reached to slap my alarm off after the first obnoxious siren sounded. I always set my alarm for 4:15 so I could sleep for another fifteen minutes. After my fifteen minutes of grace were up, I would drag my ass out of bed, shove my sports bra on, and pull up my leggings. Getting out of bed was the hardest part of getting up. But once I was out, I was good.

You just gotta get your feet on the floor.

Sitting up in bed, I rubbed my eyes before dragging myself out from under the covers. I grabbed the workout gear I had laid out for myself the night before and pulled them on. I loved this specific brand because their bras were soft, yet supportive, and their leggings did something for my ass that no other pair of leggings could seem to do. It wasn't lost on me why I pulled this specific pair out of my drawer last night. Today was Wednesday, which meant it was leg day. I loved leg day.

Hopefully, the cute soldier at the gym loved leg day too.

It had been two weeks since he first showed up at the gym

and I'd noticed him across the weight room. Ever since that morning, he was always at the gym by the time I got there. A few times I'd caught him staring at me as I set up my rack or looked up from the pages of my book to start my next set. He thought he was being sly, but the way he whipped his head away from my direction wasn't discrete. One day I noticed how he seemed to be slowing down as he walked by me and waited to see if he was finally going to stop and say hello. Instead, he just stopped behind me, checked his phone, and kept walking. I remember pushing out my lips in disappointment and watching his back in the mirror as he walked away.

He was cute, no, he was hot. Smokin' hot, which surprised me because I didn't normally go for his type. The strong, put together, clean cut type. Normally, I went for the kind of guy who had more tattoos than he did brain cells and rarely ever showered. I was less than stellar at picking men, I knew this. That's why my attraction to the soldier was so surprising to me. While there was no doubt he was good looking, the thing that always caught my eye about him were the boots.

Who wears combat boots to the gym? And why did I find it wildly attractive that he did?

Dressed and with my hair pulled back, I snagged my Nike Blazers from the basket next to my bed and carried them out into the living room. I shared a condo with my best friend, Ophelia, who was still fast asleep in her room. You couldn't really call our living arrangements a true roommate relationship because she owned the place and was nice enough to let me live with her while I figured out my life. Unlike me, she had her shit together and made several hundred thousand dollars a year. Meanwhile, I wasn't doing much more than picking up side jobs here and there. The last two years of my life hadn't been what I expected them to be, but I was working to figure it out.

Once in the living room, I pulled the chain on the lamp next to the couch and walked into the kitchen. The condo we shared was downtown and had an amazing view of the water. While it wasn't ideal living here, seeing as how the gym I went to was north of the city, it was my only option. After my life fell apart two years ago, Ophelia invited me to live with her while I got back on my feet again and I wasn't in a position to say no. Sure, I could find a gym closer than the one I drove to each morning, but it was the gym I'd gone to before moving down into the city. It was my safe place and a place I knew. It was the one piece of my old life I wasn't willing to let go of. And while it was annoying to have to get up early and drive to the gym, the Lowcountry sunrises off the water each morning made it a little bit easier to bare.

I grabbed an energy drink from the fridge and filled up my water in the sink before sitting back down on the couch to put on my shoes. When I stood, I caught a glance of myself in the mirror that was leaning against the wall across from me and turned to look at myself.

"My ass looks amazing today," I whispered, smiling at my reflection and feeling confident.

As I walked out the door, I snatched my headphones, book, and keys off the shelf before closing the door behind me and locking it.

If Soldier didn't say anything to me today, I was going to be convinced that he was gay.

———

I WAS WELL into my lift and getting into a spicy scene in my book when I spotted a pair of shoes step into my line of view on the floor. Looking up, I noticed the shoes were connected to a man I hadn't seen before. A man who was standing uncomfortably close to the bench I was sitting on and who reeked of Axe body spray. He had said something that I couldn't hear over my music, so I hit pause on my phone and pulled one side of my headphones back.

"What was that?" I looked up at him from where I sat and tried to be friendly. It wasn't easy though, I'm not usually one who likes to talk to other people so early in the morning. If it was Soldier, I would've been fine with it. But it wasn't, and I was trying not to be annoyed.

"I said, what are you reading?" he asked, pulling his lips back in one corner and giving me an overly confident grin for a guy who smelled like a seventh grader.

"Just a book a friend recommended," I lied. I wasn't going to tell him the title or show him the cover because it would give away the fact that I was reading a trashy romance novel. I wasn't ashamed of the books I read but I didn't want to give this guy any reason to linger longer than neccesary.

"I noticed you were doing back squats today. You need a spot?" He took a step forward and was now within the realm of way too fucking close. He licked his lips as he looked down at me and I felt my face morph into a grimace. *Girl you better fix your face right fucking now.*

"Nope. I'm good. I've got my safety catches in place. Thanks though." My lips pulled together into a tight line, faking a polite nicety.

"Nahh, come on. It's good to have a spot when you squat. If you fall out of it, I'll be there to catch you." *The way I'd much rather fall and let the barbell crush me than let this guy touch me.*

He lifted one leg and set his foot up on the bench, bending it into a ninety degree angle, with his hips facing me. Still sitting on the bench, his crotch was now at eye level. A very unwelcomed sight at only five thirty in the morning.

Not wanting to continue to have his dick in my face, I stood up and hoped that as I did, he would take a step back and give me space. He didn't.

"Really, I'm okay. Thanks though. I'm going to get back to my set." I stood up and tried to step around him but he didn't move.

"Come on, baby, let me catch you. I promise I'm strong enough for it." He was dangerously close and I could smell whatever sports drink he'd had on his breath. I tried to calm the panic that was building in my chest. This wasn't the first time someone had gotten too close and the last time it happened, I ended up in the hospital filing a police report.

As my brain was trying to come up with something smart to say back, I noticed Soldier walking towards where I was currently trapped by the Axe soaked douchebag. He had his head down and was looking at his phone, but he wasn't wearing any headphones. I decided that this was my out and I needed to take it.

"Hey, sweetie, there you are! Can you spot me please?"

5

HANK

I heard her before I saw her and was surprised by the sound of her voice. It wasn't what I expected her to sound like. It was better. Like sweet honey, smooth and rich.

I looked up from my phone and knew it was her. I'd spotted her from the other side of the gym and was walking this way specifically so I could walk by her. The last few weeks I'd made sure I was at the gym right as they opened so I could watch her come in. I'd watch the door waiting for her to walk in like a dog waits for its owner to come home after work each day. I always knew it was her when she walked in, her blonde hair was a distinct shade of golden yellow that I could spot from anywhere. When she would finally walk in, I'd watch her as she walked around, found a space to stretch and then start her lift. Then, I would intentionally make laps around the gym, slowing down as I passed her just so I could be close to her, before going back to my workout.

Could I have gone up to her and said hello?

Yes.

Was I too much of a chicken shit to do so?

Also yes.

Instead, I dubbed her as 'Blondie' in my mind and fantasized about her way more than a man should fantasize about a woman he's never even said hello to.

But here she was now, looking at me expectantly while some jacked up dude who reeked of Axe stood a little too close for comfort. It shouldn't make me as angry as it does to see him so close to her seeing as how I don't even know what her name is. But it did and it made me even angrier seeing how uncomfortable she clearly was because of it.

"Sweetie...did you hear me?" She forced a smile and her eyes darted back and forth between me and the guy caging her in.

"Oh, yeah. Sure, I'd love to, babe." *Babe? Where the fuck did that come from? You don't even know her name you fuckwad.* I took a step between her and Axe guy and offered my hand for him to shake.

"Thanks so much for lookin' out for my girl, but I got it from here." I gave him the smuggest smile I could. One that said *"back the fuck up before I lay you out"* while also still trying to not cause a scene.

"Uhh...oh, yeah," he sputtered. "Sure, no problem." This guy must be a complete idiot because he couldn't form a full sentence as he shook my hand. Once he was gone, I turned towards Blondie. She watched Axe guy until he was clear on the other side of the gym before audibly exhaling.

"Oh my god, thank you," she breathed. "He wasn't taking the hint and normally I would just tell him to fuck off but he's like, twice my size. I really appreciate you playing along and helping me out." When she smiled at me, the entire world stopped spinning.

The mix of her golden hair, big smile, and slight

Southern accent had halted everything around me and had me completely transfixed. There was nothing I wanted more than to see her smile or listen to her talk.

You are so fucked my man, I heard the voice inside my head say.

"Hey, it's no problem, blondie. That guy was a tool and way too close. I would have laid him out if you asked me to."

"Blondie?" Her voice perked up and she raised an eyebrow at me.

"What?" *Oh shit, I didn't mean to let that slip.*

"You called me blondie." She had a smirk on her face as she finally stepped away from me, walking behind the bar of her weight rack.

"Oh yeah, uhh..."

"It's Bailey."

"What?" She laughed as she slid a plate onto the end of the barbell and I had to try to keep my dick from giving me away. Hearing her laugh was like music to my ears.

"My name is *Bailey*." Her eyebrows were arched and she was still giving me that wide smile of hers that would cause any sane man to drop to his knees in front of her.

"Oh." *Oh? Dear god man, you need to pull it together. Why are you so flustered, you've spoken to women before.*

"You got a name, soldier?" her southern drawl teased.

"A name? Yes! I have a name. My name is Hank. Hank Martínez." I jutted my hand towards her. When she took it, sparks of electricity shot up my arm and into my heart. *Fucked. You are so fucked.*

"Bailey Brown." She smiled at me before dropping my hand. "Well, I'm going to finish my set now. Thanks again for helping me."

"Yeah, no problem." I tried to think of something else to say to extend the time I could spend next to her but came up with nothing. I was starting to head back to my own space when I heard her call out to me.

"Hey, soldier." I turned to see her leaning against the bar, her lips pulled up in the corner and her feet crossed in front of her. "Those are some nice boots you got there."

I looked down at my feet and smiled at the dusty, worn in combat boots I had on. Suddenly, I was glad I decided to keep wearing them.

"Thanks, blondie." She shook her head with a smile and pulled her over-ear headphones back on and I took that as my sign to leave.

"Bailey Brown," I whispered to myself, the warmth in my cheeks growing as I said her name.

Bailey Brown.

Blondie.

My girl.

I liked the way it felt on my lips.

6

HANK

"**G**od dammit," Malcolm hissed under his breath. Conrad and Kolbi laughed from their seats at the table.

"You just had to roll a two." Conrad sucked on his lips and shook his head disapprovingly. Kolbi breathed out a laugh and rubbed his chin which was a sure sign that shit was about to go down.

"I didn't roll the goddamn two, the dice did! All I needed to do was not roll complete trash and I would have totally bribed the guard into letting us in without having to pay the fucking toll fee." Pursing his lips, Malcolm scrubbed his face with both hands.

I chuckled at my friends and tried to stay focused on our campaign instead of where my brain had been drifting all day.

My interaction with blondie at the gym this morning and learning her name.

Bailey.

It felt like every time I blinked her face sprang to my mind and filled it up with the image of that hundred-watt smile she gave me behind the barbell this morning. While I know it was only to get that douchebag away from her, I loved how she called me sweetie and I wanted to be able to call her 'my girl' for real.

"Auffroy, it's your roll," Kolbi directed at me, calling me by my character's name and pulling me out of my thoughts. He gave me a look, "You okay? You seem distracted tonight and you were distracted at work today."

"Distracted? Nah man, I'm good. Just getting into the swing of everything, you know." I picked up the die and gave it a toss.

Growing up and before I left for bootcamp, my friends and I had a standing Wednesday night hangout where we'd play Dungeons and Dragons. Our longest campaign ran for three years and was the last one we'd played before I enlisted in the Army. We always kept it under wraps in school because playing Dungeons and Dragons was the fastest way to be pegged as a nerd and a loser, which none of us wanted.

As grown ass men though, we couldn't care less. Now we got to play and drink beer and it gave us an excuse to get together every week and shoot the shit. Kolbi was our Dungeon Master and Malcolm, Conrad, and I played the characters in the game. Reinstating our weekly campaign was something we all agreed on immediately upon my landing back in Charleston and I couldn't be happier with the decision. My friends were my lifeline in high school. A few times, they probably did save my life. They definitely saved me from going to prison when the idea of offing my deadbeat father started to sound like too good of an idea.

After I rolled, I played through my part and listened as Kolbi weaved the story of our characters flawlessly. He was an amazing storyteller. Growing up in a Gullah Geechee family ensured him of this. I'll never forget growing up and listening to his grandparents tell incredible stories about his family whenever I went to his house, in awe of how they spun the tales. It was no different now as we listened to him craft the harrowing story of our characters. This weekly ritual was the best part of my week because I got to spend time with the three people who mattered most to me.

The three guys who would drive me home after school because my dad spent all his money on booze and strippers so we couldn't afford a car. The three guys who would let me crash on their couch after my dad and I had had it out for the fourth time in a week. My three best friends who supported me when I told them I was enlisting, yet got misty eyed at my swearing in ceremony and hugged me goodbye before I got on the bus to leave.

We were inseparable growing up—Kolbi, Malcolm, Conrad and I. We met for the first time in third grade when we were all in the same class. The misfit boys who all came from fucked up households and lived on the outskirts of town while everyone else wore brand new clothes and got new backpacks every school year. Once we got together, our teacher Mrs. Krazminski never stood a chance.

Malcolm was the smart one, always reading a book and occasionally bringing the newspaper to school. Where he got it, we never knew, but he would go into detail about the latest headlines at lunch without any of us asking.

Kolbi was the resourceful one, mostly because he had to be. His family didn't have much and lived in a small house just outside of town that most of the kids in our class cruelly called a "shack". His deep brown skin and twisted hair always made him a target for nasty names and he constantly had a target painted on his back. He kept his nose down though and the three of us always stood up for him when needed.

Conrad was always the shy one outside of our group, but in it, you could never get him to shut up. For the longest time the teachers and principals in school thought there was something else going on with him developmentally because he literally never talked. That was until he met the three of us. Turns out he just doesn't like very many people and is highly selective on who he spends his energy on.

Then there's me. In our group, I'm the serious one. The one who was always looking out for everyone else and who always talked the other guys out of the stupid ideas they came up with. Don't get me wrong, we still did stupid shit growing up, a lot. But, because of me, the stupid shit we did never got us in too much trouble. The last thing I needed was to get caught doing something stupid and have to face the hands of my father in return.

The four of us did everything together once we met at just eight years old. These guys weren't just my friends, they were my brothers.

"So, Hank, how are you liking being home?" Conrad asked as he grabbed another beer from the fridge.

"I'm liking it enough. I like where I'm living, it's right next to the gym I go to in the morning. Work doesn't suck, thank god my boss isn't a complete prick." I smirked at Kolbi and he rolled his eyes.

"That bike you bought is sick," Malcolm said, blowing a long breath out between his lips. He wasn't wrong.

After getting my sign-on bonus, I immediately went out and bought myself a Suzuki GSX-R1000 sport bike and had it customized with a matte black finish, black leather covers, and even got myself a custom helmet to match the paint of the bike.

Sure it cost me my entire bonus to get, but it was a sick fucking bike.

"Thanks man. I'm happy with how it turned out." I clapped Malcolm on the back and took a swig of my own beer.

"Alright boys, I have my refill, let's continue with the quest." Conrad sat back down at the table, fresh beer in hand.

We all sat around a round marble table in Kolbi's downtown home and played until the sun had set and we could hear the sounds of summer nights engulf us. Frogs humming. Dragonflies buzzing. And the faint sounds of tourists who were stumbling out of bars and heading back to their $300 a night hotel rooms. With the windows open, the breeze of the mid-June evening blew through the room. Life in downtown Charleston always came alive during the summer with an influx of tourists and travelers coming to the historic city to learn about plantations and hear ghost stories. The allure wasn't there for me anymore as I'd always lived here, but I understood why people loved to visit.

"Alright boys, I hate to be the one who calls it, but I'm beat. Get the hell out of my house," Kolbi joked after a few more hours of gameplay, stretching his hands above his head and rolling his neck.

"Holy shit, it's after midnight already," Conrad exclaimed. "We always did get lost in the game growing up, didn't we?" he laughed.

"Hey boss, mind if I come in late tomorrow? I'm going to need the extra sleep." I looked at Kolbi with a grin.

"If I have to be up and at the office by eight in the morning, then so do you." He slapped me on the back.

"Thank god I have the closing shift tomorrow at the bar.

I can sleep in however long I want." Malcolm shot finger guns at all of us as he got up from the table.

"Another solution for the group to consider: just work for yourself," Conrad offered. He worked as a freelance software engineer and could set his own hours. Something he never seemed to be able to remind us enough about.

"I do work for myself you moron. I just also happen to have about twenty employees who work for me and expect me to be in the office. Including this idiot." Kolbi flicked his thumb at me as I pulled on my shoes.

"¿Qué chingados?[1]" I cursed at my friend. I rarely spoke Spanish as over the years I'd trained myself to keep it in my own head. The fear of being seen as different growing up had embedded itself into my brain. But my Mexican roots still came out from time to time around people I felt comfortable with. "You offered me the job. If you didn't want us to know whether or not you were going to work on time you shouldn't have hired me." I slung my backpack over my shoulder and flipped him the bird.

"I'll see you fuckers in another week. Maybe sooner. We should grab a beer this weekend. Let's post up and harass Malcolm at the bar on Saturday while he's working," Conrad suggested as we all spilled out of the house.

"I'm there," I laughed. The thought of hanging out with my friends and giving Malcolm a hard time sounded fun. I didn't realize how much I missed them until now.

"Oh good, I can't wait for that." Malcolm rolled his eyes as he got in his truck. He and Conrad pulled out of the driveway first and I watched from my bike as their headlights disappeared down the road.

---

1. What the fuck?

"I'll see ya tomorrow, brother." Kolbi waved from the front porch.

"Yeah, see you tomorrow." I pulled on my helmet and popped up the kickstand as I inserted the key. Pushing the starter, my bike sprang to life as I flipped down the visor of my helmet.

As I backed out of the driveway and made my way down the road, I started to calculate the number of hours I had until I had to be awake again.

Four. More like three and a half because it was going to take me half an hour to get back to my apartment.

Three and a half hours until I have to be up again.

Three and a half hours until I get to see Bailey again.

7

BAILEY

"So he hasn't said anything else to you? At all?" Ophelia looked at me through the mirror on her vanity as she put on her makeup.

"Nope. We've made eye contact and I've tried waving to him, but he never comes up and talks to me. Not since I had to use him as a decoy a few days ago. Maybe I freaked him out." I worried my bottom lip as I searched Ophelia's closet for something to wear.

"Maybe he's just shy. You are stunningly sexy. If I were a man, I'd be intimidated by you too. Maybe you should try to be more ugly," she quipped before laughing at her own joke.

It was Saturday and a couple days had passed since Hank and I spoke at the gym when he saved me from the creep who had gotten too close. Not even a hello. There were times where I would catch his eyes on me in the mirror or feel like someone was watching me. When I would swing my head around to look, I would catch him looking away once I found him. I would smile and start to wave at him just as he would hurry to look away or walk in the other direction.

Maybe he had a girlfriend, a voice in my head said.

"Well that would be a real fuckin' bummer," I grumbled to myself.

"What was that?" Ophelia asked, looking at my reflection again in the mirror.

"Nothing. Just talking to myself. What about this?" I pulled out a daisy printed sundress and held it up in front of me.

"Cute! You should totally wear that tonight." We were heading to one of the bars on the water for a drink. Since the majority of my closet was workout gear, she was letting me borrow something from hers.

"Okay, I'm going to go put it on," I added, heading to my own room to change.

"And put some makeup on. Not that you don't look incredible without it, but think about how drop dead, boner inducing you could be with some blush," my friend yelled at me through the walls.

I rolled my eyes and ignored her comment. Makeup wasn't something I ever got into. Not that I had any issue with women who enjoyed wearing it, I just thought it was a waste of money. And whenever I tried to wear some I always ended up looking like a drunken circus clown.

I stripped out of the loungewear I had been wearing and pulled on the dress. It hugged my hips and fell just above my knees, showing off my muscular, defined calves. Doing a spin in the mirror, I looked at myself and leaned in to study my face. I pouted at myself and ran my fingers through my shoulder-length hair. I felt pretty. Hell, I looked pretty. And I knew it.

"If only Hank wasn't so fucking shy. Maybe I could be

getting a drink with him instead of Ophelia," I whispered as I turned to look at myself one more time in the mirror. I slipped on a pair of brown strappy sandals and grabbed my bag off the bedpost.

As I exited the room, I caught my reflection one more time in the mirror. Without warning, the image of my bloodied lip and bruised eye flashed in front of my eyes and the sounds of me crying rang in my ears. I felt my feet stop where they were as my hands covered my face.

"B, are you okay?" Ophelia's concerned voice pulled me out of the memory.

"What? Yeah. Yes, I'm fine." I gave her a fake smile I hoped was convincing. "A bug just flew into my face."

"Oh my god, I wish they would spray for those. The last thing we need is a god damn bug infestation in here." She rolled her eyes and grabbed her purse off the bar before turning to me. "You ready?"

"Yep," I chirped, trying to push the flashback out of my head for good.

Tonight was about having fun with my best friend, not about digging up past traumas and dwelling on them. She was going to be with me the whole time. I was safe. Nothing was going to happen.

And besides, even if anything did happen, I would be ready. I had been working hard to get stronger over the last two years for a reason.

To be able to protect myself. To be able to fight for myself. To make sure that no one would ever be able to hurt me again.

———

As we walked into the bar, the loud pumping music filled my ears and Ophelia turned to me with a grin. This was definitely more her scene than mine but the view was pretty and I knew how excited she'd been when I told her I would go out with her tonight.

We found an open hightop and took our seats. Looking around the bar, I could understand why it was so crowded.

The place sat right on the water and had a wall of opened doors leading out to the patio which then led to a dock that you could pull your boat up to. The white walls and plush chairs gave it a modern look, while the worn wooden floors and decorations paid homage to the history of the place. They were playing country music through the speakers and there was a live band out on the patio for people sitting outside. It had a luxe feel to it while still maintaining a homey atmosphere.

"This is my favorite place to come for drinks. The bartenders are amazing here and the food is so fucking good," Ophelia hummed, looking at the drink menu. "What are you drinking?"

"Uhhh...." I wasn't much of a drinker so I didn't really know what to get. "Maybe just a mule?"

"Oh come on, not a mule, you always get those. Get something fun for once. First drink is on me, so the price doesn't matter." She gave me a wink and bumped her shoulder into mine. We had been friends for over five years, meeting at an event I was organizing at my old job. She came up to me to complain that none of the servers were cute and we had been friends ever since. She was there for me after the night that changed everything and I was grateful for her friendship. She never made me feel bad for being between jobs and always offered to help me when it came to money.

Some people might be embarrassed to be in my position, but I was grateful. I didn't have any family here and Ophie had become more like my sister over the last few years. Plus, I would be paying her back for everything plus a little more on top once I figured things out again.

We both ordered our drinks, Ophelia ordering me some $14 fruity cocktail I would most likely hate, and were chatting as music played loudly over the speakers. The weather was perfect for this time of year—hot but not stuffy. With the patio doors open and being right on the water, a warm sea breeze passed through the crowded bar, mixing together all the scents and smells of the drinks and people inside of it.

Ophelia was telling me about some guy at work she thought was cute when my eyes glanced over to the bar. All the stools were filled and people were crowded around it, attempting to order a drink. My time as an event planner made me keenly aware of people and how they interacted. Watching people like this was one of my favorite things to do. When someone stepped away from the bar, my eyes caught the image of someone I'd seen before.

Someone I'd seen in the early morning hours of the day for the last couple weeks, hoping he would come up to me and say hi. There, sitting at the bar with two other guys, was Hank.

He was wearing dark faded jeans and a black T-shirt that showed off his strong, caramel toned arms. The tattoo on his left arm flexed as he spoke with his friends. When one of the guys he was sitting with said something, he threw his head back and laughed deeply, causing my thighs to squeeze together in response. There was nothing I wanted to do more than go and run my fingers through his dark curls that had grown out over the last couple weeks. I couldn't peel my eyes away from him until Ophelia's voice cut through my brain like a knife.

"Bailey...hello? Are you even listening to me?" She gave my arm a shove which pulled me from the trance I was in. She followed my gaze to see what I was staring at. "Holy shit, what a beautiful specimen of a man HE is."

"*Ophie*," I hissed at her. She was nearly yelling and the people seated around us had all turned to see what she was looking at. The last thing I wanted was for Hank to notice and realize I had caused everyone in the bar to stare at him.

"What? He's so cute," she leaned in and whispered, wiggling her eyebrows at me with a smirk.

"That's the soldier," I explained, a smile blooming across my face. He *was* a fine specimen of a man and seeing him out of the gym and in normal clothes continued to prove that to be true.

"No fucking way." Ophelia's mouth fell open and her eyes grew into large, round saucers.

"Yes fucking way." I rolled my lips under my teeth before taking a sip of my drink with a smile.

"Girl..." she fanned her face with one of her hands and I couldn't help but laugh.

"I'm gonna go say hi." I wiggled my eyebrows and gave my friend a sly grin. My belly did a flip as I thought about approaching him with his friends around. I don't normally get nervous like this around guys, but something about him was different.

"That's my girl," Ophelia encouraged as I hopped down from our hightop and headed towards the bar. I made sure to swing my hips a little more dramatically as I approached him.

Hank had his back to me so he didn't notice me coming.

As I got closer, one of the guys he was with noticed me and gave me a smile. *Not here for you buddy but I appreciate it.*

"Hey there, soldier," I hummed once I was close enough.

"Soldier?" the guy to the left of him exclaimed, "Hank, do you know this beautiful woman?"

He turned around in his chair and when he saw me, his face morphed into a stunned expression, surprised to see me standing behind him in the restaurant.

"I'm Bailey. Bailey Brown," I stuck my hand out to the guy who had just spoken and shook his hand. "Soldier and I go to the same gym. Don't we?" I smiled at him and waited for him to say something.

He didn't.

Instead, the guy to his right slapped him on the back which seemed to snap him out of whatever thought he was lost in.

"Sorry our friend here is being rude, I'm Kolbi." The man who just slapped Hank on the back extended his hand towards me and I shook it. "The moron on the other side of Hank is Conrad."

"So Conrad, Kolbi, and Hank," I said as I pointed to each of them. "It's nice to meet you both, and see you again Hank." I looked at him again and waited for him to say something.

Anything.

He didn't.

After an awkward pause, a bartender from behind the bar came up behind the guys and looked at me.

"Who is this beautiful woman? And why is she so close to you idiots?"

I blushed and tried to stifle a smile. Never in my life had so many men called me beautiful all at once.

"This is Bailey. She knows our Hank here, who seems to have forgotten how to speak," Conrad chaffed, looping an arm around Hank's shoulder and shaking it. Hank was still staring at me, his mouth slightly ajar.

"Well, I'm Malcolm and these three idiots are my best friends." He reached across the bar and shook my hand. "They like to come here on the weekends and bust my balls while I serve them drinks and slip them free food."

I smiled at the group of guys who I could tell were close. I thought it was nice that Hank and his friends would come and visit their friend at work.

"That sounds fun. I'm actually here with my best friend Ophelia." I flipped my thumb over my shoulder towards our table. When I looked over my shoulder, I saw her watching the entire exchange go down. She wiggled her fingers in a wave as the five of us looked towards her and took another sip of her drink with a flirty smile.

"You look really nice tonight, blondie." Hank finally spoke, breaking his vow of silence. I turned back to look at him and he had a small, shy smile on his face. His eyes were flashing between my dress and his shoes.

My heart squeezed at his words and how sweet he was. He's hot as fuck but still shy. *Who would have thought such a man existed.*

"Blondie?" Conrad barked from his seat. Kolbi smiled at his friend.

"Thank you, soldier." I reached out and brushed my fingers across the top of his knee. I felt him stiffen as the pads of my fingers brushed along his jeans. "You look nice tonight too."

I didn't miss the slight color change in his cheeks and how his eyes flashed back to his shoes.

"Welp, I'll let you boys get back to your drinks. I just wanted to come and say hi. Will I see you in the morning?"

"Y–yeah. Yes, I will be there." He finally looked at me and when he flashed me a smile, my insides began to burn.

"I look forward to it. I'll see ya later then. Gentleman." I gave the group a small nod before turning from them to head back to my table.

As I walked, I swung my hips back and forth and stood with my shoulders pressed back. I knew they were all watching me, but I only cared about one pair of eyes.

When I reached my seat, Ophelia was already starting to ask me a million questions. My eyes peeked back to where he sat and I found him looking back at me. His eyes burned into me and brought a warm feeling to my core that I hadn't felt in a long time.

I picked up my drink, took a sip, and winked at him before turning back to my best friend to answer all of her questions.

8

HANK

*O*kay man, you can do this. Just walk up to her and ask her if she wants to go to dinner. Shit, if nothing else ask her for her number. Or at least say hello. It's time to stop pussyfooting around and be a man. You've been to war for Christ's sake, you can ask a pretty girl for her number.

But that's the thing, she wasn't pretty.

She was stunning. Breathtaking. Drop to your knees and kiss the ground she walked on gorgeous. I don't know what God was thinking when he created a woman like her, but he really laid it on thick.

After seeing her on Saturday at the bar, my friends wouldn't stop hounding me about her. Our group chat, which normally focused on things like work and casual hookups, had managed to come back to Bailey at least three times a day. When they found out I didn't ask her out when I saw her yesterday morning at the gym, they threatened to cut my dick off and force feed it to me. Malcolm asked me which gym I went to because, as he put it, 'a beautiful woman like her needed to be taken out and shown off' and if I wasn't going to be man enough to do it, he would do it himself.

I told him to fuck off and that I would knee cap him if he even tried.

Now it was Monday, and the words of my friends calling me a moron and a wimp were ringing in my ears as I watched the entrance of the gym. She normally came in ten to fifteen minutes after the doors unlocked, so she should be here any minute.

Not that I kept track of when she showed up or anything.

She was just a creature of habit and a few times as she came in, I *may* have also checked my watch at the same time. Now her arrival time was in my head as if it had been branded into my brain.

I pulled my phone out of my pocket and checked the time: 0509. She should be here soon.

As I slipped my phone back into my pocket, I looked up from the bench I was sitting at just in time to spot her golden blonde hair across the gym. She always wore it pulled back and there had been plenty of times over the last couple weeks where I'd fantasized myself behind her, pulling her hair, while I sunk myself deep inside of her as she moaned out my name. Most of the time, I helped myself along in the shower as I pictured her blonde hair falling behind her back as she rode me until we both fell apart together.

My dick suddenly started to grow under my shorts and I had to fill my brain with images that would kill the massive hard on I was fighting. *My great aunt Carmen. Musicals. Sweaty fat men playing baseball.*

Every man had things they thought about to kill a boner. These were mine.

I tried taking a few breaths and watched as Bailey started to set up her rack. This girl was dedicated to her lift and I found it wildly attractive just how much she could take. The last couple weeks I'd watched as she would come in, turn on her headphones, and pull a book out of her bag before setting up her rack. She would lift, pause her music, then take a seat and read until she started her next set. She followed this routine almost exactly each day and I loved watching her move through it.

When she finished with her first set and grabbed her book, I saw my opening and took it. As I walked towards her, I tried to hype myself up as best as I could.

You can do this man. You're a good looking dude, any girl would love to go to dinner with you. Plus, she came and talked to you in front of your friends on Saturday. Clearly she's into you. Just go up to her and ask her out. Don't be a dicklicker and wimp out, just do it. ¡Sé un hombre![1]

You've been to war, you can ask a girl out!

When I finally reached her, I saw her eyes glance to my feet, but she didn't look up from the pages of her book. She just kept reading. I stood there, waiting for her to look up and acknowledge me, but she didn't.

"Those are some nice boots you got there," she finally said after a long pause, still not looking up from her book or moving her headphones from her ears.

"Uhh, thanks."

She finally looked at me, a devilish grin started to spread across her face.

"You know it's rude to interrupt someone who's reading?" *Shit maybe she's not interested in me.*

---

1.   Be a man!

"Oh, I'm sorry. I won't bother you then." My feet turned away quickly until I heard her start to laugh.

"Wait, I was only teasing. Come back here." I turned to see her closing her book and looking at me with a smile that reminded me of pure sunshine. With her head cocked to one side, her ponytail swished behind her.

"You ever gonna ask me out, soldier?" she teased. The look on her face caused my dick to press against my shorts. *Don't you fucking dare*, I thought to myself.

I chuckled and took a few steps closer to her. Of course she would call me out for my bullshit. This woman has me wrapped around her finger and we hadn't even gone on a date yet.

"Well, blondie, that's actually why I was coming over here. You kinda stole my thunder though," I teased back and grinned. *Smooth.*

"Well I'm sorry, but I was starting to think you didn't have enough thunder to do it. And I would very much like to go out with you if you wanted to go out with me." She had a slight Southern drawl to her words that made them sound like honey to my ears. Sweet and thick. I stared at her lips as she spoke and wanted nothing more than to bend over and find out if they tasted as good as they sounded.

"Are you always this straightforward with people?" I asked, attempting to be cool and not overthink things. She was the most beautiful girl I'd ever laid eyes on and she was asking *me* on a date.

"Only with the people I really like." She crossed her legs in front of her on the bench and tucked her hands between her legs. She looked up at me with admiration and tease, and I was eating it up like free candy.

"Alright then. Would you like to grab dinner with me sometime?" I placed my hands on the bench in front of her legs and leveled my eyes with hers. Our faces were just inches apart and I took it as a good sign when she didn't move away from me.

"I'd thought you'd never ask." Being this close to her made me keenly aware of the fact that she smelled as sweet as she sounded—the scent of honey and vanilla filled up my nose as I breathed her in.

Aren't you supposed to smell bad when you workout? Why didn't she smell bad?

"How do you feel about Italian food?"

"I love Italian food." She leaned in when she said the word 'love' and our lips were so close that if I had leaned in at the same time they would have met.

"Italian food it is. How's Saturday?" *Good job man, keep it up. Lock it in.*

"Saturday is perfect. Pick me up at six?"

"I look forward to it." I stood up and started to walk away, feeling my pride start to swell because I had asked her on a date. When I heard her laughing, I panicked that I had just been punked, and turned to look at her.

"What are you laughing at?"

"How are you supposed to know where to pick me up if you don't have my number?" *You fucking idiot, you didn't ask for her number.*

"Riiiight....here give me your phone." She unlocked it, handed it to me, and I sent myself a text before handing her back her phone.

"Very smooth." She chuckled and shook her head as she read the text.

"What, am I wrong?" I teased. Somewhere in the depths of my soul I managed to conjure enough confidence to text, *'I am the luckiest girl in the world to get to go out with you, Hank Martínez. I can't wait for our date on Saturday.'*

Since I had texted myself from her phone, it looked like she had sent it.

"No, you aren't wrong, not entirely. I don't know if I'm the luckiest girl in the world *yet*, but I am excited for our date." She looked up and winked at me.

Looking down at my phone, I texted her back.

> I can't wait either, blondie.

She looked down at her phone, read the text, and I didn't miss the change of color in her cheeks and how her lips pushed into a soft smile.

"I'll let you get back to your lift." I gave her a wave and walked back to my own side of the gym feeling confident. My puffed up ego and pride carried me through the rest of my workout as if it was nothing. Nothing could stop me and nothing could hold me back.

I had a date with Bailey on Saturday and nothing felt better than that.

9

HANK

Group: Dungeons and Dickheads

CONRAD:

We still good for tonight?

KOLBI:

It is Wednesday brother.

CONRAD:

I'm just making sure no one fucked up their plans. It's been a long time since we had a standing campaign time. Knowing you idiots, someone is bound to forget or schedule over it.

MALCOLM:

I'm going to be twenty minutes late. Sorry guys.

CONRAD:

This is why I ask.

KOLBI:

MALCOLM:

Sorry I have a JOB that requires me to stay
late sometimes. Our closing bartender is
running late and I have to cover until he gets
here. I'm coming straight from work. You
fuckwads can wait.

> Lay off, Conrad, we can't all be comfy
> asswipes like you who work for themselves
> and lay at home all day pretending to work.

> I will be there though. And on time, unlike
> some people.

MALCOLM:

KOLBI:

Hank, aren't you supposed to be working
right now? It's not lunch, you shouldn't be
on your phone.

> Probably but my boss sets terrible examples
> for his employees and is on his phone all the
> time at work. Plus he's a huge dick.

CONRAD:

Yeah I've heard he's a major ass wipe. And
that his dick is only an inch and a half long.

MALCOLM:

I've heard that he sucks in bed and hasn't
gotten laid in months. Poor sap.

KOLBI:

You can all go fuck yourselves. And for the record, my dick is much longer than an inch and a half and I can promise you, I do not suck in bed. The girl I went home with last weekend can attest to that 😊

CONRAD:

I just threw up in my mouth

KOLBI:

Speaking of getting laid, Hanky boy, how's it going with that girl from the bar last weekend? Get her number yet?

MALCOLM:

I swear to Christ if you haven't I'm going to cut your dick off, make you eat it, and then get her number myself.

CONRAD:

Malcolm we should really talk about how violent that was.

> I will fucking cut you off at your knees if you get anywhere near her.

CONRAD:

Again with the violence.

KOLBI:

Wooahh, down boy. Someone's protective.

MALCOLM:

I'd like to see you try Hanky. You might be an ex soldier or whatever but I have a good three inches on you and could take you out if I needed to 💪

You're on dumb ass.

CONRAD:

Can we bet on who would win? My money is on Hank.

MALCOLM:

Fuck you Connie.

KOLBI:

Hank, you didn't answer my question brother.

CONRAD:

Alright I'm doubling down on Hank. Fuck you Malcolm, you know I hate when people call me 'Connie' 👆

Yes, I got her number. I'm taking her to dinner on Saturday.

MALCOLM:

Oh look, Hanky boy does have a penis. Way to finally man the fuck up dude.

CONRAD:

Alright Hank!

KOLBI:

I'm proud of you brother.

CONRAD:

Where are you going?

MALCOLM:

Do you need me to buy you condoms? They only sell those to real men.

KOLBI:

Do you want to borrow my car so you don't
have to go on your bike?

Sorry boys, I have a job to do and don't
have time to play 20 questions right now. I'll
see you idiots tonight.

CONRAD:

Way to be a buzzkill.

MALCOLM:

Fuck you dude.

KOLBI:

What a model employee you are.

———

"S o where are you going for dinner?" Malcolm asked
as we sat around the table that night.

"Haven't decided yet," I replied, not looking up
from the game board.

It was Wednesday night and we were all together again
for our weekly Dungeons and Dragons session. As expected,
Malcolm was twenty minutes late which irritated Conrad.
He was always such a stickler for schedules and routines.

"Can we please focus on the game? We're already
behind," Conrad muttered, rubbing the back of his head.

"Dude, *relax*. You need to chill out. Being so uptight all
the time isn't good for you." Kolbi slapped him on the back
and laughed.

"I am relaxed, I just wish we would all pay attention to
what's going on."

I laughed at my friend and rolled the die. When it landed, we continued to play through the story as it was woven for us. We played a few more rolls before Malcolm asked me about my date again.

"You should take her somewhere downtown. There's lots of bars you could bounce around from. No shortage of good food options either."

"The entire city is full of good food options, moron." Conrad rolled his eyes, annoyed that we had veered away from the game again.

"I was thinking of taking her across to the island, over to Penelope's. It's right on the water." I had searched for a place to take her over my lunch break. The place was small, intimate, and the menu was full of incredible looking Italian food. I remembered how she said she liked it at the gym and I wanted to make sure I took her somewhere she would enjoy.

"Never heard of it." Malcolm furrowed his brows.

"Just because you work in the restaurant scene doesn't mean you know every restaurant," Kolbi pointed out.

Conrad rolled the die and we continued to play. It never ceased to amaze me how we could easily flow between real life and the made up world of our campaign. This was how the four of us communicated best. Through games.

"Aha, fuck you guys!" Conrad laughed as his character advanced and Malcolm and I were stuck to figure out our next moves on our own.

"Do you have the proper precautions for after the date?" Malcolm raised his eyebrows at me with a sly smirk and Conrad pretended to gag from his seat.

"I don't plan on sleeping with her dude," I huffed.

"Why the hell not? She's a fucking dream. I would love

to see what she looks like under her clothes," Malcolm shot back. Kolbi sat back in his seat and shook his head, watching us go at each other like small children.

"Because it's only the first date. Real gentlemen don't expect to have sex on the first date." I threw my bottle cap at him and he swatted it to the floor. It's not that I hadn't thought about it and I had run into the drugstore after work to buy a box of condoms just in case. But I wasn't that kind of guy.

"I'm not saying you should expect it, I'm just saying you should prepare for it." Malcolm shrugged his shoulders.

"An accidental pregnancy would be a real bummer," Conrad added. I rolled my eyes at both of them.

"Yes, I have precautions for after the date. I'm not holding my breath on needing them though. If she wants to, I won't tell her no. But I am not going to insinuate that it needs to happen or should happen."

"I think that's very noble of you," Kolbi noted, standing from the table to grab another beer.

"But if you do get her in bed, be sure to wrap it up," Conrad quipped.

"And when you get her in bed." Malcolm took a pull from his beer. "You'll need to let us know how it is."

"I'm not telling you fuckers anything." I rolled my eyes again.

We continued our playthrough for the night without anymore talk of my date. As we played, I tried to keep my mind on what was happening in front of me instead of where it was trying to sneak away to.

Towards images of Bailey in my bed with me on Saturday.

I wasn't holding my breath that it would happen and I

wasn't going to push her to do anything she didn't want to do. But if she was interested in coming home with me, I would be ready.

What kind of gentleman would I be if I wasn't?

10

BAILEY

The rest of the week came and went as fast as June was flying by, and by Saturday morning I was nearly shaking with excitement for my date with Hank. The feelings of nervous energy and excitement churned in my belly every time I thought about him picking me up.

The last two days at the gym when I came in, he'd come over, said hello, and told me that he was excited for our date. He even called it a date which I thought was cute. Guys don't normally label things so quickly, but he did, and I liked that about him.

Ophelia was excited for me when I told her he'd finally asked me out and immediately asked when the last time I had gotten waxed was.

"Ophie!"

"Don't 'Ophie' me, you haven't gotten any in a long time and you don't want to scare him away by bringing a jungle to bed."

While I didn't love the comparison of my pubic hair to a jungle, she wasn't wrong. I hadn't gotten any in a long time and had stopped tending to that part of my body. I didn't see the need to trim around the edges if no one would be seeing them anyway. The waxing appointment I booked for Thursday was less than enjoyable to say the least.

I didn't even know if it would be worth it either, getting waxed. I wasn't normally one to sleep with someone on the first date. Plus, Hank is so shy I don't think he would try anything even if I wanted him to.

Even though I *do* want him to.

I couldn't put my finger on it, but something about him pulled me in. I've dated my fair share of men, but I never had the same level of attraction towards them that I do towards Hank. When he looked at me it was as if the entire world stopped spinning. When I'm at the gym, I can feel his eyes on me. And when he finally asked me to dinner on Monday, and took my phone to give me his number, it took everything in me to not turn fifty shades of red.

My phone buzzed and pulled me from my thoughts. When I looked at it, I smiled without even meaning to.

<u>2 New Messages: Soldier</u>

> I'll be there to pick you up in 30 blondie.

> I'm really excited to take you out tonight.

He sent the second message quickly after the first, almost as if he'd forgotten to send it with the first one. I'd never had a guy tell me he was excited to take me on a date so many times before.

I finished doing my hair and slipped into the dress I bought yesterday after getting done helping at a small event Ophelia was running at work. She and I walked down the main stretch of King Street looking for something that I could wear and when we walked by this one in the window, I knew it was the one.

It was a mid-length dress that flared in the skirt and the fabric was lightweight, making it perfect to wear for a summer dinner date. I loved the floral pattern and how the blues and oranges made my blonde hair and blue eyes pop. I also loved how the front of the dress was cut low but wasn't too revealing. The way the top tied around my shoulders was my favorite part of the entire thing.

It was perfect for a first date.

After slipping on my dress, I checked my hair and the small amount of makeup I had put on in the mirror. My eye caught something dark behind me and a wave of fear hit me. I spun around to see what it was only to discover it was my gym bag hanging on the hook by my door. A memory flooded my brain as I stared at it.

"Just shut up and be quiet. I won't hurt you if you don't make a sound." I was crying and laying on the cold, wet concrete. It reeked of rotting food and booze. My head moved to one side as I tried to get out from under him. The black hoodie covered his face as he overpowered me. Somewhere in the distance, people laughed as they walked home from the bars and nightclubs.

"Bailey?" Ophelia's voice pulled me back to the present. "You okay?"

She was standing in the living room just outside my bedroom and was studying me with a concerned expression. I blinked a few times and shook the memory from my head.

"Yeah...I'm okay. What do you think of my dress?" Doing a twirl for her, I painted a smile on my face. The flashback lingered in my brain and I did my best to try and push it away.

"You look stunning, as always. He isn't going to be able

to keep his hands off of you." She wiggled her eyebrows at me and gave me a smirk.

"Oh, stop it." I waved my hand at her and checked my phone. He should be here any minute.

"Seriously, B, if he doesn't try and get in your pants tonight, there's seriously something wrong with him."

I laughed her off and grabbed my heels from the closet. Sure, wearing heels was probably a little much, but I wanted to make a good first impression. As I sat on the couch and put them on, there was a knock at the door. Our heads shot towards it before we looked at one another with surprise.

"He's picking you up at the door? Wow, he is a good one." She smiled.

My shoes finally on, I walked towards the door and grabbed my purse off the kitchen counter as I passed it. When I swung open the door, my breath caught in my throat.

Hank was standing in my doorway wearing loose fitting dark jeans, a collared shirt, and a deep navy suit jacket. Casual, but still dressed up for our date. In his hands was the most beautiful bouquet of flowers I'd ever seen. He reached out his arm and handed them to me as soon as I opened the door.

"These are for you, blondie. I grabbed them from the shop across the street."

"Thank you. And hello to you too." I gave him a smirk and took the flowers from his hand, smelling them once they were in my arms.

"Oh, right, hi," he said in one breath. I watched as his eyes traced my body from head to toe, and didn't miss when they lingered just a few seconds longer on my semi-exposed chest.

"Hi. Let me just set these down and we can go."

I turned around quickly and handed the flowers to Ophelia who had her arms extending towards me to take them, and waved goodbye to her. We walked down the hallway in silence and when we reached the elevator, we both went to push the down button at the same time. Our fingers hit the button and when I felt his fingers brush mine, a shiver ran down my spine. He pulled his hand away quickly as if he had just touched an open flame.

"Sorry," he said shortly, shoving his hands into his jacket pockets and looking towards the ground.

So shy, I thought to myself with a smile.

"Thanks for picking me up at my door." I bumped his shoulder playfully as we stepped inside the elevator. He let me go ahead of him so I pushed the button that would take us to the lobby before he had a chance. No need to repeat the awkward button interaction. He took a step closer to me so our arms were touching.

"Of course. What kind of Southern gentleman would I be if I didn't?" The grin he gave me made my insides warm.

When the elevator doors opened, he reached behind me and placed his hand on the small of my back, leading me out. We walked through the lobby of my building and he opened the front door for me. I smiled at him as I passed through it.

"A gentleman, indeed. Very smooth."

He chuckled softly behind me.

Outside, the warm buzz of the summer evening hit my ears. It was the thick of summer and the heat was unreal. Not just the heat, but the humidity. I loved living in Charleston something fierce, but the summer months were what I'd imagined living in Hell to be like. Hot. Sticky. And constantly uncomfortable. I was grateful that I had gone with a dress instead of jeans because it helped keep me cool.

We walked together down the sidewalk, his hand on the small of my back, leading me forward. When we neared the street, he sidestepped behind me so that he was closer to the road and I was on the inside. I smirked at the move and felt my cheeks flush. After walking down the sidewalk for a few beats, he finally stopped next to a motorcycle parked on the street.

"Is this your bike?" I asked, my mouth gaping open as I took it in. It was all black and looked expensive. More than that, it was sexy as hell. I looked back at him as he started to pull the helmet off the back and unlatch its strap.

"Yeah, I have a second helmet for you to wear if you're okay riding behind me." *Boy, I would be okay riding behind you, on top of you, or in front of you.*

"Uhh..." I waved my arm in front of myself to show him my outfit. My dress would not do well on the back of a bike speeding through the city streets. It wasn't long enough to tuck under anything and I would 100 percent be giving the fine people of Charleston a free show if I wore it while riding on a motorcycle.

"Oh shit, I didn't even think about that. That's my bad. We can just take an Uber, on me. I don't even know what I was thinking."

"No, it's okay, just give me ten minutes, I have an idea!" Before he could respond, I hurried back inside my building and rushed back up the elevator.

I raced down the hall, unlocked my door, and scurried past Ophelia who was giving me a confused look from the couch. Once in my room, I threw open the drawer of my dresser, found a pair of old sweats, and shimmied them up and over my dress. Then, I moved to my closet and dug around for a pair of sneakers and swapped out my heels for them instead. Without wasting another minute, I grabbed my heels in my hand and ran back out of the apartment.

I would be wearing my new dress that made me feel sexy and confident and I would also be riding on the back of Hank's motorcycle. I might look like a freak while doing it, but I didn't care.

Nothing was going to stop me from going on a date with him. And maybe, just maybe, I would be riding something else after our date too.

11

HANK

"**T**ada!" I heard her say from behind me.

When she went running inside, I thought about following her in but she had asked for ten minutes and I wanted to respect that. How fucking stupid could I have been to bring my bike? I should have taken Kolbi up on his offer to borrow his car, but I hadn't expected her to wear such a short dress on our date.

My tongue almost fell out of my head when she opened the door. The way her dress plunged low in the front and how the colors of its fabric made the sapphire in her eyes pop made me want to drop to my knees and kiss the ground she walked on. Instead, I nearly shoved the flowers I bought for her in her face like an idiot. I didn't even say hello first, I just shoved them into her arms as soon as she took a step closer to me.

Fucking idiot.

Turning around to look at her, I saw her standing on the sidewalk facing me, her arms outstretched and giving me a smile that was contagious. She looked like Vanna White who just revealed the mystery prize on *Wheel of Fortune*. I couldn't help but laugh at her outfit. The girl was now wearing a pair of oversized gray sweatpants pulled up and over her dress, a pair of sneakers, and was holding her heels by the straps in her fingers.

"What do you think of my outfit?" She shimmied her shoulders at me and gave me a spin for good measure.

"I think you look stunning. Like the most beautiful girl I've ever seen." I smiled at her and watched as her head fell to one side and her cheeks turned a very prominent shade of pink.

"I'm happy to get us an Uber though so you don't have to wear the sweats, blondie, it's really not a big deal."

"Oh, hush," her Southern drawl came out thick. "I wanna ride on the back of this sexy bike of yours but I'm not going to give the entire city of Charleston a free show while I do."

She stepped up to my bike and I handed her the second helmet I had purchased earlier this week with her in mind. When I bought my bike a couple weeks ago, I only bought one helmet, not expecting anyone to ride with me. I bought a second helmet almost immediately after she said yes to our date.

"So," she started, slipping the helmet on over her head, "Where are we going?" The helmet was huge on her and I tried to stifle my laugh when she had to tip her head back to look at me through the visor.

"Here, let me help you with that." I moved to the same side of the bike she was standing on and adjusted the helmet for her, tugging the strap snug under her chin. Her eyes watched me intently as I got her straightened around. My heart started to beat harder in my chest and I chewed on the inside of my lip to try to regain some sense of self-control.

"Thank you, Hank," she nearly whispered through the helmet.

"You're welcome, blondie. And we're going across the island, I found somewhere on the water for us to go to." I loved how I could hear her gasp from under her helmet, telling me that a place on the water was a good idea.

Before putting my own helmet on, I opened the saddlebag on the back of the bike and pulled out the riding jacket I kept there. Since she was only wearing enough fabric to cover her legs, I wanted her to wear it in case of an accident. Wiping out on a motorcycle without proper coverage is a great way to rip your skin to shreds.

"Here, I want you to wear this." I walked behind her and helped her slip it on. Once her arms were in, I turned her around to face me and zipped it all the way up. I made sure to snag the clasp at the top that prevented the zipper from slipping.

"Hank, you should wear it. I'll be fine."

"I won't be fine if I wear it and you don't. I want you to be safe and I need to know you're protected." My voice came out firmer than I intended, but something about her kicked my protectiveness into overdrive. I wouldn't be able to live with myself if something happened to her.

"Fine, I'll wear it. But I need you to know that I have sweat running down my back already so if it's soaked through by the time we get to dinner, I'm really sorry."

"It's not a big deal. Let's get going so you can cool off as we ride." I laughed and held out my hands to her so she could give me her heels and purse to tuck away in the saddlebag. Then, I swung my leg over the seat of my bike and helped her take her spot behind me. When she slipped her arms around my waist as I turned on the bike, I had to take a deep breath to keep my dick from growing any larger beneath my jeans.

"You ready?" I turned to ask her through my helmet.

"I'm ready." She gave me a thumbs up and I laughed again before pulling away from the curb.

We whipped through downtown together, flying around cars and carriages. Her arms tightened around my waist as we flew over the bridge that took us across to the island where we would be having dinner. Her chest and body pressed against my back made my insides buzz and I had to fight to keep my focus on the road and not on how much the bulge in my pants was growing. The last thing I needed was to have a raging hard-on when I stepped off my bike once we got to dinner.

When we pulled off the bridge at a light, I turned my head and flipped up my visor to look at her.

"You okay? I'm not going too fast am I?" I knew I was, but I wanted to make sure she was okay. There was just something about having a beautiful girl on the back of your bike that made you wanna break every law there was.

"Oh my god, no! This is so fun!" Her warm laugh made me grin and I felt myself start to relax. Going out with her had made me nervous even though I wasn't normally one to get nervous. There was just something about this girl that had me all out of sorts.

When we got to dinner, I hopped off the bike first then helped her off. We took off our helmets simultaneously and she handed me hers before I unzipped the leather jacket, helping her out of it with a spin. I couldn't hold back my laugh when I watched her shimmy her sweats down her legs, step out of them, and then swap out her sneakers for the heels we had stowed away in the saddlebag.

I watched in awe as she went from wearing baggy sweats

and sneakers to transforming into a true Southern beauty in less than thirty seconds. She flipped her head over, shook out her hair, and flipped herself back up, smiling at me when she was standing upright again.

"What's the face for?" she asked as she stuffed her sweats and sneakers into the saddlebag on my bike.

"What face?" I felt all the muscles in my face fall. Had I been making a face?

"You were giving me a look." She laughed as she slung her purse that I'd handed to her over her shoulder. One of the straps of her dress was starting to slip and I reached out to fix it. When my fingers brushed the curve of her shoulder, our heads snapped to where our skin had made contact, then back at one another.

"I was just looking at you. It's hard not to look when someone is as beautiful as you are." She was standing within a few steps of distance from me and my voice came out low and gravely. Her eyes were locked on mine and I didn't miss when she licked her lips. It took everything in me not to close the space between us and press my lips to hers right there in the parking lot.

I suddenly felt very aware of how much I wanted to kiss her and took a step back, afraid to cross a line I wasn't sure if she wanted to cross so soon. Who was I to think that someone as gorgeous and outgoing as her would want to kiss someone like me? A man who hadn't been on a real date in over ten years and hadn't even been with a woman in almost just as long. I was lucky she'd even said yes to going to dinner with me. The last thing I wanted to do was fuck it up by trying to kiss her before I knew she wanted me to.

"Let's go get some food," was all I could think to say before turning and heading towards the restaurant. While we walked, I wanted to take her hand and hold it but wasn't sure if that would be okay either. Without saying anything, she took my hand and pulled herself into me, looping her arm around mine and smiling up at me. I couldn't help but smile down at her in return.

Dinner was amazing when I wasn't acting so fucking shy. I wasn't a shy guy really, but she made me second guess everything I said or did. Multiple times she had to repeat herself because I had been distracted by her. Not that she was doing anything abnormal, I was just completely awestruck by her.

How she carried herself. How she spoke. The way she laughed. The way she watched me so intently as I talked, clinging to every word I said. She was kind to the servers and complimented a random woman's shoes as she passed our table. She wasn't just beautiful on the outside, she was beautiful on the inside too.

"So while my family moved away, I'm still here living in Charleston. I've loved this place ever since we came here in second grade as a family for my dad's job," she explained.

We had been talking for over an hour, our empty plates sitting abandoned because we had gotten lost in the conversation we were having.

"Have you ever thought about leaving?" I asked, leaning my elbows on the table and staring at her intently. Talking with her was easy because she told every story as if it was happening for the first time and made you feel like you were living in it right along with her.

"I did, for a brief moment, but I love it too much to leave. I grew up here, went to school here, got my degree in hospitality at the College of Charleston. This city is my home, I don't think I could leave it without missing it too much."

"Do you like what you do for work?"

She paused and I saw the joy in her eyes falter for the

first time since sitting down for dinner. She took a sharp inhale in and dropped her head before giving me an uneasy half smile.

"I'm kind of just working odd jobs here and there, planning small parties and functions for people around the city. I used to work at an event hall downtown but left two years ago..." her voice trailed off. She wrapped her lips around her teeth and tucked a piece of hair that had fallen into her face behind her ear without looking at me. I got the sense that there was more to this story but I didn't want to pry.

"What about you? What do you do for work?" She perked up in her seat and looked at me expectedly, ready to change the subject.

"Oh, me? I work in security for one of my friends. He owns a big security firm that covers businesses and private residences around Charleston. He was nice enough to give me a job when I came home about a month ago." Her eyes beamed at me with admiration.

"I think that's so cool that he helped you out like that. Your friends seem really important to you."

"My friends are everything to me," I said earnestly, nodding my head. "They're like my family and have been since we met in third grade. Those guys are more like my brothers than my friends. They were there at my swearing in ceremony after I enlisted once we all graduated from high school."

That is a day I will never forget. How I stood at the front of the room standing next to several other kids my age and recited the Enlistment Oath back to the officer standing before us. How, when I turned around, I saw my three best friends standing in the pews with proud smiles. How they all drove me to the bus stop and dropped me off as I left for bootcamp and we all pretended to not be crying when we all actually were.

"That's really special. Your parents weren't there?" She reached across the table and tucked her hands into mine. I tried to not laugh too loud as she asked the question.

"No. My dad wasn't there and I wouldn't want him there anyway." The words tasted bitter on my tongue as memories from my childhood started to float to the surface of my brain.

"What about your mom? Is she not in the picture?" I could tell she was trying to be delicate, but I had learned quickly over the last few hours that this girl wanted to know everything about you if she could.

"My mom passed away when I was nine. It's just been my dad and I ever since." Thinking about my mom always put a sour taste in my mouth but I tried my best to not sound angry. My mother wasn't around because of my shit-hole of a father and I had never forgiven him for it. Bailey squeezed my hands tighter in hers and rubbed the backs of them with her thumbs.

"I'm really sorry, soldier."

After a while, we decided to head out and I helped her back into her helmet and my leather jacket before we took my bike back over the bridge. She scootched her hips forward on the seat, making her entire body flush with mine, and it took everything in me to not come in my pants. Even with her back in her sweats and sneakers, feeling her pelvis pressed against me almost had me completely undone.

I walked her back to the front door of her condo and we stood facing each other for an awkward moment in the hall-way. I wanted to kiss her goodnight, but I didn't want to be too forward. *Stop being such a chicken shit and just do it. You've kissed a girl before, just do it!*

"I had a really good time with you tonight, blondie." My hands were shoved in my pockets as I looked down at my shoes, my nerves so high that I could hardly look at her. If there was going to be an end of night kiss, now would be the time to make it happen.

"Thanks for taking me out. I had a really good time too." She leaned down and caught my eyes with hers, a playful smile on her face, and we both laughed at the palpable awkwardness between us. *Come on man, kiss her. Do it now, she looks like she wants you too. Just do it!*

"Hey, soldier," she said in a hushed tone. I pulled my eyes up to look at her again as she took a step closer to me.

"Yeah, blondie?" My breath hitched in my throat as I spoke, because as I did, her hands reached out to grab either sides of my jacket and pulled me into her.

"Are you always this shy?" she whispered, bringing her face closer to mine. Her eyes flashed between mine and my lips. The smirk on her face was almost devilish.

"Only with women as beautiful as you."

I'd hardly finished speaking when she pulled me in with a sharp tug and pressed her lips to mine. I wrapped a hand around the side of her neck and gently pulled her closer to me, not wanting any distance between us. My other hand found her waist and held her where she stood. I had kissed women before, but none of them even remotely compared to kissing her.

The way her lips felt on mine, it was as if a missing piece of me had finally been found.

When we pulled away from each other, she ran her thumb along the bottom of my lip, wiping off the small amount of lip gloss that had rubbed off on my chin. She giggled and pressed her other hand to the side of my face.

"It's a good thing I don't mind 'em shy." She smiled at me and turned away to unlock her front door. My heart sank knowing that my time with her was coming to an end. It felt too soon and I wasn't ready for it to be over yet.

"Hey, blondie?"

"Yeah, soldier?" She turned around before opening her door and faced me again. With her back facing the door, I summoned up enough courage to reach my hand around her neck and pull her in for another kiss. I needed to taste her lips on mine one more time before the night was over. I needed another taste to tie me over until the next time I got to do this.

If there would be a next time.

When I pulled away from her, her face was frozen in stunned silence. While she seemed surprised by my sudden act of courage, she also didn't seem upset that I'd kissed her. She almost looked....intrigued.

"I'd really like to take you out again if you'll let me." My hand was still holding her face close to mine, our breath mixing together between our faces.

"I would very much enjoy it if you did." Her lips pulled back into her signature smile that always made my heart skip a beat. I was quickly starting to get an endorphin hit every time she blessed me with one of them.

"I'll call you." I swiped my thumb across her cheek before taking a step away from her.

"Will I see you at the gym tomorrow?" she asked, opening up her front door at last.

"Bright and early, just like always." I waved and watched her close the door, waiting to hear the click of the lock before walking towards the elevator.

As it took me down to the lobby, I replayed the kiss in my head over and over again on a loop.

Not only had I taken her out to dinner, on my bike, and kissed her, but I'd also gotten her to say yes to another date with me.

When I reached my bike, I pulled the leather jacket out of the saddlebag and slipped it on. Not that I needed it over my other jacket, but because I wanted to feel close to her. As I zipped it up, I didn't miss the familiar scent that I was starting to long for.

Vanilla and honey. Sweet and soft.

Just like the girl I knew I was falling for, hard and fast.

12

HANK

Hey soldier

Bailey's text came in right before I was about to head to lunch. It was Tuesday already and I've wanted to text her several times since our date on Saturday. There were multiple times over the last two days that I had picked up my phone, opened a new message, typed something, then deleted it. We'd seen each other at the gym the last few mornings and I waved to her when I caught her looking at me, but beyond that, we hadn't really spoken.

Why are you being such a dicklicker about this? I'd thought to myself several times. I wasn't normally like this with women but something about this one was throwing me off my game. My brain struggled to string together any logical thought when it came to her. I smiled at my phone, grateful she had taken the initiative. Again. Just like she did with our kiss on Saturday. The kiss that I had been replaying in my head ever since it happened.

I focused on my phone again, pulling my brain away

from the thoughts of her plump, pink lips on mine, and texted her back.

> Hey blondie.

Are you ever going to call me?

This girl doesn't hold back any punches, does she?

> Who's to say I wasn't going to call you today? You could be stealing my thunder again.

I was starting to think you didn't have enough thunder in you to ask...again 😜

Would you like to get a drink with me tomorrow?

She added the second text before I could even recover from her jab.

I thought about her offer. It was Tuesday, meaning tomorrow was Wednesday, which meant it was campaign night. The guys would kill me if I canceled on them since we had just started this campaign a few weeks ago and were still laying the storyline. But I wanted to see her. Hell, I was starting to feel like I needed to see her for my own survival. There was this undeniable pull between us and having not been close to her in a few days, my body was starting to physically ache.

> How about I do you one better. Let's meet tonight if you can?

I would love that 😊

Does 6:30 work?

She sent her response back quickly. A smile formed on my face knowing I was going to get to see her sooner than I thought I would when I woke up this morning.

> 6:30 it is. I'll pick you up then.

> You don't have to pick me up, soldier, I can meet you wherever you want to meet.

> I'm picking you up, don't argue.

There was no way I was "meeting her there". A true gentleman picked up his girl from her house and took her out. This "meeting you there" bullshit was not something I would be participating in. Especially with her.

> Okay then, if you really want to, you can pick me up.

> I'll see you tonight at 6:30.

> You'll see me tonight at 6:30.

> Hey blondie?

I sent the message off quickly before my courage disappeared.

> Yeah?

> I can't wait to see you again.

> I can't wait to see you either :)

———

Right on the dot and as promised, I knocked on her door at six thirty. After we settled on drinks tonight, I'd looked up bars around her place so we wouldn't need to drive anywhere. I didn't want her to have to repeat the wardrobe change if she decided to wear a dress again. And damn was I hoping she would be wearing a dress again. The way her legs looked in the last one set me on edge in the best way possible.

After knocking once, I'd waited for a minute or so and started to wonder if she'd forgotten about our plans when she didn't answer the door. *Okay don't panic, just knock again and see if she didn't hear you the first time.* My hand reached towards the door again and knocked, a little harder than I had the first time.

"Hold on a second, I hear you!" I heard her call from behind the door along with the sound of a loud crash and things falling to the floor.

"Bailey, are you okay?" I leaned into the door and shouted through it, slightly worried that she had fallen and was hurt. I was about to reach for the door handle and see if it was unlocked when it swung open.

"Holy shit." She was standing in the door frame panting, a wide smile growing on her face. Behind her an entire bookshelf was toppled over and books were strewn all over the floor.

"That thing just tried to kill me." Her thumb jabbed behind her, motioning to the fallen bookshelf.

"What the hell are you doing in here, blondie? Are you trying to hurt yourself?" My voice came out more concerned than I was anticipating. I stepped past her into her place without an invitation and studied the damage.

"Actually, that's *exactly* what I was trying to do. I intentionally pulled the thing down while I was running to open the door just to try and scare you." She jabbed me playfully in the arm as she came to stand next to me and I tried to ignore the feeling it created in my jeans. "The thing is super old, I found it on the curb one day and brought it home. Ophelia's been telling me we need to mount it to the wall, and now I can tell her she was right." She tried to laugh it off but I didn't find her closeness to being crushed by a bookshelf funny at all.

"Don't play, blondie. You could have gotten hurt. I'm glad you didn't." My hand reached out towards her and landed on her lower back instinctually. Her brilliant blue eyes met mine and her cheeks turned a slight shade of pink when I let my hand linger in the spot a little longer than comfortable.

"How about I help you clean this up and then we go get those drinks?"

"I would appreciate that very much, thank you." She gave me a small smile before stepping away from my hand towards the fallen books. My fingers missed her as soon as she was gone.

As I helped her clean up the books, I looked around her place. The space was nice and modern, nothing like my completely average apartment that was north of the city. There was a full kitchen, two bedrooms, and a large living room that I could see from where we were. It was clear that women occupied the space because it smelled like vanilla and lavender. The vanilla I recognized, but the lavender was new to me.

"Nice place you've got here." I lifted the bookshelf off the floor and set it upright against the wall.

"Thanks, it's not mine. My friend owns it and is letting me live with her while I figure some stuff out." She itched her forehead and sounded embarrassed.

"Well you two have a very nice place." I smiled at her and she handed me some books to put back on the shelves.

"So, how did this thing fall down?" She was sitting on her knees collecting books and handing them to me so I could return them to their rightful home.

"Well, I was in my room reading while I waited for you to get here. Then you knocked but I was at a really good spot and I wanted to finish my page, so I tried to hurry up and finish reading. Then I guess I took too long because you knocked again. I didn't want you to think I was blowing you off, so I raced out of my room and in the process of turning the corner, completely slammed into the bookshelf. Then it fell down and then I opened the door, and now we're here picking up my mess." Her face was warped into an expression that resembled a small child who had just been caught doing something they weren't supposed to do. I barked out a laugh because the image of her running out of her room to open the door, just to knock over an entire bookshelf in the process, was comical to me.

"What were you reading that had you so enthralled?" I asked as she handed me the last few books and I placed them back on the shelf. I reached my hand towards her to help her stand.

"Something hot and steamy." A wicked smile spread across her face as I pulled her up. She stood only a few inches away from me, our chests nearly touching, and it took everything in me not to grab her face and pull it into mine.

"You read hot and steamy books?" My eyes flickered between her lips and her gaze.

"It's the only thing I read." She licked her lips before chewing on her bottom one. The growing sensation in my jeans was almost hard to ignore at this point.

"Let's go get those drinks." She broke the tension that was building between us by stepping away and walking towards the kitchen island. She grabbed her bag that was sitting on the counter and turned to look at me. I was frozen where I stood and trying to recover from what she'd just told me.

It's the only thing I read. I made a mental note to figure out where to buy whatever kinds of books were considered "hot and steamy".

"You comin'?" Her head cocked to one side and her blonde hair fell in the same direction. Her cheeks were pressed into her eyes as she smiled at me, reaching her hand out for me to take.

"Yep. Let's go get those drinks." I reached for her hand and took it, our fingers intertwined. As we walked back towards the door, she pulled me closer to her and planted a kiss on my cheek.

"Thanks for helping me clean up my mess. That was really sweet of you." She looked at me for a beat and before I could respond or kiss her back, she pulled me through her front door.

I knew this girl was soft and sweet, but I had just learned she had some spice in her as well.

And that was a side of her I wanted to see more of.

13

BAILEY

W hen we got to the bar, Hank's hand rested on the small of my back as we walked through the space looking for an open table. The strength of his hand brought me a sense of safety and groundedness I hadn't felt in a long time. When we found a spot to sit down, he pulled my chair out for me and helped me into it, just like a true Southern gentleman. Sitting across from me, I studied his face while he ordered his drink.

His jaw was strong and cut at a sharp angle, making him look fierce and intimidating. It made me smile to myself because if you knew him, you knew he was a big softy and very, very shy. At least around me he was. I loved how, even though his hair was cut shorter, his curls couldn't be stopped. They were tamed and mild, but still noticeable when you looked close enough. His caramel toned skin gave him a warm presence and you could tell he worked out by the way his clothes wrapped around him. I squeezed my thighs together as I started to think about how it would feel if I were wrapped around his body.

He watched as I ordered my drink and gave me an inquisitive glance when I ordered a mocktail instead of something with alcohol in it.

"I thought you asked to get drinks?" His eyebrows furrowed together in the center of his handsome face.

"I got a drink. A drink is a drink even if it doesn't have any alcohol in it," I pointed out. He gave me a small nod, succeeding to my point.

"Do you not drink?"

"I do, but not very often and usually only when I'm home." I wanted to move away from this topic as fast as possible. I had my reasons for not wanting to drink but I wasn't ready to share those reasons with him yet.

"Fair enough." I could tell he still had questions but was nice enough to not push the subject any further. His phone was sitting on the table and started to buzz as our server came back with our drinks. He flipped it over, checked the message quickly, and set it back down without answering it.

"How's your week been?" I took a sip of my drink and glanced at his phone when it buzzed again. He didn't pick it up this time and answered my question.

"It's been fine. Like I told you at dinner, I work for my friend's security firm overseeing a team that covers high-profile events, celebrities who come to town, things like that. We have some summer festivals coming up we are working to plan and get organized for—" He stopped mid-sentence to turn over his phone that was nearly exploding on the table at this point.

"Someone's popular," I chuckled, finding amusement in how frustrated he looked looking at his phone.

"It's my stupid friends," he sighed, looking at his phone quickly. I could tell he was trying not to be rude by being on his phone.

"Is everything okay? You can reply if you want, it's okay."

"Yeah, everything's fine, they're just talking about our campaign tomorrow night." As soon as he said it, his eyes widened and he looked at me. Almost as if he'd said too much or shared something he didn't want to share. The hue of his cheeks turned a slight shade of pink.

"What do you mean, *campaign*?" I gave him a smirk and leaned over the table towards him.

He let out a sigh and took a pull of his drink before speaking again.

"You promise not to laugh?" His eyebrows were raised and he looked at me nervously.

"I promise. Cross my heart and all that jazz." I ran my finger across my chest and loved how his eyes lingered on it for a few seconds too long. He let out another deep breath before speaking.

"My friends and I, all the guys you met at the bar last time, we meet up every Wednesday and play Dungeons and Dragons. It's something we did growing up until I left for bootcamp. We started back up around the same time I came home. It's how we make sure we see one another, hangout, blow off steam, you know." He took another pull from his drink. "Some guys get together and play cards or watch football. My friends and I get together, play Dungeons and Dragons, and drink beer."

I couldn't help but let out a small laugh once he had finished explaining. Not because I thought his Wednesday night plans were lame or stupid, but because I loved how much it clearly mattered to him. Here was a guy who was an ex-soldier, went to the gym every morning for at least an hour, worked at a high-intensity security firm, but was spending his evenings playing board games with his friends.

Hank Martínez was a total nerd and I kind of loved it.

"You told me you wouldn't laugh," he teased. I felt his hand shake my knee under the table as he gave me a face.

"I'm not laughing at you, I swear. I'm laughing at how cute I think you are. This thing with your friends clearly matters to you. I think that's really endearing. Most men don't have strong friendships as adults. I love that you do." I held his hand under the table and swiped my thumb across the back of it, drawing small circles with it.

"They might be idiots, but they're my best friends. More like my brothers." He pulled his hand away from mine and rubbed the back of his neck.

"I think that's amazing. I love that you have them. And I love that you get together every week. Tell me more about this game, I've heard of it before but I don't know much about it." I took a sip of my drink and straightened up in my seat, ready to learn anything and everything about his Wednesday night ritual.

"You don't have to be nice, I know you probably don't care that much." He gave me an incredulous look.

"Uh, yeah I do. I wouldn't ask if I didn't wanna know." How dare he question my interest?

After studying me for a beat, he dove into explaining the ins and outs of Dungeons and Dragons. I had no idea how involved it was. I'd heard of it before, but Hank and his friends took it to the next level. They all had their own characters, they made up new storylines, and he told me they would sometimes play for up to four hours at a time. I couldn't even think about the last thing that kept my attention for more than forty-five minutes.

"So, do you like, use funny voices when you play?" I teased. At this point, we had been at the bar for almost two hours and had both had several drinks. He was on his third beer while I was still sticking to strictly alcohol free mocktails.

"Uh," he laughed, "yeah, sometimes. It's not normally me who does, but Conrad has been known to pull out a voice every now and then." The way he spoke about his friends made my heart swell.

"I love that. I think the relationship you have with your friends is sweet." I set my chin in my hand and propped it up on the hightop.

"Yeah, they're good guys." I watched him get lost in a thought as he finished his drink. When he set it down on the table, his eyes met mine.

"Do you want another one?" he asked, looking at my empty glass.

"No, I think I'm good."

"You wanna get out of here then?" His eyes burned into mine as we held each other's gaze.

"Sure, let's go." We both stood at the same time and he reached his arm toward me to pull me closer to him. I watched as he threw some cash on the table and as we walked through the bar, he kept his hand on the small of my back just like he had before. There was an ever present protective energy about him that I could feel as I walked closely next to him.

After exiting the bar and heading back down the street towards my apartment, Hank suddenly pulled me around the corner of a building and into a small alley. For the briefest of moments, my mind flashed to a different time that I had been pulled into a dark alley, just like this one. My eyes squeezed shut as the sound of my cries rang in my ears and I felt my body tense up as the weight of a stranger held me down. My heart started to race and my breath was starting to catch in my throat when the sound of his concerned voice pulled me back to reality.

"Hey, are you okay?" When I opened my eyes and they focused, I realized that his arms framed my face and my back was against the wall. I glanced around the alley, realizing where I was and who I was with and could feel my body started to relax again.

"Yeah, I–I'm okay." My hands found his ribcage and pulled him closer. I wanted to feel his body on mine. I needed the protective energy I felt with him to surround me.

"Are you sure? I didn't mean to scare you." His voice was steeped with concern and the look on his face mirrored that of someone who had just harmed a small child.

"It's okay, you didn't scare me. You just surprised me is all," I lied. It wasn't that he'd scared me, but the move reminded me of a different time that fear had taken over my entire body. A time where fear and hopelessness were all I felt.

"A good kind of surprise I hope?"

"A very good kind of surprise." My voice was low and my eyes flashed between his eyes and his lips. I wanted him to kiss me. I needed to know that feeling once more.

He paused for half a second before he finally pressed his lips to mine. When our lips met, all the memories that were fighting for a space in my head disappeared. I leaned into him and he pushed back into me. It was as if we couldn't get close enough to one another, our tongues clashing together like waves off the shore. My hands grabbed at his shirt, pulling him closer, and with no effort at all, he looped his arms under my legs and hoisted me up in his arms. He held me there, between his abdomen and the wall as I wrapped my legs around his center. When he pressed against me, I could feel him through his jeans. A sudden heat washed between my legs and I coiled my legs around him even harder. I loved how his hands wrapped around the side of my neck and held me in place. He was strong but soft, a shy man finally taking his shot. And he was doing it like a pro.

He held me against the wall without wavering until someone walking by noticed us and whooped. We both laughed into each other's mouths, breaking away from each other just long enough to catch our breath. I loved how his eyes were all fire and passion, that he wanted this as much as I did. He dropped his forehead to meet mine and took a breath.

"Should I put you down now?" He leaned in and kissed my neck, sending a shot of lightning down my spine.

"Not unless you want to," I played.

"Do you want me to?" He kissed the other side of my neck.

"Mmmm no." I laughed as he nipped at my ear.

"Then we can stay like this forever."

"I don't think my legs can manage that." I laughed into his neck. My thighs were starting to burn from holding myself between Hank and the wall.

"Alright, let's put you down then." When my feet reached the ground, his hand met my chin and tipped it up to look at him. A small smile was spread across his face and the way he looked at me changed something inside of me forever.

It was as if he saw me for everything I was, but didn't mind all the things I lacked.

"I just need you to know, I think you're the most beautiful girl I've ever seen. Thank you for coming out with me tonight." He leaned in and kissed me softly, a stark difference from the hard and passionate makeout session we'd just shared.

"You make me feel like the most beautiful girl. Thanks for taking me out tonight and telling me about your friends. I hope that I can get to know them more. I hope I can get to know you more."

"I think we can make that happen," he promised before pulling me out of the alleyway.

He walked me home, hand in hand the entire way, and once he dropped me off, I couldn't wait for another chance to see him again.

14

HANK

"**A**lright boys, settle in."

We were all sitting around the now familiar dining room table once again for another week of gameplay. Somehow I'd made it through the work day without any major issues seeing as how my brain couldn't focus on much of anything other than what had happened last night. The feeling of her lips still lingered on mine and I could smell the scent of her hair as if she were still pressed against me.

After getting back to my apartment last night, I'd taken a shower and gotten myself off at the thought of her legs wrapped around me and what I'd imagine she'd feel like against me in bed. I thought about how her blonde hair would fall behind her as she rode me, her back arching and how she would sound as she moaned out my name. The thought of my cock inside of her, feeling the tightness of her around it sent me over the edge quickly. I hadn't been laid in a long time so it didn't take much to get me off. After cleaning myself up in the shower, I fell asleep thinking about her, wondering when I would get to see her again.

"Hank, brother, you listening?" Kolbi's hand landed on my shoulder and gave it a shake. "You good dude?"

"Yeah, why wouldn't I be?" I blinked a few times and looked at my friends who were all staring at me.

"You had some stupid fucking look on your face, that's why," Malcolm chuckled at me with a devious expression.

"I did not." I took a sip of my beer and shifted in my seat. My friends knew Bailey and I had gone out last week, but I hadn't told them about last night.

"Yeah, you actually did. It looked like this." Conrad made a face that was a cross between someone having a seizure and someone taking a massive shit. *Did I really look like that when I thought about her?* My other two friends busted out laughing at his impression of me.

"You guys are fucking assholes. Can we play now please?" I looked at Kolbi as he was the Dungeon Master and controlled the game. He gave me a small nod and started weaving tonight's story.

We were deep in the throws of playing when I felt my phone buzz in my pocket. While we had a strict no phone rule while playing, I needed to know if the reason my phone was buzzing was because a pretty blonde was texting me. I pulled it out of my pocket just enough to see the screen and smiled to myself when I read the notification.

1 New Message: Blondie

I played my turn and waited for the guys to be talking before reading the message. Holding my phone at my waist, I read her text.

BLONDIE:

Hey, soldier. I know you're with your friends right now, but I can't stop thinking about last night. I hope we can have a repeat sometime soon 😉

The winking emoji in her message immediately set me on edge.

I would love a repeat. I can't stop thinking about it either.

I sent it off quickly, trying to fight the smile I felt growing on my lips, and slid my phone back into my pocket. When I looked up, three sets of eyes were locked on me.

"It's back," Kolbi said.

"The stupid fucking look," Malcolm added.

"This boy is so fucked," Conrad finished.

My three best friends all started laughing in unison. I chewed on the inside of my lip to stop from scowling. I wasn't in the mood for a ball-busting tonight. Not from them.

"Who's the girl Hanky? Is it that hot blonde chick from the bar?" Malcolm took a swig of his beer.

"She's not *'some chick'* Malcolm. You might go through women as if they're dirty napkins, but not all of us are like that. Some of us care enough to treat them like real people."

"So it *is* a girl." Kolbi gave me a knowing look. He was always like the big brother of our group and the tone of his voice made that clear.

"Yes, it's a girl. We're moving on now." I reached for the die and started to roll when Malcolm reached across the table and grabbed it out of my hand.

"Oh, no, Hanky boy, we are not moving on from this so quickly. Tell us. What's happening there?" Malcolm crossed his arms in front of himself, the die tucked away in his fist, and leaned back in his chair staring at me. I looked around the table and all three of my friends were waiting for me to speak. I took a deep breath and let it out slowly.

I guess I was telling them after all.

"Nothing is 'happening there'. We went out last night, we had drinks. It was a good time. That's all." *And that's all I'm telling you fuckers. That's all you're getting.*

"And?"

"And what?" I looked at Malcolm since he had asked the question.

"And," he started, "Did you finish the deal? Were you man enough to get her naked? Tell us what she looked like." He waggled his eyebrows at me and I wanted to punch the smirk off his face. I loved Malcolm, but his style was not the same as mine. He loved women, we all knew that. But he would love them and leave them before they even knew what happened.

"Malcolm, come on man," Kolbi sighed.

"What? I wanna know if our Hanky here was man enough to get her in the sack. It's been a long time, I assume? Since you've gotten any?" Malcolm was the only one at the table who laughed.

"Malcolm, don't be an ass," Conrad chastised.

"What? How am I being an ass?" Malcolm shrugged his shoulders and looked around the table. Kolbi was shaking his head and Conrad was rolling his eyes. We loved Malcolm, but he sometimes pushed things a little too far.

"You're being a dick, dude. Stop," Kolbi scolded.

"Whatever man. I was just bustin' his balls. Do whatever you want Hank, sleep with her or don't sleep with her. What the fuck do I care." He rolled his eyes and tossed the die he was holding hostage back onto the board, annoyed that my other two friends hadn't joined him in trying to get me to talk.

"Can we just focus on the game, please?" I don't know why I was being so secretive. These guys were my best friends, my chosen brothers. I could tell them about Bailey and it wouldn't be a big thing. Part of me knew that, but another part of me wanted to keep what we had just between us. I liked Bailey. A lot. More than I had liked any other girl I'd been with. And there was something about her that I wanted to keep to myself.

I wanted her to be mine. Only mine.

And for now, I intended to keep it that way.

15

BAILEY

I was laying on my stomach on my bed, book in hand with my hair pulled back into a messy bun, when I felt my phone buzz under me. Normally by this point in the day I would be asleep, but my book had sucked me in and I couldn't put it down. The sexy cowboy had come home to realize he loved the girl and was racing to stop her from getting married to the douchebag from the city.

These books were always so overdone and dramatic, but I loved every single one of them. I'm weak for small town romance stories and this one had all my favorite things. Cowboys, spicy sex scenes that only ever happened in books, and the happily ever after you could only ever dream about. Nothing about these books were real, and I was okay with that. Sometimes you just need to escape to another world for a few hours and get lost in someone else's drama to feel better about your own.

My hand searched around my bed while my eyes kept reading the romantic love confession and when I got to the part where she says 'I've always loved you,' I had to wipe a small tear away from my eye. Finally, I looked at my phone and smiled at the notification.

<u>1 New Message: Soldier</u>

My thumb swiped across the screen quickly so I could read the message.

> Hey, blondie. I don't know if you're still up, but I figured I would see. I just wanted to let you know I've been thinking about you since you texted me earlier.

I looked at the time and realized it was almost midnight. Damn, this book had really sucked me in.

> Hey, yeah I'm still up. Currently crying in my bed but it's fine.

> What's wrong? Are you okay? Did something happen?

> Did the bookshelf fall on you this time?

He sent the second text quickly after the first and I couldn't help but chuckle to myself. This man, so protective, so concerned for my well being. I thought it was sweet.

> Calm down soldier, I'm fine. I'm just finishing a book and it's making me weepy. Did you just get done playing?

> Yeah we did, we just got done at Kolbi's. His place is a few streets over from yours...

The ellipses intrigued me. Was this boy trying to ask me something? If he was, I wasn't going to make it easy on him.

> Oh yeah? Is there a reason you're sharing that tidbit of information with me?

I watched as the three dots danced across the screen and chewed on my lip as I waited for him to send his reply, hoping that I was reading his signals the right way. I had texted him earlier with the hopes that I'd get to see him again this week, but if he wanted to see me tonight, I wouldn't tell him no.

> Well, and I know it's late so I totally get it if you aren't interested, but I was wondering if you would wanna get together tonight?

I flipped to my back and kicked my feet in the air.

> Get together, huh? I don't know, it *is* kind of late.

I was totally fucking with him but I wanted to see what he would say.

> Oh, okay never mind then. We can just get together later or something.

Oh my god boys are so dumb. Sometimes we wanna be fought for, why don't they understand this?

> Wait!!! I'm just messing with you. When can you pick me up?

He responded in less than three seconds.

> I'm outside.

My eyes grew into saucers when I read his text and I flew out of my bed. Ophelia was already asleep with her door closed, so I tried to make it across the condo as quietly as I could. My hand reached for the door quickly, but before I pulled it open, I took a breath. I didn't want him to think I was overly excited to see him, even though I was.

I was *very* excited to see him.

When I pulled open the door, there he stood. Just over six feet, Hank was as handsome as they come. He was wearing black tailored sweats and a perfectly-fit white T-shirt, a staple in his wardrobe I had come to realize. It looked like he had just run his fingers through his hair because some of his curls were sticking out every which way. His shy smile made my heart race and I wanted nothing more than to press my lips to it.

"Hi," I whispered, trying not to be too loud in the hallway.

"Hey, blondie," he whispered back, leaning in with his hands behind his back. "I like your pj's."

I looked down and realized that I was wearing pajama shorts that had sleeping cats wearing Santa hats on them. They were my favorite sleep shorts, and in my excitement to see him, I didn't even think about what I looked like before opening the door. Thankfully, I was also wearing an over-sized, buttoned sleep shirt that covered up the fact that I wasn't wearing a bra. I crossed my arms over my chest reflexively.

"Oh you like those huh?" *Play it cool girl. You don't need to be embarrassed. Your ass looks great in these shorts.* His eyes scanned me top to bottom and licked his lips.

"They're very cute. I like the cats," he softly laughed.

"Here, come inside." I reached for his arm and pulled him in, before gently closing the front door. I pressed my finger to my lips and pointed towards the closed door across from my room. Once I had led him through the condo and into my bedroom, I closed the door behind us.

"Sorry for dropping in so late," he said, rubbing the back of his neck.

"Don't be. I was hoping I could see you again." I crawled onto my bed and sat cross-legged. I watched hesitantly as he took in my room and suddenly felt self-conscious. I'd never had a boy in this room since moving in with Ophelia. Shit, I hadn't been with a boy since that night two years ago. I wanted him here, but part of me was still uneasy having him here. I'd dated in the last two years, but hadn't let it go any further than dinner or drinks.

You're safe. Just breathe. He isn't going to hurt you.

He walked over to my vanity and picked up the frame that sat on it. It held a photo of Ophelia and me on the night we'd met. We had become instant friends that night and had asked a stranger to take our photo. I never expected to be living with her now.

But life had dealt me a tough hand, and it was Ophelia who'd stepped up to help me play it.

"I like this photo," he said, his calloused finger tracing around my photographed face, smiling, "It shows off your hundred-watt smile."

Between the spicy book, this boy showing up at my door late at night because he wanted to see me, and his sweet words, I could feel my body starting to get keyed up. I smiled at him and squeezed my thighs together, hoping he wouldn't notice when I did.

"You think I have a hundred-watt smile?"

He looked at me and grinned from a few feet away. "It's the first thing I noticed about you. Well, after I noticed that you read between sets while you workout." He walked across the room and sat on my bed next to me.

"Oh yeah? What else did you notice about me?" Never in my life had a man complimented my smile, not to mention something about me other than what my body looked like. Most men only ever noticed your boobs or your ass. But not Hank. He'd noticed my smile and the fact that I read.

"Mmm...I noticed how kind you are to everyone around you so long as they're kind to you. And how you aren't afraid to stick up for yourself if you need to." He turned so that he was facing me on the bed. His eyes flicked back and forth between my eyes and my lips.

"And I noticed how, when I took you to dinner, you paid attention when I was talking. You were interested in what I had to say and you asked questions. You were the same way last night, like you genuinely cared about what I was saying." His voice was growing husky and he was leaning in closer to me. I leaned in right along with him.

"That's because I *do* genuinely care about what you say. I think you're fascinating." Our faces were inches from one another as he spoke again.

"And last night, I noticed how you wrapped your legs around me, and how, as soon as I put you down, I missed the way they felt. I missed the way you felt against me. I don't know what it is about you, but when you're not next to me, I feel like a piece of me is missing."

I sucked in a breath.

"I hope that's not too forward." He dropped his head and I reached out my hand to frame the side of his face so he would look at me. For the first time, I noticed the deep brown color of his eyes, and how, when you looked closely, you could see flecks of ember dancing in them.

"It's not too forward," I pulled his face towards mine and closed the gap between us, "because when you're not with me, I feel the exact same way. Like a piece of me is missing."

I'd hardly gotten my words out when I felt his lips crash into mine.

And for the first time in almost two years, I let a man make me his.

16

HANK

I couldn't hold myself back from her for another minute.

Hearing her say she felt the same way I did pushed all of the worries out of my head. As I pressed my lips to hers, she met me with a force. She was nothing short of a wild spark running rampant in a dry brush. What she wanted, she got. And right now, she wanted me.

And I wanted her right back.

She held my face to hers with both hands as our lips crashed into one another. Our kisses were reminiscent of the ones we shared last night, but these ones felt deeper, more connected. Now that there was no question about how we felt about one another, there was no hesitation in acting on those feelings. I loved how her hands felt on my face, soft yet strong.

Just like my Bailey.

She pulled me in tighter and unraveled her crossed legs, inviting me to move closer. I looped one arm behind her back and slowly laid her down, bringing myself to rest gently on top of her. Holding myself up on one elbow, I brushed the hair that had fallen into her eyes out of the way. I didn't want anything blocking my view of her perfect, deep blue eyes. I wanted to see her looking back at me as we became one for the first time.

"You know this isn't why I came here tonight, right?" I nudged her face to one side with my chin so I could kiss her exposed neck. She sucked in a breath as my lips made contact with the soft spot behind her ear.

"It's okay if it is why you came here," she purred into my ear, setting my entire body on fire with just one sentence.

"Are you sure this is what you want?" I didn't want her to say no, but I also wanted to make sure we were on the same page. I believed in getting consent no matter what.

She hesitated slightly before saying, "I want this. I want you. Make me yours, Hank."

She didn't need to ask me twice.

I pushed back on my knees and lifted my shirt from my head, tossing it onto the floor. She watched as I stripped it off and my pride inflated when I watched her eyes grow with pleasure. Between my years of military training and my daily workouts, I was in the best shape of my life. Her fingers reached up and trailed down my torso, feeling every single muscle on the way down.

"Damn, soldier, I'm going to need your ab workout so I can get me some of these," she smirked as lust filled her eyes. The fact that she thought she was anything short of perfect already made me a heat rise in my core. Leaning down, I wrapped one hand around the side of her neck and stopped just before my lips met hers again.

"You're already perfect just the way you are, hermosa[1].

---

1.   beauitful

Don't ever think you need to change anything about yourself."

"I don't know what that word meant but I like the sound of it." Her lips were pulled into a smile that showed off all her teeth. It was a smile I'd seen many times before and one I came to long for when she wasn't around. She wrapped her arms around me and pulled me in with desperation. Our bodies were already flush together, but it wasn't enough for her. It wasn't enough for me either.

Our lips clashed together as our hands explored one another's bodies freely for the first time. As her hands ran down my back, I felt her hesitate for the slightest instant when they brushed over the long scars that criss crossed my skin. They had faded over the years, but the welts could still be felt when you touched them. Not wanting to ruin the moment with an explanation, I quickly flipped her over so that she was on top of me. A small laugh escaped her lips when her hair fell from on top of her head and covered us both. She placed both hands on my chest and pushed herself up so she was sitting on my lap.

As she worked to tame her hair on the top of her head, my hands rested on her muscular thighs. I watched as her body reacted as my thumbs slipped under her shorts and grazed the thin fabric of the panties she wore underneath. Once her hair was tied up, she gave me a coy look and started to undo the small white buttons that held her shirt closed. My cock was now standing at attention and my mouth started to water as I watched her undo each button at a painfully slow pace. Once the last one was undone, she looked at me and waited. All I could see was a small strip of flesh that ran from the hem of her shorts all the way up to her neck.

"Well, soldier," she started, desire dripping from her words, "you gonna take this off of me or what?"

I looked up at the woman who had come into my life just a few weeks ago and wondered how we had gotten here so quickly. The girl I spotted across the gym but was too chicken-shit to go up and say hello to. A woman I didn't even think I was good enough to be with in the first place, yet she was asking me to make her mine.

My Bailey.

My blondie.

Mi hermosa.[2]

I pulled myself up enough to slowly slip the shoulders of the shirt down her arms. When she pulled her arms from it, I tossed it onto the floor where my own shirt had been discarded. With my head resting on the pillow, I looked up and took in every beautiful inch of her my eyes could see. Her smooth, creamy skin. How her collarbone created a divet in her shoulder that I wanted to kiss. The way her waist came in to form a perfect hourglass shape. And her two perfectly shaped breasts. Not too big, but not too small, they formed a shape that my hands longed to feel. Her nipples were a soft pink color that I would remember forever.

"What do you think? You like what you see?" she asked playfully, but there was a hint of something else in her tone. Nervousness? Shyness? Whatever it was, I was going to make sure she never felt that way with me again.

"I think," my hand reached up and pulled her down so her chest was flush with mine once more, "you're perfect."

Feeling her exposed skin on my chest made me even harder than I was before. As we kissed, her hand ran from

---

2. My beautiful girl.

my chest all the way down to the hem of my sweats, gently tugging at them with her fingers. My own hands found her breasts and played with them softly, causing her breath to hitch in her throat. I swiped my thumbs across her nipples and I reveled in the sound that came from the back of her throat. My lips moved from hers and found the top of her shoulder, kissing any piece of flesh they could find. When her hand grabbed at my cock on the outside of my sweats while she bit my neck at the same time, a carnal noise escaped me.

"Someone's excited," I teased.

"Slip your hands somewhere lower and you'll see just how excited I am," she breathed.

I pulled her higher on top of me so I could reach her center. Her head was just above mine and her tits were right at eye level. I didn't want to go any longer without knowing what it felt like to consume her perfect body as my own. I brought my lips to one of her nipples and sucked the hard peak with my lips. She pressed herself up with one hand as the other roped itself through my hair. I loved how she pulled my curls harder every time I flicked her nipple with my tongue. My other hand slid down her stomach and slipped under her shorts. When my fingers reached her center, I discovered just how excited she was.

My girl was dripping.

She arched her back as my fingers slid back and forth along her center and moaned quietly as I continued to play with her breasts. Her breath was starting to labor and her head fell backwards. I loved the way the few stray pieces framed her face and how she looked on my lap as I took her this way. I continued to rub her pussy until I couldn't wait to know how it felt to be inside of her any longer. Slowly, I slipped one finger in, feeling her tighten around it as I did.

The sound of relief that came from her told me she had been waiting to know how it felt for me to have her this way too.

I pushed my finger back and forth, in and out, slowly edging her further.

"You like that, hermosa[3]?" I murmured into her ear.

"Yes...yes," she whispered back through labored breaths. Then, ever so slowly, I slid another finger deep within her and felt her quiver on top of me.

"I love how tight you feel around my fingers, it makes me desperate to know how you feel on my cock. I wanna know how that pretty pussy of yours feels as I sink myself inside of you." I had no idea where this version of me was coming from, I would never say these things normally. But something about her made me a different man. She pushed herself down and took my ear between her teeth.

"What's stopping you?" Her eyes were filled with desire and passion as they met mine.

"Not yet. I'm not done playing with you."

I pulled my fingers from her and looped my arms around her again to flip her on her back. When her head hit the pillow, I lowered myself down and gently started to pull the hem of her shorts lower. She lifted her hips as an invitation for me to remove them completely. I slipped the shorts and her panties off of her ankles carefully and tossed them onto the floor alongside our discarded shirts.

When I looked back at her, fully exposed in front of me, I saw a flash of panic cross over her face. I'd seen the look many times before on the battlefield when an ambush was starting or when citizens from far off places watched as armed soldiers rolled into their cities. You're trained to see

---

3. beautiful

this look as a soldier, because when there is panic, there is usually danger following closely behind it. She tried to cover her panic quickly, but I had seen it, and I needed to make sure she was okay.

"What's wrong?" I leaned down to cover her naked body with mine and brushed the loose strands of hair out of her face.

"Nothing, I'm fine, don't stop." Her eyes didn't meet mine and she chewed her bottom lip. When she tried to lift her hips to mine and went to kiss me, I pulled away to look at her.

"Bailey..." I encouraged.

She swallowed hard and pulled her eyes to look at me, defeat and embarrassment written all over her face. Her voice was so small and her eyes filled with shame and small tears. "There are things you don't know about me. And as much as I want this and you, I just don't know—"

"Hey." I didn't even let her finish her thought, because I needed her to know that if she wasn't ready for this, then I was okay with that. "It's okay, mi hermosa[4]." There was so much shame in her eyes and I wanted to do everything I could to erase it. To make her know that there is nothing to be ashamed of. Not with me. I brought my hand to the side of her neck and locked my eyes on her.

"There are things you don't know about me either," I promised. So many things she didn't know. Things I wasn't sure if I would ever be brave enough to tell her. But right now, I wanted her to know that she wasn't alone with whatever demons she was facing.

"Why don't we find your clothes and just hangout? We don't have to do anything more if you aren't ready." I pressed

---

4. my beautiful girl

my lips to the top of her forehead and felt her nod underneath them.

"Are you sure?" Her eyes were round and wide as they looked up at me and I used my thumb to wipe away a single tear that has fallen down her cheek.

"Of course I'm sure. You're safe with me, always. I promise I'll never hurt you."

"I trust you."

17

BAILEY

I blinked my eyes open when the sounds from the other side of my door brought me out of the best night of sleep I've had in over two years. My body was unusually warm and there was a heavy weight around my waist. My hands reached towards it and when I realized it was Hank's arm wrapped around me, the events of last night came back to me.

"You're safe with me, always. I promise I'll never hurt you."

"I trust you."

I do trust him.

For a man I only met a few weeks ago, I felt like I could trust him with so much of myself. And last night, when he didn't push me to go any further, I knew his promise was sincere. He had never struck me as the kind of guy to push any boundaries, but his suggestion to stop because he knew I wasn't ready surprised me. Not because I thought he was the kind of guy to get upset if he didn't get laid, but because I had never been with a guy who was perfectly fine not going any further after we'd already gotten past a certain point. The fear of blue balls was normally enough for a guy to need to keep going once things had gotten started.

The thing that surprised me most, though, was myself.

I hadn't been with a man since the night of my attack, but last night, I wanted to be with Hank. I didn't just want him, I was hungry for him. The way he looked at me with so much desire and care set my insides on fire. For such a reserved guy, he had a mouth on him and it turned me on something fierce. I thought I was going to pass out when he took his shirt off, exposing every fine line of muscle and ink that covered his torso. He called me 'mi hermosa[1]', which I made a mental note to look up later. I hadn't taken Spanish in school, so I had no idea what it meant. I loved the way it sounded but I loved the way it made me feel even more.

The arm wrapped around my waist pulled me closer to the body it was attached to and I gladly followed its command. I could hear him breathing softly behind me, his body keeping me warm. Carefully, I turned over so that I was facing him instead of facing away. After he handed me my clothes last night, he offered to head out so I could get some sleep.

"I thought we were going to hangout?" I had questioned. He was standing next to my bed as I slipped my clothes back on and once dressed, I pulled him towards me. I didn't want him to leave, I wanted him to stay.

"If you want me to stay, I'll stay," he said, slipping under the covers with me, possessively wrapping a strong arm around my body. I loved how his body shielded mine under the covers. We must have fallen asleep soon after because I don't remember anything after that.

Looking at him now, peacefully sleeping next to me, I

---

1. my beautiful girl

tried to commit every inch of his face to memory. His tan toned skin was darker than it had been a few weeks ago when I saw him for the first time—the summer sun giving him an almost golden look. He had long, dark lashes (why do men always get naturally long lashes?) and you could see all the laughs he had etched into fine lines around his eyes and mouth. My finger traced along his chin up his strong jawline and when my hand hit his hair, I gently ran my fingers through his dark curls. His breath was steady and slow and I twirled a rogue curl around my finger. I couldn't help but smile looking at him as his chest rose and fell with every breath.

Part of me wanted to slide my hand around his shoulder and down his back to confirm if what I felt there last night was real. It was too dark to see anything, but when my hands had explored his back, they discovered what felt like twenty or more deep scars carved into his skin. He hadn't let me feel them for long before he flipped me on top of him, cutting off my access. I was about to reach my hand towards the scarred skin when I heard Ophelia on the other side of my door.

"B? Are you still home? You aren't usually here still!" My eyes widened as I heard her footsteps nearing my room. I carefully slipped myself out from under his arm, trying not to wake him, and skipped toward my bedroom door. The doorknob was starting to turn as I reached for it and I quickly slipped myself through the door and pulled it closed behind me, coming face to face with her.

"Hi, Ophie," I gave her a big smile and tried to not seem nervous.

"Hi..." She gave me an incredulous look and studied me out of the corner of her eyes. "What are you still doing home? And why are you standing in front of your door like that?" My hands were tucked behind my back as I stood square in front of my door. I don't know why I was so nervous, it wasn't like I was doing anything wrong.

"Oh, I..." my eyes darted around, trying to come up with an explanation as to why I was still home. She and I rarely saw one another in the morning as I was typically at the gym when she left for work.

"Do you feel okay?" she asked.

"Yeah, I'm fine, never better actually." I tried to laugh but it came out as a hiccup, causing me to choke on my spit and start coughing uncomfortably.

"Oh, well good. I'm glad you're okay. Do you mind if I grab something from your closet? I think I hung my black blazer in there because I didn't have space in mine." She started to reach for the door and push past me.

"No, you can't," I nearly shouted at her and she jumped back.

"What the hell, B?"

I took a breath, bracing myself for the storm of questions that were about to be sent my way when I told her I snuck a boy into my room last night.

"You can't go in there."

"Why the hell not?" Her hands were on her hips as she studied me. I felt like a teenager who had just gotten caught sneaking in by her mother.

"Because....because there's a boy in there!" The words tumbled out of me. She gasped, surprised by my confession, and brought both hands to her mouth.

"Shut up! Who is it?" she hissed, a devilish grin growing on her face.

"Remember that guy from the gym and the bar?" I said it slowly, grimacing as I did.

Ophelia had been telling me for a year that I needed to

get back out there. Some would blush if they knew how many men she's been with. But as she says, "No one questions a man when he brings home a woman, why should a woman be treated any differently for doing the same thing?" I knew she would have a field day with me sneaking a boy into our condo and having him stay the night.

"You bagged the soldier? I'm so proud of you B!" She shook my shoulders with both hands.

"Shhh, you'll wake him up. And I did not bag the soldier, not really. I'll explain later, okay?" I wanted to slip back behind my bedroom door and snuggle in next to him before he woke up and heard us talking like this.

"Damn straight you will. Go, go be with your *man*." She wiggled her eyebrows at me. "But for real, once he's gone, check on that blazer for me. I want to wear it to a meeting tomorrow."

"Okay, sure, fine. I'll let you know." I smiled at her and turned to slip back into my room. Once the door was closed behind me, I took a quick breath. *I would just have to deal with her later.*

I crossed my room once again as quietly as I could, watching the sleeping man as I snuck back into bed. Once next to him, I carefully placed his arm back over my torso and snuggled into his warm, exposed chest. My eyes had just closed when he shifted slightly next to me.

"Why didn't you tell her you bagged the soldier?" His groggy voice startled me and I opened my eyes again to look at him. His eyes were still closed but he had a small smirk on his face.

"Oh my god, you heard that?" I burrowed my face into his chest to hide my embarrassment.

"I felt you missing as soon as you got out of bed. I knew

you were gone, I could feel it." He kissed me on the top of my head as my insides began to melt.

"Well I'm back now, let's go back to sleep." I looped an arm around him and pulled myself closer to him. I breathed in his scent and let his warm body encase me.

"I wish I could, mi hermosa[2], but I have work." He tightened his arms around me and rested his chin on my head. He was so close that I could hear his heart beating softly in his chest. A slight knock on my door caused us both to look towards it.

"Bye you two! B, I'll be back today for lunch in case you want to eat together. If you need any supplies you can find some in my nightstand. So happy for you, sweetie!" I wanted to die of embarrassment right then and there as the front door slammed shut, signaling my soon to be ex-best friend had finally left.

"Oh my gooooooood." I brought my hands to my face and covered it, rolling over on my back because I could no longer stand to face him in my embarrassment. Hank burst out laughing next to me.

"I can't believe her," I squealed. My hands covered my face as I spoke. He continued laughing next to me as he moved toward me again. This boy didn't seem to like being away from me if he could avoid it. He had one arm wrapped around my waist and brought his nose to my cheek.

"I like her, I think she's funny." He kissed me gently and pushed some loose hair away from my face.

"She's a lot and is in so much trouble when she gets home." I made a mental note to lecture her about being inappropriate when I saw her at lunch.

---

2. beautiful girl

"She reminds me of my friend Malcolm. He would do the same thing to me."

I looked at him.

"Yeah? Would Malcolm also tell you he was proud of you for getting laid? Because that's exactly what Ophie will do when she sees me later. It's embarrassing." I rolled my eyes at the thought.

"That's *exactly* what Malcolm would do. He doesn't believe me when I tell him how long it's been because it's never more than a week for him." I was shocked at his confession, both because of what he said about himself, but also because of how similar Malcolm sounded to Ophie. I scoffed and looked at him.

"Sounds like me and Ophie." We looked at each other for a beat, both of us studying the other.

"I'm really sorry for last night." I started to worry my bottom lip as my eyes dropped from his. I knew he was probably disappointed about our lack of a conclusion.

"*Bailey,*" his hand came to my chin and tipped it back so I had to look at him, "you never have to apologize for that. Ever. I will never pressure you to do anything you don't want to do. If you want to stop, we stop. You just tell me and I'll follow your lead. Got it?"

I was so taken back by the conviction in his voice that all I could do was nod.

"Good. Now," he brought his lips to mine and kissed me deeply, "I don't want to have to do this, but I do have to go. If I am late, my boss will ask me questions I don't want to have to answer. And since he's also my best friend, he will ask me questions that would probably get him sent to HR if we weren't friends and if he didn't own the entire company." He chuckled before pulling away from me and rolled out of bed.

I missed him as soon as he was no longer next to me.

He grabbed shirt that had been left on the floor overnight as I sat up in bed. I watched his muscles flex as he pulled it over his head and had to nearly roll my tongue back into my mouth. Between the tattoos and the muscles, I was suddenly warm all over.

"I like the way you're looking at me, blondie." His voice was low and he had a smirk on his face. He took a step toward the bed and leaned over it to bring his face next to mine. "I hope you always look at me like that. Like you wanna know what it feels like to have yourself wrapped around me, to have me deep inside of you, begging me for more." My breath caught in my throat at his words. *The mouth on this man.* He brought his hand to the side of my neck and pressed his lips to mine with a fury. I would have thought it hurt if I didn't like how it felt so much.

"Walk me out?" My brain was trying to reconnect itself after his kiss and I could only nod in response again.

We both walked out of my bedroom and when we reached my front door, I had the sudden need to feel him on me one more time before he left. Before he could open the door, I pressed him against it and brought my mouth to his. His hands found my back and he dipped down to loop them under my legs. Following his lead, I jumped up and wrapped my legs around him as he stepped away from the door. I let him slip his tongue into my mouth, loving the way he tasted. He carried me towards the kitchen and set me down on the counter. I kept my legs around his torso and tightened myself around him like a boa constrictor when he pressed his hips into me. With his hands on the counter, he leaned in further and I could feel how hard he was through his sweats. When he pressed his cock into my center, I let out a small whimper.

"You drive me crazy, Bailey Brown," he growled between kisses. I looped my hands through his curls and pulled his face closer to mine.

"I love driving you crazy, Hank Martínez." We kissed each other deeply a few more times before he pulled away and looked at me.

"I would stay here with you all day if I could, but I really have to go." My lip jutted out, disappointed that he had to leave. He chuckled at the face I gave him and tapped my lip with his index finger.

"It's okay, I get it. I have things around here I need to do anyway." It was a lie, I didn't have anything to do today as I wasn't needed at any of my current side gigs. Maybe I'll spend the morning looking for something more permanent. He helped me off the counter and I walked him towards the front door again.

"Thanks for opening the door last night," he said, looking down at me with his deep brown eyes.

"Thanks for coming to see me." I smiled at him and brought my hand to his cheek. He leaned into it when I did.

"I'll call you."

I nodded before he leaned down and kissed me again. When our lips met, I felt a tingle in my belly that I hadn't felt in a long time.

One that made it feel like a thousand butterflies had taken flight.

One that made me excited for his call.

But most importantly, one that made me feel safe and one that told me I could trust him with anything.

18

HANK

After running home to shower and change, I immediately hopped back on my bike to head downtown and try to make it into work before my absence was noticed too much. As I slipped in, I peered across the hall towards Kolbi's office to see if he was in yet, but it looked empty. I took a breath as I sat down at my desk to check in with my team, grateful that I had escaped the third-degree for being late. I had just started to go through my email, trying to act as if I didn't show up almost an hour late, when my best friend's voice came from behind me.

"Care to share why you were late this morning?" His voice came out low and smooth next to my head and I could feel his breath on the back of my neck.

"Jeezus dude." I flinched in my seat. "Don't sneak up on me. You do remember that I've been trained to be able to snap someone's neck, right? You just seriously put your life in danger."

"Even if you could snap my neck, it wouldn't get you out of explaining why you were late this morning. You're never late. Ever. You're the golden boy of rule following, it's why you made such a good soldier." He moved to the front of my desk and set both hands down on its edge, leaning in so his face was level to mine. "Spill it, Martínez."

I pursed my lips together, internally debating whether or not I should tell him about my night with Bailey. I loved all my friends equally, but out of all of them, I knew I could talk to Kolbi about this and he wouldn't give me a hard time or ask stupid questions. He was the kind of friend you went to when you had things like this to share. You went to Malcolm for an ego-boost and to Conrad for a logical brain to talk things through with. I was the one you went to if you needed someone to help you get out of a tough spot. We all had our roles in the group and we all played them well.

"Hank?" He leaned further on my desk, pulling me out of my thoughts.

"Listen, we're at work, and I would really appreciate it if we could not talk about personal things while we're here, Kolb. Can we talk over lunch?"

He gave me a look out of the corner of his eye, standing up from leaning on my desk.

"Sure. Everything okay though?" Leave it to Kolbi to always act like the concerned older brother.

"Yeah, everything's good."

"Alright, over lunch then."

He walked away and headed towards his office. Once he was gone, I took a deep breath and finally started to get into my work for the day.

———

IT HAD BEEN several hours and I was deep into setting up schedules for security teams for the different events around the city when Kolbi walked up to my desk and tossed a brown paper bag down in front of me.

"Time for lunch, brother." I looked up at him and saw his signature smile on his face. The one he gave you when he knew you were about to spill your guts to him. I hadn't seen it since I told him I had enlisted. He was the first of my friends I told because I knew that he would be quickest to get on board with my decision.

"Hang on let me—"

"Now. I'm the boss, remember? Let's go." He walked away from my desk, leaving me with the brown paper bag he'd dumped on my desk.

I guess it was time for lunch.

I followed him down the hallway and into the elevator, neither of us saying anything the entire ride down. We exited the building our offices were in and walked down the street. Once we hit the park that faced the water, he took a seat on one of the benches. I was thankful he chose one under a large oak tree that created a fair amount of shade because in the mid-June heat, sitting in the sun would have been unbearable.

"So, how's Bailey?" He took a bite of the sandwich he'd pulled out of the bag and kept his eyes fixed on the water. I looked at my friend and could feel my mouth hanging open.

"How the fu—"

"I've known you since the third grade, Hank Martínez. Not once in your entire life have you been late for anything. I knew there had to be a good reason, or a good person, for you to be late today." He took another bite of his sandwich. "Plus, I put a tracker on your bike and looked her up to find out where she lives after we met her a few weeks ago at the bar."

I looked at my friend, stunned by what he had just told me.

"Don't worry, I have a tracker on Malcolm and Conrad's cars too. I don't do it to be a creep, I do it to make sure you're all safe. You guys are like my brothers and I like to know none of you are out doing anything stupid. I never look at where you are unless you aren't where you're supposed to be. Like this morning, when you were late to work. I waited half an hour and then pinged your tracker. When it pinged from the same street her condo is on, I put two and two together." He took the last bite of his sandwich and glanced over at me with a grin.

"Do the guys know you lojacked us?" I couldn't believe my friend was tracking all of us. I guess it makes sense, he does own a security firm. But damn.

"No, and I would appreciate you not telling them. I only told you because I knew I could trust you not to flip the fuck out about it like a child. And don't go thinking you can remove the tracker. If you do, I'll know and just install a new one."

I looked at my friend warily.

"So," he continued, "How's your girl?"

My lips pushed up as the thought of her being 'my girl' filled my head. No one had ever made me feel the way I do like she does. Just the thought of her made me smile.

"She's good." I nodded, taking a bite of my sandwich. I wanted to talk to him about her, but what we had still felt so new. I didn't want to overshare or make a big deal about it too soon. But last night she had told me she felt the same way about me that I felt about her, so maybe talking about it wasn't a bad idea.

"Just good? I checked how long you were at her place. You went over there after the campaign last night and didn't leave until this morning. Please tell me things were more than just *good*."

"They were..." I started. The moment of panic I remembered seeing on her face flashed in front of my eyes. My eyebrows pushed together and I chewed on my lip, thinking about what could have caused her to suddenly feel that way when everything was fine up until that point.

"But...." He noticed the face I was making and gave me a questioning look.

"But, I don't know man. Things were good, we were... connecting." I wasn't going to give him the details while families and tourists were walking around us in the middle of a Thursday afternoon. "But something seemed to spook her. I don't know what happened. I asked for her consent, she seemed into it, but once we hit a certain point she just...froze."

"And what did you do?"

"I told her we didn't have to go any further than she wanted to go. She tried to tell me she was fine but I could tell she wasn't. I don't know. I know there's more to her that she isn't ready to share with me yet and I won't force her to. When she's ready to share, I'll be ready to listen." I finished my sandwich and crumpled up the brown paper bag in my hands. My eyes looked out towards the water, trying to understand what had caused her to freeze up like she did.

"Are you going to ask her about it?" he asked. "I'm assuming you're going to see her again."

"I don't know if I can yet. We've only gone out a few times and going to her place last night wasn't exactly planned." My mind went to what I would say to her when I called her like I promised. I wanted to see her again, hell, I longed to see her again. I hadn't been lying when I told her that it felt like a piece of me was missing when she wasn't around.

"She knows about the scars," I added, keeping my eyes on the water. I could see him look at me quickly out of my periphery.

"Did she ask about them?"

"No. But I didn't really give her a chance. I didn't want to ruin the moment by explaining them to her. It's part of the reason I feel like I can't ask her about what happened last night. There are things about me I haven't shared with her either." As I spoke, the deeply embedded scars on my back seemed to throb, as if they knew I was talking about them and they were reminding me of the pain and anger that plagued my past.

No one knows about the scars on my back except for me, my friends, and the man who put them there. When I was on active duty, many of the men I went to war with saw them, but no one ever asked where they came from. We all seemed to have our own scars, visible or not, so no one asked about anyone else's because they never wanted to have to explain their own.

"Well," his strong hand clapped me on the shoulder, "I think you're a good man for not pushing her to do anything she wasn't ready to do. And I think, if you feel the way I think you feel about her, you should share a little bit of yourself and maybe that will make her feel safe enough to do the same. Good relationships are about mutual trust."

"Says the man who has secret trackers on each of his best friends," I say, rolling my eyes.

"I trust you guys as my best friends but I don't trust you fuckers to not go out and do something stupid. It's for your own good." He laughed and stood from the bench. I stood with him. "For real, brother, I'm happy for you. I think if you share this piece of you with Bailey, she might do the same. I don't know her very well, but she seems like a good one."

"She is a good one. Thanks for talking, Kolb. I won't tell the others about the trackers if you don't tell them about last night. I'm not ready for everyone to be in this yet. I'll tell them when I'm ready."

"Your secret is safe with me, brother."

19

BAILEY

It had been a few hours since Hank left and I was sitting on the floor of the living room scrolling job listings on my laptop. The TV was on in the background because I never liked to sit in pure silence for too long. My fingers swiped the trackpad on my computer as my eyes sifted through the sea of job openings based here in the city.

My heart sank as I continued to scroll because I missed the job I used to have. I had gone to school for hospitality and tourism, and had scored a major events director position at one of the largest banquet halls in the city. My job was chaotic, had insane hours, and I had to deal with crazy-ass people at least every other week, but I loved it. I loved how fast paced it was and the satisfaction that came with an event going off without a hitch. There was nothing more fulfilling than seeing the final event take place and hearing how much the attendees enjoyed themselves. I smiled, recalling all the fantastic events I had directed, when my mind took me back to the night that changed everything for me.

"Shut up and stay quiet and I won't kill you," the man had growled after he pulled me down to the ground by my pony-tail. He'd come up from behind me as I was taking out the trash for the night. I was trying to help the caterers clean up so they could go home sooner and was alone in the back alley of the event hall. I had just turned the corner to head towards the dumpsters when my neck snapped behind me and I fell to the ground. He was on me before I could even process what was happening. *"Now be a good little bitch and lie still for me, this won't take very long."* I crushed my eyes closed trying to push his voice out of my head. I fought as hard as I could to get him off of me and had bruises for weeks after to prove it. When I wasn't strong enough to escape him, he stripped me of my dignity and stole a piece of my soul in less than twenty minutes.

The sound of the door being unlocked pulled me out of my memory. I looked towards it to see Ophelia coming home for lunch as she had promised when she left this morning. I waved at her from my spot on the floor and waited to say hello as she was on the phone.

"Sure. Okay. Yes, Dale, that's fine." She looked at me and rolled her eyes as if the person on the other end was annoying her. "Mmhmm, okay well I'm home now and it's my lunch hour so we can pick this up when I am back at the office. Goodbye, Dale."

"Dale being a pain in the ass?" I laughed as she threw her bag down on the counter and kicked off her heels.

"He's always a pain in the ass. But I pay him to be a pain in the ass, so it's fine." Ophelia was the head of a marketing firm and Dale was her second in command. She complained about him constantly, but deep down, I knew she appreciated everything he did for her.

My eyes went back to my computer, still searching for

something to apply to so I could stop jumping from one side hustle to another, as Ophelia started to make her lunch in the kitchen. Our condo was split in the center with an open kitchen that looked out over the living room with our bedrooms on either side of it. It was the perfect size for the two of us, even though she hadn't bought it with me living with her in mind. After I was attacked, I quit my job, too ashamed to go and work where it happened, and she offered to have me move in with her while I got back on my feet.

Two years later, I was still here trying to figure my shit out.

Walking over with her lunch, she sat on the couch behind me and looked at my computer screen. "Job hunting?"

"Yeah, I'm tired of working all these odd jobs and planning birthday parties. I want something stable and something that will help me get out of your hair," I sighed.

"B, I wish you would stop saying that. You know you're not in my hair. I love having you here." She nudged me with her foot and I turned to look at her.

"All the same. I still need to find something that pays me more than what I'm making, which is almost less than nothing." My current employment included picking up odd event planning jobs around the city. I'd been lucky and hosted events at my old job for some of the city's most prestigious families. After I left, a few of them had tracked me down and asked if I would organize private parties in their homes. The idea of starting my own event planning business had crossed my mind, but I didn't currently have the money to make it happen. Hence, the job search.

"I know how much you've considered starting your own business. Why don't you just let me loan you the money?"

"No way, Ophie, I'm not letting you do that." I had

shared my entrepreneurial dream with her in the past and she instantly offered to front me the money to get it off the ground. I'd already taken so much from her, though, that the thought of taking anything more was too much.

"I don't know why you have to be so stubborn. You were the best of the best at your old gig, you would smash if you went out on your own."

"Can we please drop this? I'm not taking your money, period."

"Fine, fine. If you don't wanna talk about job stuff, we can talk about the hot soldier who you snuck into your bed last night." A devilish grin spread across her face as she brought him up. I felt my cheeks warm as the memories of last night flooded my brain. "Oooohhhh she's blushing! Must have been a good night then."

I rolled my eyes and pushed myself off the floor to sit on the other side of the couch. She placed her lunch plate on the coffee table and turned towards me, giving me her full attention.

"It wasn't like that, Ophie. We didn't do anything." I shook my head at her as she gave me a disappointed look.

"Why the hell not? Could he not get it up?"

"Oh, he could get it up." I licked my lips remembering how hard he'd felt on top of me.

"So what's the issue? You're hot as fuck, any man would be lucky to be with you." I looked at my friend and took a breath before speaking.

"It was me. I kinda...got spooked." My eyes fell to my hands which were in my lap. I don't know why I felt embarrassed to share this with her, she was my best friend. Maybe it was because she never had any issue getting men to do exactly what she wanted them to do and was never shy about her sexuality.

"Did he hurt you? Did he try and do something you didn't want to do?" The tone of her voice was cut with a fierce protectiveness.

"No, not at all." I waved my hands in front of her, trying to calm her down. "It was me, I just...panicked for a second. He came over because he wanted to see me and then we started to, ya know. And I was into it until my brain jumped to what happened to me two years ago for a split second and I panicked. I tried to move past it, pretend like it didn't happen, but he saw it..." I trailed off.

"And then what happened?"

"Well, I tried to keep going but he told me no. He said that we didn't have to go any further than I wanted. He told me that he wanted me to know that I could trust him and that I was safe with him. So he helped me get dressed and we fell asleep. I hadn't meant for him to stay the night, that was a total accident."

"Girl, you know I don't care who stays the night here." When I caught the sly grin that had spread across her face I rolled my eyes at her for the third time.

"There's something else..." I started, unsure if I should tell her what I hadn't been able to stop thinking about.

"Oh no, please don't tell me he has a tiny penis."

"Ophelia, no. Stop, I'm being serious here," I nearly whined.

"Okay, okay, I'm sorry. Continue."

"Well last night, when he had his shirt off, I could feel what felt like giant scars on his back. I didn't see them because it was dark, but they were long and pronounced. And it wasn't just one, there had to have been at least fifteen or twenty of them." When I felt them last night, I wasn't sure what to make of them. He hadn't given me long to examine them before he flipped himself over and pulled me on top of him. When he had, I took it as his way of telling me not to ask any questions.

Ophelia let out a long breath before speaking. "Damn, did you ask him about them?"

"I didn't think it was my place. He didn't seem to want to talk about them so I just pretended not to notice. At least, I tried to pretend."

"Do you think they're from his time in the service?"

"I'm not sure. But Ophie, they were big and they felt... deep." I couldn't imagine what he had gone through to gain his scars. Just the thought of it made me sick to my stomach. The thought of anyone hurting a man like Hank so much to where they would leave marks like that made me so angry I could feel my insides getting hot.

"You like him." She gave me a confident stare, dropping her chin and looking at me over the bridge of her nose.

"I—yeah, I do. He makes me feel safe and like I can trust him." Before saying them, I hadn't realized just how true my words felt.

"Then I think you should be honest with him, sweetie. Maybe, if you're comfortable, if you share a piece of yourself with him, he'll do the same. It sounds like you both have stories. Maybe if you share yours, he will be brave enough to share his."

I looked at my friend who had never been one to share more than her physical self with a man in total shock. As her words sunk in, I knew she was probably right. Maybe if I shared more of my story with him, he would feel comfortable to do the same. I reached across the couch and pulled Ophelia into a hug.

"I think that's a great idea, Ophie. Thanks for talking."

"I am always here for you, B. Hank seems like a good guy and I love how happy he seems to make you." She pulled away and placed both her hands on my shoulders, looking at me with a smile. "And just so you know, you can always find a stash of condoms in my bedside table in case you sneak the sexy soldier back into the condo late at night again. What's mine is yours."

I pushed her away from me and we both burst into a fit of laughter.

———

A FEW HOURS and multiple job applications later, I was lying on the couch reading a new trashy romance novel I had swiped from Ophie's bookshelf when my phone buzzed on the coffee table. I reached for it, reading the clock on the wall as I did. Without realizing it, it was already five thirty. I swiped my thumb across the screen and checked my messages.

1 New Message: Soldier

Hey blondie.

I smiled at his text, loving how he always called me that.

Hey soldier.

I haven't been able to stop thinking about you today. I'm lucky my boss is also my best friend because after getting in late and then only doing about half of what I needed to do today, any other boss would have fired me.

The thought of him sitting at work thinking about me

made my cheeks warm. If I was honest, I hadn't really stopped thinking about him either.

> The feeling is mutual.

I want to see you again. Would you make me a lucky man and let me take you to dinner this Saturday? I found somewhere new on the water that I think you'll love.

> How do you know I'll love it?

Call it a feeling.

> Someone's feeling confident 😉

> I would love to go to dinner on Saturday.

I'll pick you up around five if that's okay?

> I'll see you then.

I can't wait.

20

HANK

"**H**ey, thanks again for hookin' me up, Kolb. I wouldn't be able to do what I have planned for Bailey if it weren't for you since I can't take my bike." I slapped my best friend on the shoulder as I stood next to the all black Ford Bronco he was letting me borrow for the night.

"It's no problem. But, just so you know, it's a company car, so don't have sex in it or anything please. We use this to transport high-security clients around the city when they don't want to use the sedans." He laughed as he said it and I rolled my eyes. I had no plans of having sex in the company car. He grabbed my chin and moved it back and forth as if I was a child. "I love seeing our little Hanky boy all mushy over a girl."

Pulling my chin from his hand, I took a few steps away and opened the front door. Slipping inside, I noticed how clean and new the inside looked, the new car smell filling my nostrils as I buckled my seatbelt.

"I'll bring it to the office on Monday, if that's okay?" I asked after starting the car and rolling down the window.

"Yep, totally fine man. Have fun tonight. And remember, if you do something dumb, I'll know about it. Company cars are lojacked too," he admitted with a satisfied smirk on his face. I hadn't told Conrad and Malcolm about the trackers he had on all of us but I had found the one on my bike. I don't know when he placed it and considered ripping it off once I found it. But his words rang out in my ears, *'If you take it off, I'll know and just put on a new one,'* so I left it alone. If he wanted to know that the three places I go are my apartment, the gym, and work, so be it.

I waved at my friend as I pulled out of his driveaway and headed for Bailey's. As I drove, my insides buzzed as I thought about being with her again. I hadn't seen her since I left her place early Thursday morning with the exception of when we made eyes at each other at the gym. We'd exchanged some playful texts while we were both there but hadn't actually spoken to one another. Instead, we both stayed in our own areas and watched one another from afar. There was more than one occasion when I would finish a set and look over to find her licking her lips or staring at me with her mouth open. The way I wanted my girl was something fierce and if I wasn't mistaken, she felt the same way about me. The sexual tension between us was so strong I'm pretty sure everyone in the gym could feel it too.

Since Kolbi lived downtown, it didn't take me long to reach her building. I sent her a quick text letting her know that I was heading up before locking the car door behind me. I waved hello to the doorman who let me in and headed towards the elevator. Anxiously tapping my leg in anticipation of seeing her again, I stood in front of the elevator waiting for the doors to open. When they did, a wave of blonde flew into me before I even knew what happened. She had her arms wrapped around my neck and without even thinking, I lifted her up around her waist and spun her around. The giggles that fell from her mouth as we spun were ones I wanted to remember forever. I carefully set her down but didn't remove my hands from her waist nor did she remove her arms from around my neck.

"Hey there, soldier," she hummed, her wide smile proudly stretched across her face.

"Hey there, blondie." I leaned in and kissed her on the cheek which she responded to with a pleasant 'hmph'. "Why did you come down? I was going to come up and get you from your door like I always do."

"Because I couldn't wait any longer to see you," she said as if it was the most obvious thing. We were still locked together, our faces mere inches apart, as people in the lobby glanced at us as they passed. I didn't care if they looked. Let them see how much my girl has me wrapped around her finger. She pulled me into a hug and I breathed in her vanilla and honey scent that I've grown to associate with the feeling that everything was right in the world.

"I missed you, hermosa[1]," I hummed into her ear and she wrapped her arms a little tighter around my neck.

"I missed you too." She pulled away from me and I could see her cheeks were the faintest shade of pink. "Where are we going tonight? I'm starving!"

I looped my hand into hers and laughed, pulling her towards the front door of her building. As we walked towards the car, I noticed that she was wearing a pale blue dress and brown sandals. The color of her dress made the deep blues of her eyes pop and her golden hair shine unlike anything I'd ever seen. She was perfectly dressed for the hot summer heat which was good because my plans for us were

---

1. beautiful

outside. We walked together in silence but when we got to the car, she stopped short and gave me a confused look.

"Where's your bike?" Her face was scrunched up and she almost looked disappointed.

"At Kolbi's. I couldn't bring it tonight because of what I have planned for our date. This is a loaner from him." I opened the passenger side door for her but she didn't move to get in.

"But you still have your bike?"

"Yes, hermosa[2], I still have my bike. What's wrong?" I gave her an inquisitive look from the side of the car. She was still standing on the sidewalk, looking at the car as if it was an old beat up clunker and not a brand new SUV. She crossed her arms in front of her chest and mumbled something I couldn't hear from where I stood. "What was that?"

"I *said*," she shifted her weight and bit her bottom lip, smiling slightly as she spoke, "I'm glad you didn't get rid of your bike because I think it's sexy as hell." Her eyes burned into me with so much desire and passion that I wanted to throw her over my shoulder and march her right back up to her bedroom. Ever since our last night together, I had been fantasizing about all the things I wanted to do with her. Once she was ready, of course.

I took a few quick steps towards her and closed the gap between us. Pulling her hips into me with one hand, I leaned down and met her gaze as she looked up at me, "I think you're sexy as hell and I hope that one day I can show you how much I mean that. Maybe even on my bike if you're lucky."

Where the fuck did that come from? This woman does something to me I swear.

---

2. beautiful

Her chest was rising and falling against mine as I continued to hold her against me, her eyes were wide with surprise at my words. I grinned down at her, continuing to play into what I'd said, and pressed my lips to hers. She tasted as good as I remember and I loved how she roped her fingers through my curls. Someone from across the street whistled at us which made us break apart from one another and laugh.

"Now get in the car," I demanded. She did what I said, but not before giving me a look. As I helped her into the car and closed the door for her, I didn't miss when she mumbled, *"God, it's hot when he's bossy."*

I smiled to myself as I walked towards the driver's side door, pride swelling inside of me. I liked knowing what turned her on, and if bossy did it for her, I would be as bossy as she wanted me to be. I finally took my seat next to her and turned the car on when she spoke.

"So, where we goin'?" she asked from the passenger seat, her blue eyes threatening to completely undo me with one glance.

"You'll see. Just sit back and enjoy the ride." I placed my hand on her thigh, moving it just to the inside of her leg and loved how she squeezed her thighs together when I did. Keeping my eyes on the road, I pulled away from the curb and headed towards our date at last.

21

BAILEY

I probably should have let him pick me up at my door but I just couldn't wait to see him any longer. After Ophie and I talked on Thursday, I decided that if it felt right, I would share a little more about my past with him. While I hadn't known him very long, there was something about him that made me feel like I could trust him. Not only with my story but also with myself. Something in my gut told me that he wouldn't hurt me or look at me any differently once I told him about what happened to me two years ago. The feeling of safety and genuine care that radiated from him was undeniable. There were a few times I tried to sneak a peek at him as we drove, but every time I tried to take in his striking jawline or strong arms, he would look over at me and I would look away, feeling embarrassed that he caught me staring.

We had been driving for almost half an hour, crossing over the Ravenel Bridge into Mount Pleasant—the next closest part of Charleston—when we turned right off of the main road. I looked at him, confused, because I knew there weren't any restaurants in this part of the city. Only a park and some old docked battleships that tourists would go and explore on their annual vacations. He simply smiled at me and gently squeezed my thigh where his hand had been resting the entire drive over. *If he slips his fingers just a few inches higher...*

When we pulled into a parking spot, he hopped out of the car and came to my side to open the door for me. Out of all the guys I had been with before, Hank was the first to open every door for me every time without fail—a true Southern gentleman through and through. He extended his hand toward me as he opened my door and I took it, letting him help me out of the car. Once he closed my door, he went and opened the tailgate. I looked around the park and took in all the people walking around and enjoying the summer evening. I loved Charleston during this time of year. Once the sun went down, the temperature was warm but enjoyable. The dress I'd picked was perfect for this kind of evening.

"You ready?" His voice behind me pulled my attention away from the people and towards him. I spun around to find him carrying a large wicker basket in one hand with a blanket draped over his other arm. I hadn't noticed them since they were in the back of the SUV behind the row of seats.

"Hank." I took a breath, my brain putting together what we were doing for our date. "What are you doing?"

"I'm taking you to dinner on the water like I promised," he mused before turning on his heels and walking towards the park.

I trailed behind him as we walked towards a patch of grass and some trees scattered around in a seemingly disorganized manner. When we reached the trees closest to the water, he set the basket down on the grass and laid out the blanket under a tree. Then, he moved the basket to one corner of the blanket and sat down. He reached his hand to me and helped me take a seat next to him. I watched as he pulled out two plates, silverware, and plastic cups from inside the basket. Under the cutlery, he pulled out plastic containers that were full of food. I looked at him and couldn't help but smile.

"You're taking me on a picnic?" My eyebrows raised and I bit my bottom lip. This was the sweetest thing anyone had ever done for me.

"I hope that's okay," he said, opening up the containers that held piping hot food. As he did, my nose was filled with the smell of spices and chili peppers. I looked in the containers and gasped. Each one was filled with what looked to be home-cooked Mexican food.

"Did you make all of this?" I couldn't hide the shock in my voice which caused him to laugh.

"Why do you sound so surprised?" He looked at me with a grin that I wanted to cover with a kiss.

"I don't know, I...I've never had a man cook me dinner before. Not to mention the whole picnic thing. I think this is the nicest thing anyone has ever done for me." My heart fluttered in my chest. Setting the container down, he leaned in and kissed me.

"You deserve to have someone be nice to you, Bailey. I consider myself lucky to get to be the one who is." I felt my cheeks get warm at his words.

"You know, for an ex-soldier, you're kinda a big softy," I teased, resting a hand on his cheek.

"Only for you," he whispered through a soft smile close to my lips before pulling away.

We started eating and he explained each dish to me as we did. I loved how he explained them in great detail but loved even more how he spoke of how he learned to make them. He told me stories about how he and his mother would spend hours together in the kitchen cooking after school. How she would help him reach the counter by letting him stand on a chair and how she would refuse to speak anything but Spanish to him as they cooked. It made my heart hurt to think of all the memories he didn't get to have with her because he lost her at such a young age. The memories he did have though, he shared with a fervor.

"And we would laugh and laugh," he said, chuckling to himself as he took another bite of his food. As he did, some of the rice from his spoon fell off, landing on the blanket and nearly missing his pants. Without even skipping a beat, I reached over, picked up the spilled food, and popped it in my mouth. What could I say? It was too good to waste.

"Blondie," he said, studying my face, "you have something on your..." He wiggled his finger near the corner of his mouth.

"Oh!" I went to wipe it away but he stopped me by grabbing my wrist.

"Here, let me get it." Holding onto my wrist he pulled me closer until my face was in front of his. Since he was lying on his side, propped up on one elbow, I had to sit on my knees to lean down to get close enough. Wrapping his hand around the side of my neck, he pulled me in and licked the side of my lips before pushing his tongue into my mouth, kissing me without shame right in the middle of the busy park. He pulled away from me and looked at my mouth, "There, I think I got it." I rolled my eyes at him as I leaned back to sit on my butt again.

"I like hearing you talk about your mom, I can tell how much you love her. I'm sorry you lost her so soon." I wasn't sure if it was my place to say it, but I wanted him to know that he was safe to talk to me about her if he wanted to.

"I do love her. Even though she's been gone for twenty years, I still love her more than anything." His eyes were cast down toward the blanket. He seemed to be lost in a memory.

"I don't mean to pry but...how did she die?" I played with the hem of my dress and worried I'd crossed a line. I didn't want him to feel as if I was trying to be nosy, I just genuinely wanted to know more about him and his story.

"She died in a car accident." His voice came out flat and void of emotion. His eyes met mine and I watched him with bated breath, unsure of what to say next. Thankfully for me, Hank kept talking. "My father killed her when he was driving home drunk. They had gone to dinner downtown and...he had too much to drink and..." His eyes fell to the blanket again. My hand reached for his in a desperate attempt to comfort him through his pain. His thumb swiped back and forth across the back of my hand but he didn't look at me.

"It changed him, losing my mother. He had never been an overtly happy man before she died, but after she was gone, nothing was good enough for him." He kept his eyes cast down toward the blanket as he shared his story and my heart squeezed in my chest. "Everything I did was wrong. Everything I did was a reason for punishment. He took all of his anger out on me, as if I was the one who killed her. Stupid bastard."

"Hank..." I started, unsure of where to take my words next.

"Even now, twenty years later, his anger is embedded into my skin. A permanent reminder of what I lost and what I gained in return. A mother who I loved and a father who would only leave me alone after he beat me until I bled." My breath caught in my throat hearing him share this about himself.

"The scars on your back..." My voice came out hardly above a whisper. I could feel the tears in my eyes as I thought about Hank as a little boy having to survive that kind of childhood.

"He loved using his belt." He pursed his lips together and shook his head, blowing out a long breath as he did. "I'm sorry, I didn't mean to dump this on you tonight. You asked about my mother, not about my scars or my childhood trauma." He tried to laugh it off but I wouldn't let him.

"Hank," I moved so I was closer to him and took both his hands in mine, "we all have scars, even me. Just because you can't see them doesn't mean they aren't there." I licked my lips and took a breath. Was I really going to tell him now? I felt like I had to since he had shared so much with me. His act of bravery had inspired me to be brave and share a piece of myself with him too. He watched me intently, his deep brown eyes never breaking away from mine. When he cocked his head to one side, I took that as my invitation to keep going.

"Two years ago, while I was finishing up at an event I was working at..." I took a deep breath, trying to calm my heart rate which was reaching an unhealthy beats per minute, "I was attacked. Not just attacked, I was raped." I couldn't look at him any longer, the shame filling my body made it impossible. I hadn't even realized I started crying until a big, wet tear splashed on the back of my hand. He gently wiped it away with his thumb, his hands slowly starting to squeeze mine with more power.

"Bailey, I—"

"No, let me finish." I needed to get this out before I

couldn't anymore. "I was raped outside of the event hall I worked at. It was the end of the night and I was trying to help by taking out the trash. The guy came out of nowhere and had me on the ground before I even knew what was happening. I tried to fight back but he was too strong. He had a knife, he...he threatened to kill me." My words broke between sobs and I tried to catch my breath. Talking about this never got easier. It felt as if it was happening all over again every time I told the story. He sat up and pulled me closer to him, wrapping his body around mine like a shield.

"Bailey..." he hushed me as I cried into his shoulder right in the middle of the park. Anyone looking at us would think he was breaking up with me and not that I had just bared the ugliest part of myself to him.

"That's why, the other night," I hiccuped, "I haven't been with anyone since that night. Not like that. I just got scared, that's all." It came out as an apology even though deep down I knew I had nothing to apologize for. For a few months after my attack, I went to groups with other women who had been through the same thing. We were often encouraged to accept and believe that what happened to us wasn't our fault. That we hadn't asked for it or deserved it. Even now, two years later, I was working on believing that.

"Shhhh, you don't have to explain." He pulled away from me and cradled my face in both of his hands, wiping my tears away with his thumbs.

"I understand if you don't want to see me anymore." The words slipped from my lips, exposing my deepest fear by sharing this part of me with someone else. That they wouldn't want to be with me because I was soiled.

Dirty.

Damaged.

The fear that I would be viewed in the exact way I felt after a piece of my dignity and soul were stolen from me.

"Hermosa[1]," his voice was low as he tipped my chin up so I had to look at him, "that's the furthest thing from what I want." He leaned in and kissed my tear-stained cheek, sending a wash of warmth over my skin. It was hot and humid outside but every piece of me felt cold and frozen.

"I think about you every day and I miss you as soon as you're gone. I would spend every minute of every day with you if you'd let me. Knowing this about you doesn't change any of that." He was speaking into my hair as he had pulled me into a hug, his arms keeping me safe as they hung onto me. "If anything, knowing this about you makes me care about you even more. You are so strong, Bailey, stronger than I even knew. Thank you for sharing this with me." I couldn't help but laugh because no one had ever thanked me for telling them about my attack. Leave it to Hank to continue to be a gentleman, even when talking about this.

"Thank you for letting me share. There aren't many people who I tell about this, but something about you makes me feel safe. Like I can share anything with you." I burrowed my nose into his neck and breathed him in.

"Can I ask you one thing?"

"Of course," I pulled away from him so I could wipe my eyes. We sat facing one another on the blanket and were so close that our knees were touching. He held my hands in his like a lifeline.

"Did they catch the guy? What happened to him?" His eyes were filled with concern. As I studied them closer, I saw something in them I hadn't seen in them before.

Anger.

---

1. Beautiful

I bit my lip before speaking, knowing that my answer wouldn't be what he wanted to hear.

"I don't know what happened to him. Once he was done with me he ran off. He was wearing a hoodie and it was dark so I couldn't see his face. I filed a police report but nothing ever came from it. Ophelia, my roommate, was the one who convinced me to file it even though I knew there wasn't much the police could do if I couldn't identify who attacked me."

Flashes of that night came back to me as I spoke. How the stranger had left me on the ground, my dress pushed up and my tights ripped. How I walked home in a haze, not even bothering to get my stuff from inside the event hall. How, after hiding in my apartment for three full days, Ophelia came pounding on the door and wouldn't leave until I let her in. When she saw me for the first time, covered in bruises and dried blood as I was still in a state of shock, she forced me to go to the police station. I'll never forget how her hand trembled in mine as she sat next to me and I told the officer what happened. How her eyes filled with tears as my own slid down my face. The words of the county doctor still ring out in my head from time to time, *'It's a good thing you haven't showered, we might actually get some evidence even though it's been a few days. You're very lucky.'*

I didn't feel very lucky.

"Hey." The warmth of his voice and his calloused hand on my cheek pulled me back to the present. "You wanna get out of here? Let's go back to my place, I'll give you something to change into and we can just hangout. What do you think?"

I searched his face to see if I could see any difference in how he looked at me now that he knew my secret. His brown eyes burned just as bright as they did before and his smile made me feel just as safe. My fear of him seeing me any differently after knowing what had happened to me was slowly being replaced by a sense of safety and comfort.

He didn't think I was damaged or broken.

He just wanted to make me feel safe.

"I think I'd like that very much, soldier."

22

HANK

When I heard the words leave her lips I thought my heart was going to stop.

'I was raped.'

I hadn't felt so hollowed out since the moment my aunt told me about my mother. Hearing her talk about being attacked gutted me and when she told me the man who harmed her had gotten away, I saw red. I was so angry I had to take a moment and remind myself it was about her, not me, and that getting angry wasn't going to help anyone. I thought for a moment about asking Malcolm if he wanted to meet up for some one-on-one sparring sometime this week to work it off.

We had been driving in silence ever since I helped her into the car, my hand protectively resting on her thigh. Unlike before, her hand was interlocked with mine, holding it tightly and running her thumb across the back of my hand. Without meaning to, my breath became synced with each swipe of her thumb and it brought me a new sense of purpose.

Before Bailey, everything I did was for the Army.

Now I was ready to flip my entire life upside down just to make sure she was okay.

After thirty minutes in the car, I pulled into the parking lot of my apartment. I looked at her and pulled our hands towards my lips, kissing the back of hers before getting out of the car. I walked around the car and opened her door, extending my hand for her to take. She took it with a look of admiration in her eyes and hopped out, never letting go of me.

Once we reached my door, I unlocked it and let her go in ahead of me. I was suddenly nervous to have her in my place but I wasn't sure why. I had cleaned up before I left and my bed was made because a soldier never left his bed unmade.

"This is nice," she commented with a polite smile, turning in a circle as she stood in what was both my kitchen and my living room. My apartment was fine but I definitely wouldn't constitute it as 'nice'. It's what I had the money for when I came home earlier in the summer and it was the closest place to the gym, so I signed the lease. Now that I had more money thanks to my job, I planned on moving to something nicer downtown as soon as I could.

"You don't have to lie," I chuckled. "I know it's not much. It's definitely not as nice as your place."

"Please, 'my place' isn't even my place. I don't know if I told you, but Ophelia owns the condo. She's just nice enough to let me live with her while I figure my shit out..." Her voice trailed off at the end and I could tell she was embarrassed. She was playing with the hem of her dress again, something I noticed she did when she was nervous. Not wanting her to feel uncomfortable, I pulled her into a hug and wrapped my arms around her shoulders.

"Let's get you something to wear," I said close to her ear.

She slipped from my embrace and took my hand into hers again. As we walked through my apartment, she swung our hands back and forth until we reached my bedroom. The small room was just off of the kitchen and only held my bed, a small desk I had found on the side of the road, and my closet. It wasn't much, but it was enough. I had learned to live with so little that the thought of having anything above the bare minimum felt unnecessary. Now that I had a beautiful woman in my room, I wished I had done something a little more with the space.

She sat down on the foot of the bed and watched me as I pilfered through my closet, trying to find her something clean to wear. After a little digging, I found an old pair of sweats and a T-shirt with the word ARMY written across the front that I somehow still had from my first few years in the service. I turned around to find her watching me with reverence.

"What are you lookin' at, blondie?" I asked with a side smile, walking towards her with the clothes.

"Just you. I like seeing you in your space, it's nice seeing you here." She took the clothes I handed to her and looked around. Assuming she was looking for a place to change, I pointed to the bathroom door on the opposite side of the room. There was nothing I wanted to see more than her stripped down to nothing but her underwear, but after what she shared with me earlier, I wasn't going to push for anything she didn't first ask for herself. I sat on the bed and waited for her, playing with my hands and trying to stay busy. *I can't believe she's in my place right now. Changing into my clothes. I wonder what she looks like as she slips off her dress...*

"What do you think? Am I ready for duty?" I spun my head towards her voice which she had deepened and when our eyes connected, she gave me the worst salute I'd ever seen. I couldn't help but laugh at her. She had her face screwed up as if she was trying to look tough and the clothes I had lent her were comically oversized. They literally looked like they could swallow her whole. But damn did she look hot as fuck wearing my clothes. *Breathe dude, just breathe.*

I stood from the bed and walked towards her. Once in front of her, I placed my hand over hers, stretching out her fingers so they were flat and bending her elbow so that her salute was now proper. Her eyes watched me with so much attention you would have thought I was doing something far more entertaining than I was. Once her form was fixed, I took a step back and returned the gesture.

"You look like you wouldn't last a day," I deadpanned before bursting into a fit of laughter.

"Hey!" She playfully punched my arm, offended. "I think I would make for a fine soldier with proper training." We were both laughing at this point. I reached for the arm she used to punch me with and pulled her into my chest.

"I think you would, too, with proper training of course." The way she looked up at me, her eyes locked on mine, almost brought me to my knees. It wouldn't take much for me to close the space between us and press my lips to hers. I missed the feeling of them and wanted nothing more than to pick her up, wrap her legs around my torso, and officially make her mine.

"Hank?" I watched her perfectly curved lips say my name, still holding her against my chest. I held her wrist in one hand and had my other arm wrapped around her lower back. If I pressed hard enough, she would definitely feel the hard-on I was trying to conceal.

"Yeah, blondie?" I hummed.

"Thanks for the clothes," she nearly whispered. Her eyes were fluttering between mine and my lips, like a silent invitation for me to lean in and close the gap between us. I took a step away from her instead but held onto her hand.

"You're welcome. Let's go watch a movie or something." I pulled her hand behind me and tried to pretend that I hadn't seen her face fall for half a second. It wasn't that I didn't want to kiss her, it's that I didn't want her to think I was taking advantage of her. She had shared something so personal with me that I wasn't sure where to go from here. I wanted her. Badly. But I wasn't going to push her into doing something she wasn't ready to do.

Walking out to the living room, I took a seat on the couch and watched as she sat on the opposite side and tucked her legs under herself. We argued for twenty minutes about what movie to watch and after three rounds of rock, paper, scissors, I lost and had to watch *13 Going on 30*. Over the next hour and a half, I learned that Jennifer Garner is one of her favorite actresses, Mark Ruffalo is considered a 'daddy', and that she had once dressed up as Jenna Rink for Halloween. By the end of the movie, Bailey had made her way over from the opposite side of the couch and was lying on her side with her head on my lap. At one point she had mentioned she was cold so I went and grabbed her a blanket. As she watched the movie, covered up and with her feet on the couch, I looked at her. I saw her quote parts of the movie word for word and laughed at bits I wouldn't find funny if she weren't around. I think I watched her more than the movie, but I was okay with that.

I could watch her like this every day and be perfectly fine with it.

I'm so fucked.

"Mmmm, that feels nice," she cooed, pressing her cheek into my thigh.

"What does?" I asked, watching her and loving how she nuzzled her cheek into my leg.

"You playing with my hair like that." Looking at my hand, I realized what I had been doing. I had a long blonde tendril wrapped around my finger, and was twisting and twirling it between my index finger and my thumb. "My mom used to play with my hair when I was little and it always relaxed me."

"Then I will keep doing it." I smiled down at her as she looked up at me.

"Let's play a game," she said suddenly, twisting herself so she was on her back and looking up at me.

"Okay, what game do you wanna play? Keep in mind, it's almost ten so starting a rousing game of Monopoly probably isn't the best idea."

"You got a bedtime or something?" she teased, giggling to herself, "Plus, do you even own Monopoly?" She looked around my place and we both took in the sheer lack of stuff it had.

"I was never a Monopoly kid. Always preferred different board games growing up."

"Like Dungeons and Dragons?" Her eyebrows raised as she asked. A small part of me worried she was judging me, the memory of being teased for playing the game as a kid still stinging years later.

"Yes," I tickled her side causing her to spasm and laugh loudly, "like Dungeons and Dragons. We just call it D and D though."

"Ahhh, I see. D and D. Interesting."

"You said you wanted to play a game?" I reminded her.

"Oh, yes, I do." She clapped her hands together in front

of her and a smile grew on her face. "Let's play twenty questions."

"Twenty questions? You wanna play twenty questions?" I asked.

"Yes, I wanna play twenty questions. Please?" She looked up at me again with puppy dog eyes that made my ability to resist her request impossible. For a guy who did eleven years in the service, I was a fuckin' softy when it came to her.

"Fine, we can play twenty questions, but only because you look so cute." Her cheeks flushed at my words and I grabbed another piece of her hair to play with.

"Okay, me first, hmmm. Okay, what is your favorite thing to cook?" she asked.

"Hmm…" I chewed on my bottom lip, thinking about all the recipes and dishes my mother had taught me how to make before I lost her. "I think my favorite is chilaquiles[1]. It's really easy to make, is perfect to eat at any time of day, even though it's meant to be breakfast, and you can share it with someone." I thought about how my mother would make me the dish every Saturday and Sunday, and then she and I would sit at the bar and eat it together.

"I hope you make it for me one day." Her lips were spread into a small smile and I made a promise to myself that one day, I would.

"Okay, your turn," she commanded.

"What?"

"It's your turn. Now you ask me a question." She spoke to me like I should have known that already.

"Oh, okay let me think. How about…what do you do when you're having a bad day?" I'm not sure where the ques-

---

1. A traditional Mexican breakfast dish consisting of corn tortillas cut into quarters and lightly fried.

tion came from but I was curious about her answer. What did she do when she was having a bad day? It felt strange to even think she could have a bad day seeing as how she always seems to have a sunny, spunky disposition.

"Good question," she gasped and swatted my leg. A sense of pride swelled in my chest. "Hmm, I think my favorite thing to do on a bad day is take a bath and read. I don't know what it is, but the hot water and a good book always seem to make me feel better."

The naked image of her in the tub hit me like a ton of bricks and I quickly adjusted how I was sitting so the growing erection I had wasn't poking her in the back of the head.

"What do you do when you're having a bad day?" She looked up at me and when she tilted her chin back, I worried I was about to be found out.

"You can't just steal my question." I chuckled and tickled her again.

"Yes I can. I asked to play the game so I can make up the rules and ask whatever questions I wanna ask. Now answer." She gently pinched my leg and I let out a gasp at the sensation.

"Okay, okay fine, just don't hurt me," I teased, tickling her slightly causing the room to be filled with the warmth of her laugh. "I guess I like to go for a ride on my bike, it helps me clear my head. Or I go to the gym. I find that a little bit of self-inflicted pain goes a long way." She 'humphed' and nodded her head in agreement. Knowing it was my turn to ask, I continued. "Do you have a favorite kind of candy?"

"Doesn't everyone?" Her eyebrows knitted together as she looked up at me. "Sno Caps are my favorite."

"Sno Caps? Are you serious? Those are like, the most

random candy." Leave it to my girl to prefer a candy you could only find at movie theaters and concession stands.

"What? They're good! I like to suck on them until all the chocolate melts and then chew on the crunchy bits." She laughed in my lap and I tried to push out the idea of her sucking anything out of my head. While I don't think she realized it, she was turning me further inside out with every new answer she shared.

"Okay my turn to ask," she started again. "How did you meet your best friends?"

"I met them all in third grade and we've been insepa- rable since. Well, metaphorically speaking. Kolbi is the one I work for, Malcolm works at the bar where you met them, and then Conrad works for himself."

"What do you mean '*metaphorically*'?"

"Well, we all grew up here in Charleston together and would spend nearly every day together. Then when I turned eighteen, I enlisted in the military. It was a way for me to get away from my dad and it got me an education, kind of. I never really did finish school. Once I was trained, I went into the field and never came back. It was only earlier this year that I decided I was ready to move on and come home."

"So that means you were gone for—"

"Almost eleven years." I finished her sentence for her and looked down to see her eyes were wide and her mouth was slightly ajar. This was the first time we had really spoken about my time in the service.

"That must have been so hard for you to be away for so long."

"It was hard to be away from them, sure. But not here. I never heard from my dad once while I was gone but my friends, I talked to them every day that I could through email or video calls. They're my real family in my eyes." My bottom lip wrapped around my teeth as I thought about how my friends got me through so much even when we were thousands of miles apart. I wouldn't be who I am today if it weren't for them.

She sat up from her spot and shifted to sit next to me cross-legged on the couch. She took my hands into hers, kissed the backs of them, and looked at me with more admiration than anyone ever has.

"Thank you for keeping our country safe all that time, Hank. I'm very grateful for you." I had been thanked by strangers for my time in the military for what felt like a thousand times but none of them meant as much to me as hers did.

"I think it's my turn for a question," I hummed, moving my body closer to hers.

"Yes, I think you're right, soldier," she replied as she leaned in toward me with a small smile.

"May I kiss you?"

23

BAILEY

May I kiss you?

This man and his manners might just be the death of me.

Never in my life has a guy ever asked if he could kiss me. He just did it. I couldn't fight the smile on my face, touched by his need for permission before just taking something I would have happily given him. I thought he was going to kiss me in his bedroom once I had changed. I wanted him to kiss me, to take me to his bed, lay me down and make me his. But then he took a step back and I took that to mean he didn't want to, that maybe he had changed his mind about me after all and he didn't like me like I thought he had.

"Yes, you can kiss me," I whispered into his lips, leaning in even closer to him. My heart surged with joy, knowing that my fears had been wrong.

"Thank god, because I've been wanting to since we got back." His words were rushed before he crashed his lips into mine. I hadn't realized how much I missed the way they felt until our lips were reunited once more. He snaked his hands behind my head and into my hair, pulling me even closer to him. Without thinking, I crawled my way onto his lap, never breaking the connection we had formed. With my legs on either side of him, I sat down only to discover that he was long and hard under the shorts he was wearing. Wetness pooled between my legs knowing how hard I was able to make him. After being attacked, I didn't think anyone would ever want to be with me again and it made me feel good knowing I had been wrong.

"You're driving me crazy doing that, *hermosa*[1]," he growled the name into my ear as my head dropped behind me. His lips pressed into the soft parts of my neck, sending a chill down my spine with each kiss.

"I don't know what you mean," I hummed, allowing the feelings he was causing with his lips to consume me.

"You, pressing your hips into me like that. It's an unfair tactic to use on a man who is trying to show some self-control." I looked down and realized I had been grinding my hips into his hard cock, enjoying the friction it was producing.

"Why are you trying to show self-control?" I brought both hands to his face and pressed my lips into his before he could answer. He pulled away from me and looked at me for a beat before speaking.

"Because I don't want to push you to do something you aren't ready to do. You shared something really personal with me not even a few hours ago and I would feel awful if you thought I rushed you into something after sharing that. I never want you to feel pressured or taken advantage of when you're with me. I only ever want you to feel safe and cherished. As you should have always been treated."

We were both breathing heavily on the couch, staring at

---

1. beautiful

one another for several long seconds. I was trying to collect my thoughts but doing so seemed impossible. He had left me speechless. Instead of saying anything, I pressed my lips to his once more. He and I consumed one another, our tongues clashing together and our breath becoming muddled between us. I hadn't wanted anyone like this in a long time but I knew I wanted him. I wanted him to fill me up, to consume me, to make me his. I didn't just want him, I needed him. Like the night sky needs the stars, I needed Hank Martínez.

"Soldier," I whispered through labored breaths.

"Yeah?" He pulled his lips away from mine just long enough to say it.

"I want you. I don't just want you, I need you. Please, Hank."

He pulled away from me and searched my eyes with his. I could tell he was thinking about what I had just said, unsure of if I'd meant it. I trusted him, and while I had gotten scared the last time we were in this similar position, I didn't have an ounce of fear in me now. Nothing about being with him in the way I wanted him made me feel scared. It made me feel alive.

"You sure? We don't have to if y—"

"Would you just hush up and take me to the bedroom?" I huffed with a playful grin on my face.

"*Gracias Dios mio*[2]," he hissed under his breath. I had no idea what he'd said but the sound of the Spanish words falling from his lips turned me on even more. Before I knew it, he was standing from the couch and holding me under my butt with both hands. My legs instinctually wrapped

---

2. Thank God

around his torso and I laughed as he said, "You have no idea how much I would love to do that."

He carried me from the living room directly to his bed like a straight-up caveman. I liked this side of him; the side that was possessive and in control. More often than not I saw the shy and kind side of him, but this hungrier side of him he was showing me now made me excited. I wanted to know just how hungry he could be.

When we reached the bed, he laid me down gently and took a step back. My eyes widened as he locked his eyes on me and pulled the shirt he was wearing up and over his head. As he did, the muscles in his arms and core flexed, causing me to almost drool like the last time I'd seen them. His eyes burned into me with so much passion my cheeks flushed. Desire and lust swirled in his eyes.

"If at any point," he started, lowering himself onto the bed, his body starting to encapsulate mine, "you get nervous or want to stop, you tell me." His lips found the soft part of my neck again causing a small moan to escape from the back of my throat. The combination of his lips on my neck and his strong body on top of mine was starting to cause my brain to go fuzzy.

"Don't worry about me. I want this, I want you." Desire dripped from my words as I ran my fingers along his back. I fought the urge to trace the scars that lingered there. He pushed himself up to where he was looking straight down at me with an intensity in his eyes.

"I mean it, Bailey, you tell me if you want to stop at any point. Promise me you'll say something." He spoke with so much severity in his voice that I knew he wanted me to feel safe and nothing meant more to me than that.

"I promise." My hands started to pull him in, walking

across the exposed flesh of his back as he lowered himself back down on top of me. "Now please, *make me yours.*"

24

HANK

I couldn't control myself any longer. As soon as the request left her lips, as soon as my name fell from her mouth, any ounce of self-control I was still hanging onto was gone. I wanted her more than anything and I knew she wanted me. Unless she asked me to stop, I would make her mine.

I crashed my lips into hers once more and relished in the heat that I felt as her hands explored my back. It wasn't the kind of heat that burned, it was the kind of heat that made you feel comfortable and safe. She made me feel safe and I would do anything to make sure she always felt the same way with me. Whether it was here in my bed or out in the open, she would always feel protected and comfortable with me. I would make sure of it.

As I continued to press my lips to hers, my hands followed the curve of her waist down to the waistband of the sweats I had given her. Fuck me for giving her pants and not shorts. I slipped my hand under the waistband and lowered it under the fabric. Instead of finding the hem of her underwear underneath, I felt nothing but exposed skin.

"*Hermosa*[1]," I begged, the feeling of her warm skin against the palm of my hand was starting to pull something primal out of me.

"Yes?" she purred from underneath me. Her hips bucked towards me as I slid my hand further down the inside of the sweats.

"Are you not wearing any underwear?" My voice came out as a growl and sounded almost like a threat as something feral and animalistic continued to grow inside of me.

She let out a small laugh before bringing her lips to my ear and nipping at it with her teeth. Then she whispered, "Why don't you take 'em off and find out for yourself?"

"*Me vuelves loco hermosa*[2]," I groaned.

"I have no idea what that means but I like the way it sounds," she giggled.

"It means you need to take these off right now." I'll tell her what it actually meant later, right now I needed to get these pants off of her. She lifted her hips up as I pulled at the elastic and pushed the sweats down her hips with ease. I pulled them off the rest of the way for her before quickly grabbing at the bottom of the ARMY T-shirt she was still wearing. She sat up from where she was lying on the bed and lifted the shirt up and over her head. This wasn't the first time I'd seen her fully exposed, but she still took my breath away.

Her blonde hair fell around her shoulders and was still curled from when I picked her up for our date. The sapphire in her eyes burned into me like a slow burning fire and part of me wanted to be able to jump into them two feet first. The curves of her body moved as if they had been

---

1. Beautiful
2. You drive me crazy, beautiful

painted by an artist and her breasts sat perfectly round on her chest. When I stood to toss her sweats out of the way, she sat up to meet me, spreading her legs wide, giving me a perfect view of her pussy. I licked my lips as I looked at it, suddenly needing to know how it tasted. The last time we had been together like this, I had only gotten to feel her on my fingers but tonight I was going to learn how she tasted on my tongue.

"You look like you're about to eat me." She chewed on her bottom lip and looked up at me through her lashes.

"I'm glad you can tell because that's exactly what I'm going to do." I wrapped my arms around her thighs and pushed her further back onto the bed, dropping to my knees and opening her up even more. When she was where I needed her, I placed both hands on the insides of her legs, opening them up and stretching them a little more. My face was hovering just above her center and I looked up towards her eyes to find her looking back at me.

"I am going to eat this pretty pussy of yours, hermosa[3], until you come undone on my tongue. Then I am going to finally get to know what it feels like to have it wrapped around my cock." She let out a shuddered breath in reply.

I am a good man. A man of honor. I had served my country with self-control and dignity. But what I wanted to do to her was anything but those things.

She was shaking with anticipation underneath me and part of me wanted to see just how long I could make her squirm before she couldn't handle it any longer. I wanted to know how far I could take her before she was begging me to give her the release she needed. But tonight wasn't that night and I didn't have a shred of self-control left in my body

---

3. beautiful

to see how far I could push her. Unable to hold myself back any longer, I buried myself between her thighs and tasted her for the first time. The taste of her on my tongue was unlike anything I had ever experienced. I thought feeling her around my fingers was good, but this was better.

My tongue ran the length of her center and once I hit her clit with my tongue her head fell back onto the mattress. This was the first time I had ever done this to a woman and I already knew I wanted to do it again. The way her hips reacted as my tongue swiped across her pussy drove me wild and I never wanted it to end. I wanted to know how it felt for her to come undone beneath me.

"Hank," her voice pleaded, "oh my god." There was a slight tremble in her voice which brought me more pleasure than I expected it to. I loved the way she dug her nails into my shoulders as I continued to eat her out and felt my cock bulging under my shorts. I flicked my eyes up towards her chest and reached my hand to one of her breasts. I softly pinched her nipple between my fingers and she convulsed under me with pleasure each time I did.

"Holy shit, you are going to make me come." She dug her nails even further into my skin and arched her back as I continued to flick her clit with my tongue and pinch her nipples with my fingers. Wanting to see just how loud I could get her, I brought one hand down to her center and slowly pushed a finger inside of her. And then two. She moaned and started to shake as I pushed and pulled my fingers from her, continuing to keep my mouth where it was while playing with her breast with my free hand. I could tell she was close to the edge and wanted nothing more than to feel her fall apart for me.

"Come for me, hermosa[4]." I pulled away just long enough to say. "I won't stop until you do. I need to know what it feels like to have you come undone on my tongue."

"Oh my god...yes...Hank, yes!" She shouted my name and her entire body quaked as I took her over the edge. Her pussy contracted around my fingers but I never moved from where I was, milking the orgasm for all it was worth. My eyes moved to take in the way her body reacted as the pleasure I caused took over, and marveled at how beautiful it was to watch her come down. Her chest rose and fell with her labored breaths and her eyes were rolled to the back of her head in ecstasy. I brought my lips to her pussy once more and kissed the now swollen and sensitive skin. As my lips met her center, she bucked her hips and pulled away from me, the sensation too much as she was still coming down.

I slowly crawled up her body, bringing my lips to her ear and nipped it between my teeth. She had her eyes closed and was still trying to catch her breath after what I had just done to her. Pressing my lips to her neck, I leaned into her ear and whispered, "Esa es mi buena chica[5]. That's my good girl." She giggled underneath me, finally opening her eyes to look at me as I hovered over her.

"I love it when you speak Spanish," she mused, bringing both her hands to either side of my face. I leaned into her palms and closed my eyes, welcoming in the sense of comfort she brought me after what I'd done to her. I loved knowing I could get her off like I just had.

"I love watching you come undone under me. I don't think I've ever seen something so beautiful before." I looked

---

4. beautiful
5. That's my good girl.

166

down at her face and couldn't believe how luminous she looked. Her skin was flushed and her eyes were dreamy. "Are you still okay?" I asked, hoping she would say yes. I wanted to know how she felt wrapped around me but if she told me she wanted to stop, I would.

"I'm very okay," she groaned. She pushed herself up onto her elbows and reached for the waistband of the shorts I was still wearing. "Now drop your drawers."

"My *drawers*?" I couldn't believe she'd just called them that.

"Yes, your drawers. Now hush up and take 'em off, I wanna see what you've been hiding underneath them." She looked hungry as her eyes flicked from where her hand was pulling on my shorts to my eyes. I liked seeing her riled up so soon after making her finish. My girl wanted me, and I was ready to give her what she wanted.

I pushed myself off of her and stood at the foot of the bed. She watched me intently as I untied the drawstring of my shorts and pushed them to the floor. Her eyes widened as she took me in. She chewed on her bottom lip and continued to stare at me from where she sat up on the bed. For half a second a wave of unsureness swept through me, worried about what she thought about what she saw. I was never embarrassed of my size but I knew other guys were bigger. My friends and I had compared sizes before, and while I wasn't the biggest in the group, I also wasn't the smallest.

"Soldier," her voice was silky and full of desire.

"Yes?" I gave her a half smile as I watched her eyes become full of want.

"You gonna come over here and give me what I want or what?"

"You want me?"

"I don't just want you," she sat up further and grabbed my arm, pulling me closer to where she was on the bed, "I need you. I need you now. I can already feel how wet I am just looking at you. You're not a want, you're a need."

Our lips crashed together again as I lowered myself back down on top of her. Almost instantly, she wrapped her legs around my torso and latched herself onto me. I could tell she wasn't lying about how turned on she was, I could feel her desire dripping down the inside of her thigh. I wrapped an arm under her back and shifted her so that she was on top of me. I wanted to see all of her and having her on top gave me a perfect view of all her beautiful pieces.

"Please tell me you have a condom. I'm on the pill, but still want to use one if you have it," she spoke into my neck, bent over and grinding her hips down onto mine. I reached my arm towards the bedside table and pulled open the drawer. I had bought some the day after I slept at her place, kept two in my wallet, and put the extras in the drawer. She leaned over and pulled one out, holding it in her hand. She looked back at me, sitting on my lap, and gave me a shy expression. "Can I..."

"Can you what?" I looked at her and tried to figure out what she wanted, my hands moved to grab her muscular thighs that were bracing either side of me.

"Can I put it on you?" Her voice was small and full of desire. I don't know what I did in a past life to have earned this moment with her, but God fucking bless.

"You wanna put it on me?" My eyebrows raised and her cheeks flushed.

"Only if that's okay..."

"Hermosa[6], it is so sexy that you want to do that. Any

---

6. Beautiful

man would be fucking stupid to say no to that." My eyes burned into her, thoroughly turned on that she wanted to put the condom on me. A naughty smile bloomed on her face and she moved to one side of me. She tore open the foil in one quick motion and slowly rolled the condom down my hard shaft. My breath hitched in my throat feeling her hand run along my cock as the condom fit around me. Once it was on, she swung herself back on top of my lap and looked down at me through hooded lids.

"Make me feel good," she mewled into my ear. I could hear the smile she had on her face even though I couldn't see her.

Reaching between us, I lined myself up with her and she met my movements. I played with her entrance, causing her breath to get caught in her throat before pushing myself inside of her at last. The way she stretched around me for the first time was something I'd remember for the rest of my life. We both exhaled deeply as I pushed further inside of her, a sense of relief and satisfaction swelling between us. We moved as one, Bailey grinding her hips down onto mine as our lips pressed into one another. She pressed both her hands into my chest and lifted herself up, looking down at me as she rode me. She ran her fingers through her hair and arched her back. Her breasts were on full display and I couldn't keep my hands off of them. I reached up and took them both in my hands, flicking her nipples as I did. She moaned and placed both her hands back on my chest, bringing herself closer to me to play with.

"You feel so good inside of me," she groaned, ripples of goosebumps springing to life on her skin.

"You feel so good around me." She pulled her hips away from me, taking me almost completely out of her, then sank her hips back down, taking me all the way to the hilt. A rush of adrenaline coursed through my veins as she did it a second time. I wrapped my arms around her back and pulled her close. "You're going to make me finish if you keep doing that, hermosa[7]."

She gave me a sultry laugh before replying with a question that wound me up even tighter, "Then why don't you?"

An animalistic moan escaped my lips and I forced her onto her back. Pushing myself back into her quickly, her head lifted from the bed and looked towards me as I did. Beads of sweat were collecting around her brows and I could feel my own slipping down my back. The way we came together was carnal, raw, and completely untamed. The way my heart raced as I made her mine made me think that it was about to burst out of my chest and I had to breathe heavily to try to keep up. I could tell she was getting close to the edge with each thrust by the way the muscles of her pussy contracted around me.

"Hank, I'm close." she moaned under me. Her breath was ragged and her words were needy. She wrapped her hands around my wrists that were on either side of her face and dug her nails into them.

"*Ven por mi, hermosa*[8]," I begged, then remembered she couldn't understand me. "Come for me, beautiful. I'm close, too, and want to feel you crash when I do." I reached my hand between us and started to rub her clit with my fingers. She started to climb, the noises coming from her becoming louder with each swipe against her clit. I continued to push in and out of her and felt myself climbing right along with her. She pulled me into her chest, wrapping her arms around my shoulders and brought her lips to my ear.

---

7. beautiful
8. Come for me, beautiful

"*Make me yours, Hank.*"

When the words left her lips, I did exactly what she asked. I felt the orgasm rip through her body and mine at the same time and we both hit our peak together. She cried out my name as I thrusted into her once more in a way that I knew the neighbors would hear. I didn't care, let them hear how good I make my girl feel.

"Eres tan, hermosa[9]," I hummed into her ear as she continued to come down.

"I'm going to need a goddamn Spanish-to-English dictionary to know what you're saying," she mused with a laugh.

"I said, you're so beautiful. You're the most beautiful girl I've ever seen. I can't believe you're mine."

"I'm yours?" She looked up at me as her cheeks slowly turned a deep shade of pink.

"Only if you wanna be." I brought my hand to her cheek and stroked my thumb across it. I knew I would never be the same after having her this way. I was ruined by her already.

"I'd like that very much." She turned her head and kissed the palm of my hand. Leaning down over her, I framed her face with both my hands and pressed a tender kiss to her lips.

"I'll be right back." I pulled out of her slowly and got up from the bed before walking to the bathroom. I quickly discarded the condom into the trash and ran some water. As it warmed up, I found a washcloth and ran it under the warm water before heading back into the bedroom. She was still lying on the bed, watching me move closer towards her.

"What are you doing?" she asked as I leaned over her legs.

---

9. You're so beautiful

"I'm taking care of you," I started, "I'll always take care of my girl." I brought the damp washcloth to her legs and wiped them clean. "If you want to take a shower, you're more than welcome too."

"While I appreciate the offer," she reached for my hand as I threw the washcloth towards the hamper, "I think I just want to lay with you for now."

I climbed back into bed and pulled the comforter over both of us. She wiggled herself into the crook of my arm as I wrapped it under her head. When she was pressed into my body, it felt like a missing piece of me had finally been returned. She looped one arm around my torso and pulled herself closer to me. With her cheek resting on my chest, I instinctually started to play with her hair. Being with her like this was unlike anything I had ever felt. I had been with other women in the past, but none of them left me feeling so whole and content as she did.

Being with her made me feel as if I was full once more.

25

HANK

<u>1 New Message: Blondie</u>

Stop it.

I looked up at her from across the gym to where she was sitting at her usual bench. She was a creature of habit and always used the same rack or sat at the same bench in the free weights section if she could. I knew exactly where to look when her message came through on my phone.

A few days had passed since I made her mine and I haven't stopped thinking about her since. The next day she headed back to her place, but not until I had one more taste of her. Now that I knew what it felt like to have her, I wanted to have her every day if I could. She intoxicated my mind like a drug and I was already fiending for my next hit.

Stop what?

Stop looking so fucking hot over there. That girl on the machine in front of you keeps checking you out in the mirror. If she doesn't stop I'm going to come over there and make her stop.

I turned towards her and she met my eyes before jutting her chin out towards the girl who was sitting at the machine in front of the rack I was at. Sure enough, she caught my glance in the mirror and gave me a sultry smile. I looked away quickly, not wanting to give her the wrong idea.

She's pretty, isn't she?

I read her text and tucked my phone back into my pocket. I then cleared my rack, cleaned it off, and walked towards where she was sitting. She watched me from her bench, her hair pulled up into a messy bun and her over-ear headphones slightly removed, and gave me a perplexed expression. Once I reached her, I leaned over the bench, placed both my hands between where her legs were straddling it, and gave her a kiss.

"Not as pretty as you, blondie. No one is as pretty as my girl." Her lips pulled back into a tight smirk and her cheeks flushed. I cocked my head to the side and pressed my lips to her cheek and she brought a hand to my jawline as I did. I was never one for public displays of affection before, but with her, I would do anything. Hell, I wanted people to know she was mine and that I was hers.

"Good answer. Wanna spot me?" As she stood from the bench, her breasts, which were well supported by her sports bra, brushed against my chest. The skin-tight, long-sleeve workout top and leggings she was wearing had been driving me crazy all morning, and now that I was close enough, I could smell her signature scent—honey and vanilla. I had to fight to not give myself away in my gym shorts.

She walked behind the rack and dipped under it so that the bar was across the back of her shoulders. As I walked to stand behind her, I counted the plates she had on both sides of her rack that she was about to squat.

"Holy shit, you know how much you're squatting right now, right?"

She looped her hands around the bar and pressed it up so it was resting fully on her shoulders.

"195, it's a new PR," she grunted as she squatted down and pressed back up. I followed her motions one for one in order to catch her if she fell out of it. Each time she made it back up, she pushed a breath out through pursed lips. I kept my arms hovering under her elbows so she knew I was there but never had to help her up.

"Come on, Bailey, one more, you got this," I encouraged as she stood in front of me, hovering with the bar across her shoulders. Her eyes were locked forward and I knew she was trying to hype herself up to get in one more rep. "You're so strong, hermosa[1], one more, you can do it. I'm right here to catch you if you need me." I kept my arms under her and took a step closer to her so she could feel me behind her. She shook her head and pushed out another forced breath before sinking down into a squat and rising to her feet before clicking the bar back into its holding spot. She ducked under the bar and turned to look at me before flexing. I couldn't stop myself from laughing at her, she looked too damn cute.

"Nicely done, blondie."

---

1. beautiful

"Thank you, thank you, I have an *excellent* spotter." She winked at me before sitting down on the bench.

"You mind if I share with you?" I flicked my thumb towards the bar and started to add some plates when she nodded her head.

"It's Wednesday, right?"

"Yesterday was Tuesday which means today is Wednesday, yes." My voice was playful but she stuck her tongue out at me anyway.

"That means you have D and D tonight with the guys?"

"Yeah, why?" I ducked my head under the bar and started to squat. She sat on the bench and watched me stand and sink back down. There were a few times I caught her licking her lips as her eyes followed my movements. After finishing my set, I racked my weights and stepped out from under the bar.

"Can I come?" Her voice was full of hope and her eyes gleamed at me.

"Uhhh..." I had to think. This was something the boys and I hadn't discussed before, bringing a girl to campaign night. It was never really an issue when we were younger since none of us had girlfriends. The guys wouldn't care if I brought her, would they? "Sure, yeah if you want to come you can. It's probably going to be really boring. It's not really a game you can join in on."

"That's okay!" Excitement teemed in her voice. "I'll bring my book and read if I get bored. I would love to hangout with your friends and just watch you play. Plus, I miss you." She gave me a sheepish grin and took a step closer to me. I couldn't control my hands as they found her waist and pulled her in. I pressed another kiss to her cheek before spotting her through her next set.

Bailey was coming to campaign night and I could only hope that my friends wouldn't want to kill me for bringing her.

26

HANK

I picked her up from her place half an hour before I was expected at campaign night. She insisted that I wait for her outside, so I stood next to my bike and waited for her to come down. As she exited her building, she came out wearing tight black leggings and a baggy T-shirt. The closer she got, the more I realized the shirt was mine. She had worn the ARMY T-shirt home after staying at my house last weekend and was wearing it now underneath a cream sweater. Her hair was curled and fell loosely around her shoulders and once she was close enough, I caught a glance of the smile that always made my day brighter.

"Hey there, handsome, thanks for picking me up," she sang, leaning in and kissing me on the cheek.

"What happened to 'soldier'?" I appreciated that she called me handsome, but I much prefer her usual name for me.

"You don't like 'handsome'?" She cocked her hip out and placed a hand on it. Her eyebrows were pulled together and she gave me a half smile.

"I like 'soldier'..." I pretended to be sad and dropped my

head down which caused her to laugh and throw her arms around my neck.

"Oh my lord, soldier it is!"

I smiled at her, unable to hold it in because the Southern twang in her voice as she said 'lord' made my heart melt. I handed her the second helmet and buckled it for her under her chin. Before moving away from her, I reached through the helmet and tapped her nose with my index finger. I then reached into the saddlebag on the back of my bike and pulled out the new jacket I bought after the first time she rode with me. I had to make a guess on the size but as she slid it on, I knew I had guessed right. She smiled at me from under her visor and climbed on behind me once I had sat down. It didn't take us long to get to Kolbi's since he lived downtown like she did.

I had texted him earlier in the day to make sure it was alright that I brought her along with me. Mostly because it was his house we met at and also because I knew I was going to need backup with the others when I showed up with a girl. He didn't give me shit for wanting to bring her and told me he was excited to see her again. I always loved Kolbi for his unwavering support.

Holding her hand in mine, I pushed open the front door and shouted down the long entry hallway toward the kitchen where I knew the guys would be.

"Alright, assholes, who's here already?"

"We're in here you dicklicker, hurry up so we can start!" Conrad shouted back. I turned to look at my girl who was laughing as she followed me.

"You wanna a beer Hanky? Hey, how's that hot piece of a —" Malcolm had his head in the fridge as he was speaking but stopped abruptly when he turned around to see who was with me.

"Hot piece of what now?" Bailey mocked as he made eye contact with her. Her head was cocked to one side and a grin was growing on her face. *That's my girl, give it right back to him.* My heart swelled with pride watching her hold her own with my friends.

Conrad took a step closer to us, looking towards the voice that didn't belong, and furrowed his eyebrows together as he looked at Bailey. "What is she doing here?"

"Conrad, that's no way to speak to our guest." Kolbi looked to Conrad from the table before standing and making his way towards her. He took her hand and pulled her in, placing a cordial peck on her cheek. "Hello Bailey, it's nice to see you again. You're looking as beautiful as ever."

She gave him a friendly smile before placing her hand back into mine and wrapping her free hand around my arm. The move signaled to everyone who she belonged to and watching my friends stunned expressions was almost too much to handle.

"Thank y'all for having me. I was very happy when Hank told me I could join you guys tonight." She looked at all of my friends before beaming back at me. I leaned in and kissed her forehead before looking back at the guys who had been my lifelong friends.

"Disgusting," Malcolm joked before pushing a beer into my chest and taking a seat at the table.

"I'm happy for you, brother." Kolbi gave us both a warm glance and headed towards the table too. The only one who didn't say anything was Conrad who gave Bailey a disapproving look from where he'd been standing at the table. I knew why he was looking at her like he was, but I wasn't going to bring it up right now. I glanced towards the table and counted only four chairs before looking back towards my girl.

"Do you want a drink or anything? Looks like there's only room for four at the table but you're more than welcome to hangout in the living room. It's just around that wall." I pointed around the dividing wall between the kitchenette and where the living room was. You could see the table the guys and I would be playing at from the couch.

"I would take a water if you don't mind. And I'm fine, I promise. I told you I would bring my book, I can read while you play. I really just wanted to hangout with everyone and be with you." She squeezed my hand and the corners of her mouth reached for her eyes.

After getting her a water and showing her where the bathroom was in case she needed it while we played, I finally took my seat at the table.

"Can we start now please?" Conrad grumbled from where he sat. His tone didn't hide how annoyed he clearly was. Kolbi gave him a shaded glance before looking back at me. Malcolm shrugged at me from his seat as he took a pull from his beer.

"Something wrong, Tolith?" I spoke to him in character because I knew part of his irritation was the fact that I brought her with me to a campaign night.

"I just didn't expect to have an uninvited companion joining us tonight for our journey. I didn't realize NPC's were welcome here," he gruffed, reaching across the board and avoiding my gaze. I don't know why he was so upset that she was here, she wasn't even playing with us. Leave it to Conrad to insult my girl in the nerdiest way possible by calling her a 'non-playable character'. You normally only heard that insult when you were playing online with random twelve year olds who were talking shit over Voice Chat.

"What are you, fourteen? This isn't a 'No Girls Allowed'

club. Besides, I asked Kolbi before coming over if he was fine that I brought her with me and he said it was."

"You asked him but not us?" Conrad jutted his hand out and waved it between him and Malcolm. I looked towards Malcolm who was playing with the cap from his beer bottle.

"Are you annoyed she's here too?" I directed the question towards Malcolm and couldn't hide the irritation that was growing in my voice. I couldn't believe Conrad was acting this way.

"Please, Auffroy, Denis de Brey is *never* upset when a beautiful maiden is around," he boasted, giving me a slick grin and bringing his hand to his chest, puffing it up as he did.

"And don't we know it, brother," Kolbi slapped his hand down on Malcolm's shoulder and all of us laughed, including Conrad. Kolbi looked around the table now that the tension had been dispersed, "We good to start now everyone?"

I nodded my head and looked at Conrad who just shrugged. I could tell he was still annoyed with me and I didn't love that I had upset him. These guys were family and I never liked being the reason they were unhappy. While I didn't get why it was such a big deal to him that Bailey came with me tonight, I still didn't like knowing he was mad at me.

Over the next few hours, my friends and I played through the storyline that was weaved for us. Every so often, I would stand and look into the other room only to find her curled up on the couch reading. A few times I looked in at her, she was already looking back at me with a smile. She looked so at home there on the couch, like she was meant to be there. Having her close to me, even if she was in the other room, gave me a sense of peace and warmth I haven't felt in a long time. She had an energy to her that I could feel even from another room.

"Auffroy, what's your roll?"

I was looking towards the living room again, wondering about what she was reading that could be causing her to look at the pages like she was. She had a smirk on her face she was trying to cover with the back of her hand. '*Something hot and steamy*' she had once told me. Maybe she was reading something hot and steamy now. Suddenly my dick twitched under my jeans.

"Auffory, what's your roll? Auffroy!" Kolbi shoved me in the shoulder, breaking my glance from Bailey and bringing me back to the table. My friends all looked at me, each of them with a varying degree of annoyance on their faces.

"Sorry," I snatched the die off the table and threw it across the board, "sixteen on the dice, twenty on the roll," I announced.

"Very nice. With that roll, you get lucky and find the sacred scroll you've been searching for inside the ancient library. With this discovery, you and your party find a map that will lead you to the city you've been searching for."

"Good shit." Malcolm slapped his hand down on the table.

"Finally. Nicely done, Auffroy." Conrad sighed. We had been stuck on this quest for over an hour, each roll setting us back a little bit. We'd battled an ogre, fought some goblins, and solved two different puzzles before getting to this point. Kolbi was putting us through it today and the dice weren't playing in our favor.

"Auffroy?" Bailey's voice came from across the table and we all looked to her. We had been so enthralled in the game that none of us noticed her walk in and stand next to the table.

"You okay, hermosa?" *Shit.* I squeezed my eyes shut before looking at my friends. The nickname had slipped and I knew I was going to hear about it.

"Yeah, I'm good. I was just going to get more water. Anyone need anything?" Her hands rested on the backs of Conrad and Malcolm's chairs. Malcolm turned his neck to look at her and I didn't miss how his eyes passed over her chest for a few seconds too long. Conrad kept his eyes on the board as if looking at her would turn him to stone.

"I would take another beer, beautiful," Malcolm mused up at her, giving her his most charming look. I wanted to punch him in the throat.

"I'm fine, thank you for asking," Kolbi gave her a warm smile which she returned.

"You need anything Conrad?" She looked down at him but he continued to ignore her glance.

"No," he grunted. She gave me a look, furrowing her eyebrows just long enough for me to see. I could tell Conrad's lack of enthusiasm towards her was throwing her off.

Before leaving the table, she walked behind my chair and wrapped her arms around my shoulders possessively and rested her chin there, "And what about you, you need anything?" She spoke directly into my ear and a shiver ran down my spine. The growing bulge in my jeans was almost too much to hide.

"I would take another beer if you don't mind." I brought my lips to her cheek and kissed her. Fuck my friends and what they thought, I wasn't afraid to show my girl affection in front of them. I would deal with the hounding I'd get from them later.

"You got it," she whispered before kissing the top of my head. As she walked towards the kitchen I whipped my head towards Malcolm.

"Don't call her 'beautiful'," I spat.

"Why? You did." He gave me a cocky smirk before crossing his arms over his chest confidently.

"How did you—"

"I took Spanish in high school you moron, I know what 'hermosa[1]' means. I might be Asian but my Spanish is quite good. It also doesn't hurt that I heard you speaking it with your dad growing up."

"Well, don't call my girl beautiful like that, or look at her like you did, it's disrespectful."

"Your '*girl*'? So you're official now?" Kolbi interjected.

"I mean, I think so. We haven't given it a name yet." My mind flashed back to her laying under me this past weekend when I had called her mine and how she told me she would like it if she was. I guess I just assumed that meant we were together. Maybe I should ask her just to be sure.

Malcolm looked as if he was about to say something when Bailey came back in with a fresh glass of water and two beers. She handed one to Malcolm before walking over and handing me the bottle. She leaned over to meet me at eye level and placed a tender kiss on my cheek.

"I'm going to go back to my book, let me know if you need anything," she hummed.

"I will for sure, thanks." Her lips being so close to mine felt like an invite and I wanted nothing more than to press my lips to them. She stood and walked down the small hallway once more and I watched her go.

---

1. beautiful

185

"That is one fine woman you got yourself there," Kolbi said quietly so she wouldn't hear.

I was too distracted by the way her hips swayed and how much she felt like she belonged in this chosen family of mine to respond. But I knew he was right.

Bailey was one fine woman.

And she was all mine.

27

BAILEY

I tapped my fingernails nervously on the coffee table, my legs tucked under it and my back leaning against the couch. Ophelia always asked me why I sat on the floor like this versus sitting on the couch. Personally, I thought it was more comfortable. When we would watch TV together, she would curl up on the couch like a normal person and I would sit on the floor. More often than not, I ended up stretching between commercials and Ophie would laugh at me while I did. It felt nice to stretch after lifting at the gym in the morning and the practice had become a habit.

Now I sat on the floor staring at yet another rejection email from a job I applied to earlier in the week. This is the fifth one I've gotten this month, each one stinging more than the last. I had my degree in hospitality and tourism management, yet I couldn't find a job in it to save my life. I was lucky that Ophelia was letting me live with her and that I only needed to cover the cost of my food and utilities or else I would be on the streets. I had some freelance events coming up, but I needed something more stable.

"I wish you would let me help you launch your own compa-ny." Her words rang out in my ears as I read the rejection letter again. I wish she was here right now, she would give me the pump up I needed to get out of this funk. She was on a work trip until Wednesday though, which meant I had the next five days to myself. Only Ophelia would offer to help me launch my own company after letting me live with her for the last two years. I don't know what I did in a past life to deserve her as a friend, but whatever it was, I'm glad I did it.

I looked around our condo, the mid-morning sun shining through the two big windows that overlooked the street. Our condo sat squarely in Harleston Village and I loved it. The location of it, how it was laid out, the design Ophie had given it. When Hank picked me up on Wednes-day, I discovered that I lived virtually around the block from his best friend Kolbi. I smiled as I thought of his friends and how they played together for several hours. I loved getting to hear them jab at one another as they played and found myself getting lost in the story they were spinning. Every so often he would stand from his chair and look in on me and I would pretend not to notice him or the way my heart sped up when I knew he was looking at me. A few times I was already looking at him when he stood to check on me and I couldn't help but swoon. The way he looked at me with a mix of admiration and protection made my heart swell.

The slight ding of a new email hitting my inbox brought me back to reality and I quickly swiped my fingers across the trackpad of my computer to wake it up. My head fell into my hands after I read yet another, *'Sorry, we're not hiring right now,'* email from another event planning company I'd contacted to check and see if they were looking for help. The feeling of anxiety and stress started to bubble in my stomach. I needed a steady, consistent job because I knew my current living situation couldn't last forever. I started to rub my fingernails with my thumb, something I do when I get anxious, when my phone buzzed on the table next to my computer. I smiled as I picked it up and read the notification.

<u>1 New Message: Soldier</u>

> Happy Saturday, blondie. What are you doing today?

Would it be too dramatic to say 'wallowing in my own self-pity'?

> Just hanging out. Ophie is out of town for the next few days.

> You're home alone for the next few days? In that big building?

> I have a doorman, soldier. No one is going to get me.

> You lock the door at night right? Every time?

> Yes, every time. It's even locked right now. Don't worry about me, I can take care of myself.

The more I texted him, the more my racing heart started to slow. His calming energy having a significant impact on me even through text.

> I just want to make sure my girl is safe.

> I mean you, you are safe.

He sent the second text immediately after the first, as if he was trying to backtrack on what he'd sent. I hugged my phone to my chest and squealed like a teenager at the fact that he called me 'his girl'.

> Am I 'your girl'?

I mean...I'd like you to be.

If you want to be...

I squealed again.

> I think I'd like that very much 😊

I sent it back and watched the screen like a hawk, waiting for the three dots to pop up again. I didn't think this is how he would ask me to be his girlfriend, but I was okay with it.

It's settled then. You're my girl.

> And you're my soldier.

I smiled at my phone and suddenly had an idea.

> Hey, do you wanna come over tonight?
> Ophie is gone so it would just be us.

I'll never turn down an opportunity to see you or that beautiful smile of yours. How's six?

> Six is perfect!! I'll see you tonight.

I'll see you tonight.

———

I STOOD from the couch after I heard the knock on the door and went to open it. Before letting him in, I took a deep breath and painted a smile on my face. I didn't want him to know I was upset, I just wanted to try and enjoy the evening with him.

When I swung the door open my jaw dropped at what I was looking at. Standing in the hallway was Hank, but he was also holding a giant pizza box and an oversized bouquet of flowers. I brought my hands to my mouth and laughed slightly, overwhelmed by his gesture.

"What are you doing?" I asked, extending my hands out to take the flowers from him. He pulled them back before I could reach them and I gave him a look.

"Wait, I need to say something." He took a quick breath and straightened his shoulders. He seemed nervous and if he wasn't holding the flowers, it would have put me on edge. "Bailey Brown, will you be my girlfriend?"

My jaw dropped again and I gaped at him, stunned by his question but touched all the same.

"Didn't we clear this up already? Isn't that what you meant when you asked me to be your girl?" My bottom lip pouted as I looked at him. It was hard to know for sure because of his caramel colored skin, but I'm almost certain he was blushing.

"I mean, yeah, but," he laughed nervously, looking down at his feet before bringing his warm brown eyes back to mine, "doing it over text didn't feel right. It didn't feel...official." His eyes met mine and the way he was looking at me almost made me pass out. I extended my hand towards him again, this time grabbing his wrist and pulled him into a hug.

"Yes, Hank Martínez, I would love to be your girlfriend. Your girl. Your blondie. Whatever you wanna call me, I'll be it."

"You forgot *hermosa*[1]," he purred into my ear, sending a shiver down my spine. *This man and his Spanish*. We kissed in the hallway before I pulled him inside and closed the door behind us.

A few hours and a whole pizza later, I was lying on the couch with my head on Hank's lap as he twirled my hair between his fingers. He asked if we could watch *13 Going on 30* again and I happily agreed. I tried to not let the multiple rejection emails from the day get me down, but as the credits rolled, the slow creeping feeling of anxiety was back in my belly.

"Bailey?" He said my name and I turned to look up at him.

"Hmm?"

"Is something wrong?" He furrowed his brows at me and gave me a concerned look.

"Uhh no, why do you ask?" I lied. I felt embarrassed that no one wanted to give me a chance but I wasn't going to tell him that.

"Because the last time we watched this movie you talked through the entire thing, quoting almost every line. You didn't say anything this time."

"Oh." I hadn't even noticed. "I just didn't want to be annoying, I guess."

"*Hermosa*[2]," he said, looking down at me, his lips pressed together in a line. "I can tell when something is wrong. Why won't you tell me?"

---

1. beautiful
2. Beautiful

I chewed my bottom lip and sat up to face him. I didn't like being dishonest with him because I would want him to be honest with me. I sucked in a breath before exhaling deeply. "I just had a hard day is all. I've been trying to get a full time job doing some sort of event planning or something in hospitality, but no one is hiring. I got three rejection emails today alone. It just makes me feel like a failure." I stared at my hands, unable to bring my eyes to meet his.

"You're not a failure," he stressed. "Hey, look at me." His fingers came to my chin and pulled it up so I was forced to look at him. "You are not a failure, not even a little. You will find something and anyone who hires you will be so lucky, hermosa[3]."

I blew out a breath and pondered his words before speaking. I knew I was good at what I did, lots of people had told me as such several times at my last job. Shit, the reason I had any money nowadays was because old clients from the event hall tracked me down and asked me to organize private events for them. I loved throwing a good party, I just wished somewhere local would hire me to do it full time. The longing in my heart to start my own event planning business was strong, but I would need to save up the money before launching it on my own.

"I'm just having a down day I guess," I confessed. Without speaking, he squeezed my hand and stood from the couch. He then walked into my bedroom and was gone for a few moments before I heard the sound of running water coming from the bathroom. When he came back out, his lips had curled into a caring smile and his eyes flickered with anticipation.

"What's that look for? What are you doing?"

---

3. beautiful

"Come here," he urged, pulling me up from the couch and dragging me into my bathroom. I followed closely behind him, his strong hand wrapped around mine until we reached what he wanted to show me. When I saw it, I felt my eyes crinkle in the corners, touched by what he had done.

"You said when you were having a bad day, you liked to take a bath and read. You're having a bad day, so I drew you a bath. If you want, I'll read to you while you soak." He motioned towards the bath that was now half full of piping hot water and then looked down at me, his lips pulled into a warm grin.

"You'll read to me?" My voice trembled and was so small I didn't even think he could hear me over the running water. Not only had he remembered what I liked to do on a hard day, but he also offered to read to me. I thought the flowers he brought me were sweet, but this was better.

He pulled me into his chest and wrapped his arms around my shoulders. An instant wave of safety and security flooded my body as I breathed him in. I nestled my nose into his chest as he flexed his arms, squeezing me a little tighter. "I'll do whatever I need to do to make my girl happy, and if that includes reading to her, then that's what I'll do." When he kissed me on the top of my head, I squeezed my thighs together and was happy he couldn't see the big stupid smile that had spread across my face.

"The book I'm reading is out on my nightstand, can you grab it for me?" I asked, pointing to where the book was lying. He released me to go and grab it as I started to undress and climb into the tub. I caught him watching me as I slipped out of my bra and panties and slowly lowered myself into the hot water, wrapping my arms around my legs once I was safely inside. He set the book down on the bathroom counter and left the bathroom quickly before returning with a chair from the dining room table. He carefully set the chair next to the bathtub, grabbed my book off of the counter, and took a seat.

"What page are you on?" he asked, carelessly flipping through the pages.

"Careful, careful," I said hastily, "there's an old receipt in there that I'm using as a bookmark. That's where I'm at."

"An old receipt? Why don't you get a proper bookmark?"

"I have one, I just don't know where it is right now. I think it's in another book and I had the receipt, so I'm just using that."

"How many books are you reading right now?" He gave me an inquisitive look and I smirked.

"Right now? Just three. I usually have four or five going though," I confessed, shrugging my shoulders into my ears.

"Damn, blondie, you never cease to amaze me," he marveled, shaking his head at me. Then, he opened the book and started to read.

I loved listening to him pronounce each word with care and laughed when he tried to do voices for the characters. As I soaked in the hot water, allowing myself to relax and destress, I watched as he turned the pages of my book and read to me. The story sounded so much better coming from his lips, especially when we got to a spicy part of the book. Since I had read hundreds of romance books, I knew when the story was about to get risqué and I waited with excitement to see how he would handle it.

"He bent down and," he paused and brought the book closer to his nose and his eyes went wide as he read the next part in his head. He lifted his eyes to me where I sat in the tub, watching him with anticipation. "Is this what women want? For us to do....this?"

"I don't know what he's doing, my narrator has stopped narrating," I teased, giving him a sly grin. He took a sharp inhale and blew it out between pursed lips. He almost looked uncomfortable and I half expected him to tell me the reading was over, but instead, he leaned over, placed his elbows on his knees, and started reading again. Reading these scenes on your own was never a bad time, but holy shit listening to a hot Latino man read them to you was unlike anything else. As I sat in the tub, listening to him read one spicy sentence after the next, I could feel the heat inside of me starting to rise.

"Damn," he said after finishing the chapter and clearing his throat, "now I know why girls read those things." I couldn't help but laugh because he wasn't wrong.

"They're not a bad time, are they?" I joked, looking up at him as he continued to sit, leaning over on his knees.

"No, they are not. You ready to get out or do you wanna soak some more?"

"Let me wash my hair really quick and then I'll get out."

"Okay, I'm going to go get some water while you do that, I'll be back." He gave me a wink and stood from his chair, quickly turning away from me when he did. As he passed the mirror I noticed why he had been sitting hunched over himself as he read. The large bulge in his pants was undeniable. I brought my hand to my mouth to stifle my laughs until he was gone and quickly washed my hair under the faucet. A few minutes later, he returned more relaxed than he had left. "Where do you keep your towels?"

"Under the sink," I explained, pointing to the cabinet he could find them in. He pulled one out, unfolded it, and held it up for me. I stood from the bath and let him wrap the towel around me before carefully stepping out. As I tied the towel around me, he leaned over the tub to pull the plug to let the water drain out. I grabbed another towel and wrapped it around my head. He stood behind me like a bodyguard and watched me in the mirror as I washed my face and put on moisturizer. I then let my hair down and grabbed my brush.

"Can I do that?" he asked, staring at the brush that was in my hand.

"You," I paused for a beat, looking down at my brush and then back to him, "you wanna brush my hair?"

"If that's okay. I love your hair, it's one of the first things I noticed about you when I saw you at the gym that morning." My heart started to melt as I gazed at him in the mirror before turning to hand him my brush.

"Sure, you can brush my hair, but please be gentle. I have a very sensitive head."

"I promise to be gentle."

And he was.

He stood behind me and ran the brush from the crown of my head all the way down the end of my blonde locks. I watched him as he carefully ran the brush through my hair, his eyes locked on my head with focus and attention. As I stared at him in the mirror, watching him take care of me and knowing he was doing it because I'd had a bad day, I could feel something growing in my belly. A feeling I hadn't ever felt before for another man but one I had read about time and time again. The feeling they write songs about and make movies about. The feeling you knew instinctively, because it's a feeling we all long for until we have it. The feeling I never felt worthy of having after being attacked two years ago because I felt so ruined and broken.

My breath caught in my throat when our eyes locked in

the mirror and he gave me the big goofy smile I had come to long for, and I knew.

I was falling in love with Hank Martínez.

28

HANK

I f I could stop time whenever I wanted, I would push the button right now to freeze in this moment with her forever.

She was standing in front of me, wrapped in a towel, and watching me in the mirror as I pulled the brush from the top of her head down to her shoulders with as much care as I could. I never had sisters growing up, so this wasn't something I'd ever done before. I'm not sure what prompted me to ask to brush her hair, but when she had released it from the towel she had wrapped around it, I knew I wanted to. As I brushed through her damp hair as gently as I could since she had told me she had a sensitive head, I felt her eyes studying me in the mirror. I rested my hand on her waist to hold her still, and she laid her hand over mine. After I'd finished brushing, I leaned over and kissed the top of her shoulder before handing the brush back to her.

Once she was dressed in her sleep shorts and an oversized shirt, I moved towards the front door to head home.

"Where are you going?" she asked in a small voice,

standing in the doorway of her bedroom with wide, longing eyes.

"I was going to head home so you could get some rest." I took a few steps closer to her again and brought my hands to her elbows as she grabbed onto my shirt.

"Can you stay?" She looked up at me and gave me puppy dog eyes which I think she was starting to discover that if she used them on me, I would give her whatever she wanted. I felt my mouth pull into a smirk and pressed my lips to her forehead.

"Of course I will."

We both slipped into her bed after I stripped down into just my boxers and she pressed her body into mine. For a while, we just lay next to one another, enjoying the feeling of having the other close. She had her head on my shoulder and was running her fingers lightly across my chest. I could feel my heart rate starting to slow and my eyes getting heavy when she spoke.

"Have you ever thought about what animal you would be if you were reincarnated?" She spoke with so much intention that I could tell she wasn't joking. I tried to hold back the laughs that came because of how surprised I was by her question.

"Uhhh, not really, no. Have you?" I tucked my chin into my neck to look at her.

"Of course I have. I think about these types of things all the time." Her voice came out even and she acted as if this was a totally normal question to ask. I tugged on her shoulder and she followed my lead by moving even closer into my chest. My fingers started to run along it and she kissed my pec.

"So, what animal are you reincarnating into in your next life?"

She looked up at me with a confident smirk. "A fox."

I barked out a laugh and shook my head at her. "A fox?"

"Yeah, a fox. They're smart, and cunning, and know how to hold their own. Just like me." I looked down at her with reverence and loved that she saw herself in this way. My girl was headstrong and confident and I loved that about her.

"You would make for a very cute fox," I said before leaning down and kissing her nose. She scrunched her face at me and pushed some of the hair that had fallen into her face away.

"I think you would reincarnate into a bear." She said it so matter-of-factly as if she'd thought about this before. She probably had.

"A bear?" I exclaimed, surprised by the animal she had assigned to my reincarnated self.

"Yeah, a bear. Cute, cuddly, and shy, but will completely rip your face off if you threaten them. You give off big bear vibes."

I laughed next to her and she bounced on my chest. This girl always seemed to surprise me by the things she said.

"I could also see a wolf." She pushed out her lips and nodded her head, enjoying the thought. "You're a pack animal for sure, just like a wolf. They're shy too, just like you."

"I'm only shy around you, blondie, you make me like that." She propped herself up on her elbow to look at me.

"I make you feel shy?"

"You make me more than shy, you make it hard for my brain to function. Ever since meeting you, it's like you've filled every crevice of my head and are the only thing I can think about. When I saw you for the first time at the gym I felt my heart stop. You bring me life and steal my breath away with just one smile. I've never felt this way about anyone before." I placed my hand on her cheek and she nuzzled into it.

"I've never felt like this with anyone else before either, soldier."

————

I ROLLED over on my stomach and extended my arm across the bed, waving my hand back and forth searching for her. As I lay in her bed still half asleep, my mind fell back to the memories of last night. How she looked as she stripped and sank into the tub. How I offered to read to her and had to hunch over my lap to cover the erection I got as I did. It's no fucking wonder women read those books, they're unreal. I tried not to develop a complex but made a mental note to try some of the things I'd read last night with Bailey if she'd let me. I loved how she let me brush her hair and how it felt between my fingers. Getting to care for her that way meant everything to me. My eyes sprang open as my head caught up with the fact that she wasn't next to me like she was when we fell asleep last night.

I pushed myself up and looked around her room. We had fallen asleep after she got dressed and climbed into bed. We stayed up until almost two in the morning talking and laughing together. It was funny to me how easy it was to be with her. We'd only known each other for roughly a month, but when we were together, it was as if we had known one another our entire lives. As I looked around the room, I noticed my shirt that I had thrown to the floor was gone and her bedroom door was slightly ajar. The more coherent I became, the more my senses started to pick up on the aroma of bacon cooking; I could hear it popping and sizzling on the other side of her bedroom door. Bringing my feet to the floor, I pushed up from the bed and walked out towards where the smells were coming from.

Once my head peeked around the corner of the door, the most devastatingly beautiful sight came into view.

Bailey stood at the counter wearing nothing but my shirt and a pair of lacy underwear. Half her hair was tied up on the top of her head in a bun, and she was dancing around the kitchen while holding a pair of tongs. I watched her from the doorway, taking in everything that she was, in awe of how carefree she looked as she spun around, unaware that she was being watched. She shimmied her shoulders along with the soft-playing music, flipping the bacon every few beats. I couldn't hold back my laughter when she grasped the tongs in her hands and used them as a mic, quietly singing along to the song that was playing on her phone. She jumped when she heard me laugh and found me quickly with her eyes.

"Oh! Oh, Hank, you scared me," she breathed heavily and brought her hand to her heart. "I didn't wake you did I? I was trying to be quiet."

I moved closer to her and wrapped my arms around her waist, pulling her into my chest. She looked up at me, her eyes growing wider the closer I brought my face to hers. "No, hermosa[1], you didn't wake me up," I assured her before bringing my lips to hers.

I couldn't help myself—she was like an energy source for me that I needed to get my daily refill of, and seeing her in the kitchen like this made my need for her that much stronger. My hand sank below her lower back and rested on her ass. When I squeezed, she let out a sound that was a mix between a groan and a yelp. She set the tongs down on the

---

1. beautiful

counter and brought both her hands around my neck. With both hands on her ass now, I lifted her with ease and set her down on the kitchen counter, leaning into her lips with force. She roped both of her lean legs around my torso like a koala and held me in place with her muscular thighs. We kissed, our tongues clashing into one another, as I pressed my hips into her center. When she felt my cock pressing into her, she moaned loudly on the counter. My hands couldn't help themselves as they slid from her ass to the inside of her thigh and she bucked her hips towards me when my fingers grazed the outside of her panties. I was about to slip my fingers underneath the purple, lace fabric until the kitchen started to fill with smoke and the smoke alarms went off.

"No! The bacon!" she shouted, pushing me off of her and hopping down from the counter. The damage was already done though and the once juicy bacon she had been cooking was now black and charred. She turned the burner off and threw the pan in the sink, dowsing it with cold water to dispel the smoke.

"This is all your fault," she teased, snapping the tongs at me.

"My fault? How is this my fault?" I brought my hands to my chest, shocked that she was blaming me for this.

"Yes, your fault. If you hadn't come out here lookin' all hot with your dark curls and exposed chest, I wouldn't have gotten distracted and burnt the bacon. I blame you." She scrunched her face up at me and crossed her arms over her chest next to the oven, trying to look annoyed. I took a step closer to her again since she'd moved away to clean up the mess.

"You like my curls?" I asked, bringing my hands back to her waist. No one had ever complimented my hair before, I always just saw it as average.

"I mean, yeah. I think they're pretty cute," she mumbled under a grin as I pulled her closer to me.

"And my, 'exposed chest', as you called it. You like that too?" I picked her up and set her back on the counter next to the sink that was now filled with the burnt pan and still smoking bacon.

"Yeah, I like that too," she mused, her eyes flickering between my lips and my chest. I pulled my shirt she was wearing up so it was resting on her waist, exposing her ass and thighs to me. As I did, her hands started to explore my chest. As her fingers grazed across it, a fresh wave of energy rippled through me.

"You know what I like?"

"What's that?"

"I like the sight of you wearing nothing but my shirt, dancing around the kitchen in your underwear as you sing and cook breakfast." I kissed the side of her neck as her head dropped behind her. "I also like the way your hair looks after you throw it on top of your head like this, like you're too busy doing bigger and better things to be bothered by it." I brought my lips to her neck again and nipped it softly. She sucked in a breath. "But you know what I like most?"

"Tell me," she begged as I nipped at her neck again. I pressed my hard cock into her center as her legs straddled either side of me.

"I like the taste of your sweet pussy on my lips and I will have it right now for breakfast. Spread your legs for me, hermosa², let me have you." She did as I asked, opening her legs wide for me as I pulled at the seam of her panties. She lifted her hips for me as I pulled them off, then tossed them

---

2. beautiful

to the kitchen floor. Placing my hands on her ass once more, I pulled her to the edge of the counter so I could have every part of her with ease.

She watched as I dropped to my knees and brought my face between her legs. Her eyes widened as I kissed her knee, and the top of her leg, then her inner thigh. I hovered just above her center and brought my eyes to her to see if she was still watching me.

She was.

And knowing she was drove me crazy.

Unable to stop myself from tasting her any longer, I brought my lips to her pussy. She groaned as I held her on the counter and pressed my tongue to her clit. Flicking it back and forth, I could hear her starting to breathe heavier. I craved to have more of her, so I slipped my hand under her shirt and reached her breasts. When my fingers found her chest, I realized she wasn't wearing a bra and was instantly more turned on than before. I played with her nipple as I continued to suck and lick her center. She started to shake under me and roped her fingers through my hair.

"Ooh my god," she moaned, her voice trembling as I helped her climb. "Please don't stop."

"I'm not stopping until you come on my tongue, hermosa[3]. Vente para mi, bebé[4]," I begged before bringing my mouth back to her. I meant it when I said I wanted her for breakfast and I wasn't going to stop until my girl fed me properly.

I slipped a hand beneath my mouth and pushed a finger inside her. Her muscles instantly contracted around it and she shouted out in pleasure. Her fingers tugged harder in

---

3. beautiful
4. Come for me, baby.

my hair as I moved my tongue faster back and forth on her clit. I pulled my face away from her and brought two fingers to the outside of her pussy, moving them back and forth across her clit and her head shot up to watch what I was doing to her.

"You're gonna make me come. Please, *please...*" she couldn't finish her plea before her eyes rolled into the back of her head and her head dropped behind her again. I continued to work her like this until I knew she was about to fall over the edge. I wanted to feel her finish on my mouth, so I brought my lips back to her as she screamed out my name and fell over the edge completely. Her breath was labored as she propped herself up on her elbows. Her hips bucked every time I swiped my tongue across her clit, still sensitive from the orgasm I'd just taken from her.

Nothing has ever tasted so sweet.

Her eyes fluttered back to where I was crouched between her legs and were filled with lust and desire. "For a guy who was once too shy to tell me his name, you really know how to make me scream it now."

I pushed to my feet and brought my lips to her ear, "Hearing you scream my name is something I'd like to do every day. I'd like to hear you scream it again right now if you'd let me."

"Yes, *please.*" She flung her arms around my neck and the animal in me grabbed her as if she were a fresh meal to be had. I had just eaten her once, but I was already ready for another meal. I pulled her towards me and looped my arms under her legs as she wrapped them around my torso. Our lips meshed together the entire way from the kitchen to her bedroom. I set her down gently on the bed and took a step back to look at her. I consumed everything she was with my eyes and tried to commit every piece of her to memory.

"What are you lookin' at?" she purred, her slight Southern twang coming out thick.

"Just the most beautiful woman I think I've ever seen who is quickly becoming my everything," I confessed. Her lips pulled up into a shy smile and she reached her hand towards me.

"Make me your everything Hank," she whispered, pulling me down on top of her.

And that's exactly what I did.

Who was I to deny a beautiful woman?

29

HANK

Leaning back in my desk chair, I stared at the clock, wishing it would move faster so the work day would be over. My mind bounced from the work I should have been doing to the time I spent with Bailey yesterday.

For a girl who was once apprehensive in bed, I could tell her walls were coming down with me. After carrying her into her bedroom, she let me have my way with her in ways I'd only ever dreamed of. She was wild when she let go and I loved being on the receiving end of it. After having her in the kitchen, and again in her bed, we showered together and she let me wash her hair. I'll never forget pulling her into me as the soap and warm water washed over us. With her in my arms, I could feel broken and scarred pieces of me starting to mend. Bailey was mending me each time she gave that big happy smile of hers or called me 'soldier'. I just wish there was something I could do to help her in return.

During our hours-long discussion at her place Saturday night after I read to her in the bath, she confided in me how she sometimes has flashbacks of her attack. *'I feel like I'm haunted by it. Knowing he's still out there...it feels like I haven't gotten closure yet. It's like I can't move on from it,'* she shared. I admired her bravery when she told me she had gone to a support group for a few weeks after her attack and told her as much as I laid next to her under the covers. My heart ached knowing she hadn't gotten the closure she needed to feel safe or like she could move on. Anger and rage boiled inside of me every time I thought about the piece of shit who hurt her walking freely down the street. I knew how often rape cases went unsolved, but knowing my girl was one of those cases didn't sit well with me.

As I recalled how she told me that the police never found the man who attacked her because she had waited a few days to report it, an idea sprang to my mind and I stood from my chair. I moved across the hallway in a few swift strides and pushed open the two glass doors that led into Kolbi's office.

"I need to talk to you about something." Kolbi looked up at me from his desk as my voice echoed through the vast, high-ceilinged office.

"Woah, brother," he started, giving me a concerned look as he sat back in his chair, "What's wrong? What happened? Why do you look so pissed?"

"I look pissed?"

"You look more than pissed. You look like you're ready to put someone's head through a wall." I felt like I was ready to put someone's head through a wall. Thinking about her attacker and his lack of recourse for what he did turned me inside out in the worst way.

"It's about Bailey," I fumed.

He motioned towards one of the chairs on the other side of his desk for me to take. "Take a seat. What's going on, did you two have a fight? Is she okay? Last time we talked things seemed good. You were both disgustingly adorable when she came to D and D on Wednesday. What—"

"She was raped," I blurted, unable to hold it in any longer. My eyes darted around the room and I tried to take a few breaths for fear that if I didn't, my anger would explode out of me. Just saying it out loud made me sick.

"What?" he urged, standing from his chair. His fists clenched at his sides as if he was ready for a fight. "Where is she now? When did this happen?"

"A couple years ago," I started, trying to calm him down. The last thing we needed was for both of us to get fired up in the middle of the work day. "It's why she was hesitant the first time I stayed with her. She only just told me a week ago. Remember when I borrowed the car to take her on the picnic? She told me then."

He stared at me with a stunned expression as he lowered himself back into his chair. I felt a strong sense of appreciation for my friend seeing how he was just as upset about this as I am. It meant a lot to me to see how much he cared about my girl. "I'm so sorry," he said, blowing out a breath.

"She's opening up to me Kolb, sharing things with me more freely. The more she does, the more I want to help her, to protect her. It kills me knowing that the son of a bitch who did this to her is still out there."

"He's still out there?" he bristled.

"Yeah, that's part of what I wanted to talk to you about," I explained before telling him my idea. I wanted nothing more than to be able to help her heal from this and I knew that a big part of that was finding the man who attacked her and giving him the justice he deserved.

"So do you think you can find it?" I pressed.

"I mean, I have some buddies who work down at the station and I have an in with the city. I might be able to see if we can find any security footage or something from a red light camera from that night. But if the police didn't find anything then, I don't want you to get your hopes up that I'll be able to find anything now. I know you want to help your girl, but two years is a long time in terms of stored footage. There's no telling if the city even still has backups from then."

"Kolbi, you run a multi-million dollar private security firm. I find it very hard to believe you can't dig something up or find anything. Even just a sliver from that night that might have the guy on camera would help." I looked at my friend as he studied me intently.

"I'll do my best, that's all I can promise. I'll call my guys down at the station and see if they can pull the file from that night. Maybe someone remembers her coming in to report it or has any leads they can share with me."

"That's all I can ask of you." I sighed and stood from my chair. He stood with me and shook the hand I had extended to him. I had started to walk back to my desk to finish my workday when he called out to me.

"Hank," I turned to face him once more, "does Bailey know you're asking me to do this?"

His question hit me square in the chest because no, she didn't. She had no idea that I was asking my friend to dig into her past and I wasn't ready to think about how she'd take it if she found out I had shared her secret. She had entrusted me with it and I had blatantly broken that trust in an effort to help her.

"No, she doesn't. I'd really appreciate it if you didn't tell her you knew. And the guys, they don't need to know about this either," I pressed.

"Of course, brother, whatever you want. But, if we find something, what are you going to do?"

I looked down at my shoes for a beat and thought about it. I would do what I thought was best for her and tell her what we found. She was strong and I knew she would be able to handle it if we found her attacker.

I just hoped that she wouldn't hate me for breaking her trust all in the effort to help her heal at the same time.

30

BAILEY

The timer I had set went off and I jumped from the couch to pull the tamales from the pot to check and see if they were done.

I had asked Hank to come over for dinner tonight after checking to make sure Ophelia was okay with it. She rolled her eyes at me and reminded me that it was Saturday and she would be heading out for the night with some work friends.

"And if I have to come home, that means I will have failed to make a man fall in love with me and ask me to go home with him," she cooed at me with a wink. I love my friend with everything I am, but sometimes I worry about her decision making skills.

Earlier in the week, I had reached out to Amanda, an old caterer I knew from back when I worked at the event hall, and asked her if she could teach me how to make authentic Mexican tamales. Hank had made them for me when he took me on our picnic, so I wanted to try and make them for him in return. As I carefully pulled the steamer basket from the pot of boiling water, I pulled back the husks on a few of them to check to see if they were done. After rewrapping the ones I checked, I lowered them back into the boiling water and set the timer again for another five minutes. Amanda had told me to steam them a little longer than I thought they needed to make sure that all the masa had cooked through and you could easily eat them.

Just as I covered the pot back up with the lid, a knock came from the front door. Excitement and anticipation grew inside of me as I hurried towards it, stopping only for a moment to check myself in the mirror. I had my hair wrapped and secured behind my head with an oversized claw clip and a few pieces had fallen around my face. I smiled at myself because of how genuinely happy I looked. I hadn't looked, or felt, like this in years and it was all because of my soldier. I reached for the door and swung it open to find him standing in the hallway holding a stunning bouquet of deep blue hydrangeas.

"These are for you," he stated, handing me the bouquet as I took a step towards him. "I saw them and they reminded me of your eyes and I knew I had to get them for you."

Unable to hold myself back from him, I flung my arms around his neck, smashing the flowers in between us. I hung onto him tightly, breathing him in and letting the sense of safety and security he brought wash over me. He gently laid his hand on the side of my waist, his other trapped between us still holding the flowers.

"Uh," he muttered into my ear as I continued to squeeze him, "I think you're smashing your flowers."

"Oh!" I pulled away from him quickly and our eyes fell to the now slightly smashed petals. "Oh, I'm sorry! I was just so happy to see you I couldn't help myself. I have a surprise for you!" I grabbed his hand and pulled him into the condo.

He took a deep inhale as he stepped inside and I carefully took the bouquet from his hands, setting them on the counter as I walked into the kitchen. "What is that smell? It smells amazing."

"Yeah?" I chewed on my bottom lip, hopeful that I had gotten the dish right. I wanted to show him how much I loved his history and culture, which is why I tried so hard to get the meal right. It might have taken me almost five hours to make because I had to start over. Twice. But god damn if these weren't the best tamales ever. "I...I made tamales."

"You did?" He looked at me with a dreamy expression, almost as if he couldn't believe what I had said.

"Yeah. You made them for me that night when you took me on a picnic and I loved them. I wanted to make them for you because I know how much you love to cook. I can't say mine are as good as yours but, I tried to get them right." I shrugged.

He took a few steps closer to me and wrapped his arms around my waist, pulling me back into him. He looked down at me, his dark brown eyes fixated on mine. As I looked back into them, the ember flecks that scattered the edges of his irises caught the light and seemed to dance.

"This is the nicest thing anyone has ever done for me, hermosa[1]. Thank you." He pressed his lips to my forehead and then lifted my chin with his fingers and pressed his lips to mine. I felt the blood rush to my cheeks and couldn't fight the shy smile that grew across my face before he said, "Let's eat, I'm starving."

We served up our meals, which included tamales, red rice, refried beans, and some fresh salsa Amanda had made and brought over for me. We both made our plates and took

---

1. beautiful

a seat at the small dining table that Ophelia and I normally ate at together when we were both here for lunch or dinner.

As we ate, I couldn't help but picture what my life would look like if this is how it always went. Hank and I, sitting across from one another, eating delicious food and talking about our day. I loved the idea of him coming home to me after work and the two of us cooking together. I hadn't even realized I was smiling at the idea of it all until he pointed it out.

"What are you smiling about?"

"What? Oh, nothing," I chuckled. I didn't want to tell him what I'd been daydreaming about in case he didn't feel the same way. I thought I knew how he felt about me but I didn't want to scare him off by telling him that I liked the thought of us living together and having every night be like this one. We had only really been dating for a little over a month and it felt too soon to share this with him.

"So," he started, taking a big bite of rice, "I wanted to ask you something." I laughed as a piece of rice fell from his mouth back onto his plate.

"Why don't you finish your bite first and then ask me, soldier?"

"I would but this food is so good, I can't stop eating it," he gushed, causing my insides to swell with pride. He chewed his food, swallowed, and then started again. "So I wanted to ask you something."

"You said that already," I teased.

"There is a veteran's benefit here in the city in a couple weeks and I would like you to go with me as my date. A couple of my buddies from my time in the service will be there and I would love to show off my girl if you'll let me." He gave me a sheepish look from across the table. "So...what do you think?"

"Is this the one held at the library downtown each year?" I had heard of the benefit before but had never attended. It was a big deal around town as many of the city's wealthiest families attended to donate and support the troops.

"Yeah, that's the one. Will you go with me?" he asked again, waiting for me to answer his question. It wasn't that I didn't want to go, it was that I hadn't been to this kind of event since the night I was attacked. The thought of going to any event of this caliber brought up emotions I had trained my body to ignore and push down over the last two years. But looking at him, I knew I couldn't say no.

"Of course I will. When is it?" I asked, swallowing my apprehensions and fears.

"It's in two weeks, the first Saturday of August." The words spilled out of him with so much relief and excitement that I knew I had made the right choice.

The thought of going to a major event like this one opened up old wounds, but seeing how happy it made him made dealing with it bearable. I knew that as long as I was with him, I was safe.

As long as he was with me, I would be okay.

31

HANK

The next two weeks—between the time I asked Bailey to attend the veterans benefit and it actually happening—flew by. Work was insane preparing for the event since Kolbi's firm was running security and half the VIP client's my team catered to were attending. I asked him several times if it was okay that I attended, since I was the person who typically oversaw these kinds of events, but he assured me it was.

Knowing I couldn't take us to the benefit on my bike, Kolbi lent me a company car again so I could drive us both there. I knew Bailey liked my bike, but there was no way I was going to be able to drive us both to a black tie event on the back of it. The Annual Veteran's Benefit was one of the city's largest fundraisers for veterans and this would be the first time I would be attending. My insides buzzed with excitement because I got to see some of my old Army buddies again who were traveling to the city for the event.

When I asked Bailey to come with me as my date, she seemed nervous to say yes. I tried not to dwell on why that was and tried to focus more on the fact that she had agreed to come with me. While we had only known each other since the start of June, it felt like we had known each other forever. She completed me in a way I didn't know I needed and I couldn't wait to show up with her on my arm. How I had managed to score such a beautiful woman I will never know, but I'm not one to look a gift horse in the mouth.

I was sitting at my desk waiting for five o'clock to roll around so I could head out for the day. I still needed to pick up my uniform from the dry cleaners for the benefit and get home to shower and shave so that I wouldn't have to do it tomorrow. It felt nice to pull out my dress blues from the back of my closet after not seeing them for a few months. When I came home, I carefully packed all my uniforms away for safekeeping. Yesterday I had dropped off my service uniform to get dry cleaned so it was pressed and up to standards. As I stared at my computer, checking off all the last minute details for the event, my phone buzzed. I looked down at the screen and read the notification.

1 New Message: Blondie

I think I found the dress.

I smiled at her message and started to type back. She told me she was worried about finding something to wear to the benefit because she didn't want to embarrass me. I assured her time and time again that she would never embarrass me and that I felt nothing less than the luckiest man to have the opportunity to take her with me.

Oh yeah? Send me a picture.

No way, I want it to be a surprise.

> Come on, just one peek.

Not a chance.

> Can you at least tell me what color it is?

...fine I'll tell you what color it is.

It's red.

> I'm sure you look stunning in it.

> And sexy as hell.

Hopefully not too sexy, I don't want to embarrass you.

> I've already told you that's not possible. I can't wait to show up with you on my arm and show you off in front of everyone.

> You're going to be the most beautiful woman there, I already know it.

Thank you, soldier.

I'm still not showing you the dress.

I laughed at her second message and could picture the face she was making as she sent it. My girl was hard-headed when she wanted to be and I loved that about her. There were many things about her that I loved. But really I just loved that she was mine.

Mi hermosa.[1]

———

---

1. My beautiful girl.

I PULLED up in front of her building promptly at 6:15 p.m. as promised. Before getting out to walk to her door, I reached across the center console of the company Bronco I'd borrowed and grabbed my jacket. Once out of the car, I slipped my navy blue dress coat on and buttoned it in front of me. I nodded to a couple walking past me as I walked towards the front door of her building and headed inside. It wasn't very often you saw people in their dress uniforms, so I wasn't surprised by their stares.

The elevator took me up to her floor and I stepped into her hallway brimming with anticipation. This was the first time I would see her all dressed up, and ever since her texts yesterday, I had been visualizing what her dress could look like. I loved how casual she was in her day to day life, but part of me was salivating at the thought of seeing her in a sexy red dress all done up. My arm reached for the door and knocked a few times. Ophelia opened the door with a wide grin on her face.

"You're gonna die. I hope you brought yourself an extra pair of clean pants because if Bailey doesn't make you come immediately upon seeing her, you don't like her enough," she quipped without even saying hello first.

"Ophelia!" I heard her shout from her room. "Stop it right now! Hank, I'm so sorry, just ignore her. Ophie, get away from him before I come out there and beat your ass for saying things like that." The volume of her voice grew as she moved closer to the door. As soon as she stepped out of her room and into my line of sight, my heart nearly stopped and I fully understood why Ophelia had made the comment about my pants.

She looked stunning. Not just stunning, she looked drop dead gorgeous. Her dress was sexy as hell but still inside the realm of appropriate for the evening. Deep red and floor-length, it had a slit that ran up her thigh, showcasing her strong, toned legs. She was wearing a pair of strappy heels that matched the bejeweled neckline of her dress. The way it hugged her neck made me jealous. My heart rate increased as she smiled and posed for me, absolutely radiating.

"What do you think, soldier?" she remarked, holding her arms out away from her body. When she spun around and exposed how deep the back of her dress fell, I nearly dropped to my knees in front of her. I must have waited too long to answer because Ophelia smacked me hard on the back.

"Well, Hank, what do you think of our girl?"

"I think she looks stunning. Like the most beautiful thing I've ever seen," I sputtered, tripping over my own tongue as I stared at her. She giggled before taking a few steps closer to me. She rested her hands on my arms and brought her face close to mine.

"You don't look too bad yourself," she hummed as her lips pulled back into a warm smile.

"Here, let me take a picture of you both and then you can go." Ophelia took Bailey's phone from her hand and positioned us in front of the wall. I felt like I was back in high school having my prom pictures taken. Unable to keep my eyes off of her, I looked down at her and felt my lips pull into a smile. She continued to look at the camera, putting my favorite smile of hers on full display. She shined as she stood next to me and with every picture taken, I could feel my heart falling for her even further.

"Okay, I think I got some good ones," Ophelia exclaimed, handing the phone back to Bailey. She slipped her phone into the small silver purse she was holding and turned to me.

"You ready to go?" Her sapphire blues pierced straight through every logical thought I was trying to form. Just one look from her turned me inside out. Unable to hold myself back from her, I pulled her into my chest, wrapping my arm around her waist and pressed my lips to her cheek.

"Yes, hermosa[2], I am." Ophelia let out a soft sigh at my words and looked at us with hearts in her eyes.

We waved goodbye and headed out towards the car hand in hand. As the elevator doors closed, I pulled her into me again, pressing her hips into my side. I tucked my lips behind her ear and growled.

"I just need you to know that the sight of you in that dress is the sexiest fucking thing I've ever seen. You're an evil woman for thinking it's fair to make me sit next to you all night wearing that when you know I can't have you until after we leave." Her breath hitched in her throat and I loved how an evil, knowing smirk grew on her face. "You knew this dress would drive me crazy, didn't you, mi diablita[3]?"

She turned her face to meet mine as our bodies got closer together in the elevator. "I *was* hoping it would get that kind of reaction out of you."

I grabbed her chin with my hand and forced her to look at me. "You're a naughty girl and I promise to make you pay for this later. I hope you aren't planning on wearing this dress again after tonight because I fully intend on tearing it off of you once I get you back to my apartment." Her eyes burned into me with desire and I didn't miss how her chest was rising and falling more quickly.

"I hope you do," was all she could say before the elevator doors opened.

---

2. beautiful
3. little devil

As we walked towards the car, I tried to focus on all the things I knew would help to kill an erection. Part of me knew, though, that I was fighting a losing battle.

32

BAILEY

"You ready?" Hank looked at me from the driver's seat and I could tell by the look on his face that *he* was ready to go. I chewed my bottom lip, excitement and nerves building in my core. I looked at him for another beat before he dipped his head at me, his dark curly hair bouncing as he did. "Blondie? You ready to go or what?" he teased.

"Yeah, mhmm, yep, I'm ready." I sat in my seat and waited for him to come around and open my door for me. I learned the last time we were in this car that he preferred it if I let him be the one to open it. I watched through the window as he buttoned his suit jacket—the move causing my face to get warm—and walked to my side of the car. When he opened my door, he held out his hand towards me and helped to lift me out of the Ford Bronco he'd borrowed to drive us tonight. I swung my legs out of the car, my ass making the leather interior squeak as I moved, and tried to cover my laugh at the sound. Once he had me standing, he laced a strong arm around my waist and pulled me into his side.

"You know, I totally heard that. You didn't fart, did you?" he played.

"No, Hank, I didn't fart, oh my god," I scoffed jokingly. "It sounded like a fart though didn't it?" I tried not to laugh too loud as I spoke. He turned his face towards my neck and laughed with me. I love how, even when at a high-caliber event like the Annual Veteran's Benefit, he was still the goofball I knew I was falling in love with. I loved how easily he made me laugh and how quick he was to laugh right along with me.

"Even if you did, you'd still be the most fucking gorgeous woman here tonight. That dress is sinful," he growled into my ear as we walked up the steps of the library. My breath caught in my throat as he dropped his hand just below my lower back and landed square on my ass and gave it a squeeze.

"Careful there, if someone spots you doing that I'm sure they'll come over with a whistle or baton and scream at you to drop and give them twenty," I purred into his ear. The sexual tension between us was almost palpable. An instant heat grew between my legs when I saw him standing in my entryway wearing his dress uniform when he came to pick me up.

"For you, hermosa[1], I would drop and give them a million," he whispered so close to my ear that his lips brushed against it just enough to send a shockwave down my spine. *Calm down girl, you aren't wearing any underwear, soaking through this dress is not an option.*

As he led me inside, we were met with a sea of gazes from the people in the lobby. All eyes were on us as he said hello and saluted different men he passed. Part of me

---

1. beautiful

wanted to believe I was making it up, but I couldn't help but notice that many of the men in the room were giving me the once-over. Maybe wearing this dress was a mistake, maybe it was too sexy, too inappropriate, for this kind of event. I'd never been to a benefit like this before as an attendee, only ever as someone running them. In that role, I only ever wore simple black dresses and flats in case I needed to get somewhere quickly or spilled food down my front as I tried to help the caterers.

When I saw this dress in the store, I knew it was the one. It was a long, semi-formal gown with a slit up the front of my thigh that didn't go too high according to the sales girl. Its high neck was bejeweled with crystals that caught the light of the old chandeliers in the hall. My favorite thing about it was the back. It plunged low and was completely open, showing off the strong, toned muscles I had been working so hard on at the gym. Ophelia helped me pin my blonde locks up into a twist and even did my makeup for me. This was the most gussied up I had gotten in years and I couldn't lie, I knew I looked good.

We walked through the hall, talking with other couples, and he proudly introduced me as his girlfriend to some of the men he knew from his time in the service. Everyone was cordial and I did my best to smile and be interested in what they were saying. As we moved around the room, talking to different people along the way, he kept his hand on the small of my back and just the feeling of it there made me feel more at ease.

After forty minutes of making the rounds, a voice came out over the speakers asking us to take our seats inside the main hall as the benefit was about to begin. Hank took my hand and squeezed it gently as we made our way through the crowd. When we reached our table, he pulled my chair out for me and helped me take my seat before taking his own next to me. Butterflies took flight in my belly when he casually reached under the table, grabbed the base of my chair, and moved me about five inches closer to him. Once he was seated, he unbuttoned his suit jacket and rested his arm across the back of my chair. He was close enough to me that I could smell him and I wanted nothing more than to lean over, bury my nose into his neck, and inhale deeply. The tingling between my legs was back and I squeezed my thighs together. *Don't think about it. Don't think about how insanely hot he looks right now and how badly you want him. You aren't wearing any underwear and people will know you're hot as fuck if you don't calm down.*

He leaned in to say something and my heart started again as his lips brushed my ear for the second time in the last hour. Damn this man and him knowing what that does to me.

"You okay?" A coy grin was on his face as he whispered into my ear.

"Yes, why wouldn't I be okay?" I tried my best to keep a straight face, giving a polite smile as some of the other guests at our table were glancing over towards us.

"Because for the second time since sitting down, you've squeezed your legs together as if you're trying to hide something." He turned away from the table, his lips fully on my ear now as he spoke, "If I were to slip my fingers up your dress, just how wet would you be for me?"

My eyes rounded and my jaw dropped just enough to be noticed. I couldn't believe what he'd just said as we sat around a table full of his old Army buddies. *God dammit if I wasn't turned on before, I sure as fuck am now.* I took a deep breath before speaking in an attempt to steady my voice.

"I don't know, why don't you try and find out?" My words

came out almost breathless and I was on the verge of panting like a dog in heat. Still, he kept his lips where they were, brushing against my ear. The sane part of me wondered how appropriate it was to be acting like this in such a public setting. The feral part of me who wanted him like a starving animal didn't care.

"Trust me gorgeous, if half the men in this room weren't staring at you right now, I would." My head jerked to look around the room and sure enough, half a dozen men were watching us. I brushed a few stray hairs out of my face and tried to look like I wasn't totally ready to hike up my hemline and ride him right here and now in a room full of veterans.

Someone on the stage started speaking and he turned away from me finally to listen. Half and hour later, I wasn't sure who was talking or what they were saying because I was too preoccupied with what was happening under the table. Not even ten minutes into someone taking the podium did Hank slide his chair forward and then reach between my legs to pull mine forward too. As soon as our laps were covered by tablecloth, he slipped his hand between the slit of my dress and was rubbing the inside of my thigh while never breaking eye contact with the person on stage who was talking about what an honor it was to serve our great nation. Deciding to be just as evil, I rested my hand on the top of his dress pants and was rubbing his very hard cock. Every now and then I would glance around the room and check to see if anyone was looking. Thankfully, no one ever was.

"Come on," Hank suddenly growled in my ear. He stood from the table and held out his hand for me to take. Not knowing what was happening but also not the least bit interested in what was being said from the stage, I fixed my dress before standing and took his hand.

He pulled me through the old library and I had to nearly trot to keep up with him because he was moving so quickly. Once outside, he looked around the front lobby and pulled me down the hallway.

"Hank, where are we going?" I asked, laughing and trying to keep up. I had on four-inch heels and while my dress had a slit, it still wasn't the best thing to run in which is what he was trying to do.

He found a door with a plaque on it that read JANITOR and pushed it open. Once we were both inside, he pushed the door closed and jimmied a mop under the handle so no one from outside would be able to get in.

"I couldn't sit there any longer with you playing with me like that. I almost came in my pants three times because of you." He was breathing heavily and unbuttoning his jacket and shirt. "You, in that dress, is evil. Pure evil, blondie. And I think you knew how much it would drive me crazy when you bought it. No man, no *sane* man, would be able to keep his hands off of you while you're wearing that dress."

"I didn't buy it with the hopes it would stay on all night," I confessed with a smirk.

"Good, because it's coming off. *Now*." He swung his coat and shirt off in one fell swoop and pulled me to his lips. My hands landed on his chest and I could feel his heart racing as our tongues clashed against one another. He cupped my face with both of his strong, callused hands, not letting me catch my breath even for a moment.

"Turn around," he commanded and I did what I was told. Once facing away from him, his hands made quick time with the clasp that held the halter neckline of my dress together and once it fell, he grabbed my waist and spun me around to face him again. My whole body shivered when I saw his eyes meet my half-naked image in the tiny janitor's closet.

"You," he reached forward and took both my breasts in his hands, "have the greatest tits I've ever seen." My head fell backwards once he brought his lips to my nipple and his fingers played with the other. I couldn't stop the groan from escaping my mouth as he played with me. "Let me hear you, cariño[2]."

"Hank...people in the hallway..." I whimpered.

"Let them hear you too. Let them hear how good I make you feel." My fingers dug into his chest before one traveled down to his waistline and then to his crotch where I could feel just how badly he wanted me. I lifted my head and started to grab at his belt, needing to free him. After struggling for a moment, he reached down and helped me finish what I had started. As soon as he pulled his dress pants down far enough, his cock sprang free and was standing at attention. My eyes locked on it and I don't think I've ever wanted something more in my life.

Before he could get his mouth on me again, I hiked up the skirt of my dress and dropped to my knees in front of him. I placed both hands on his hips and wrapped my mouth around his throbbing cock, a low, audible moan escaping him as he towered over me. Slowly, I thrust him in and out with my mouth, occasionally looking up to find him watching me take him with lust and desire.

"Gracias Dios mio por hacerme el hombre mas afortando[3]. You're so good at that." His hand gripped the sides of

---

2. sweetheart
3. Thank you god for making me a lucky man.

232

my head and I felt him grow a little more as he spoke. With each new pull, I took him deeper and deeper in my mouth.

"If you keep doing that, I'm going to finish in that gorgeous mouth of yours," he murmured. To show him how badly I wanted that, I wrapped three fingers around his cock and continued to suck him off while also sliding my fingers up and down his shaft, twisting my wrist as I did. He met my rhythm and I could tell he was getting close. I was ready to take him like this, I *wanted* to take him like this, but he pulled away from me before I could bring him his release. He reached down and looped his hands under my arms, pulling me to my feet and he grabbed my chin with his hand, forcing me to look at him.

"I'm not finishing like that tonight, I'm finishing inside of you. Deep and hard. And you're going to stay nice and quiet or else we might get in trouble." While some women found the whole commanding thing to be off-putting, I found it incredibly hot. Seeing him take control like this turned me on something fierce. "Now spread your legs and let me feel that pussy of yours. I'm sure you're tight as fuck and drip-ping for me already."

Reaching towards the hem of my dress, I pulled it up further and let him reach for what he wanted. He wasn't wrong, there was no denying that I was wet and ready for him to take me. My hands rested on his shoulders as he reached in between my legs and started to rub my center. When he flicked my clit with his finger, my breath shud-dered and my hips bucked towards him, begging for more. He continued to play with me with one hand and used his other to play with my breast again. My lips found any exposed flesh they could find and I kissed, sucked, and bit at his skin. Reaching down for him again, I took his still hard cock into my hand and started to play with him.

"Hands up," he hissed, his voice coming out shaky and low. We were standing against a metal shelving unit full of cleaning supplies and miscellaneous hardware. He looked around and found a bundle of rope sitting on the shelf and grabbed it before turning back to me. "I'm not asking you again, hermosa[4], hands up."

Lifting my hands above my head, I watched as he started to unwind the rope. Before doing anything, he looked at me with a fierce expression. "Do you trust me?"

"Yes," I whispered with a small nod.

"Do you feel safe?"

"I always feel safe with you."

"Are you okay if I tie you up and fuck you senseless?"

"*Please*," I begged.

Reaching above my head, he tied the rope around my wrists and then around the frame of the metal shelf behind me. He double-checked to make sure I had space to move my wrists and free myself if I wanted to before dropping onto his knees. He bunched the skirt of my dress together in one hand, pinning it to my waist, and brought his lips to my center. If it weren't for the rope holding me up, I would have dropped to the floor as soon as his tongue swiped my clit. I was so close already that the motion and sensation it created inside of me was almost too much.

"Hank..." I groaned as he flicked and nipped my clit. He circled my pussy with his tongue over and over and the pressure building inside of me made me want to cry out. He was taking me to the edge and if he didn't stop soon, I was going to finish right here and now.

"Baby...please," I begged between shallow breaths. "You're going to make me finish." I felt him nod his head

_____

4. beautiful

without breaking contact with my clit. Trying to muffle my moans, I let him take me over the edge. He slipped two fingers into my already tight pussy and I couldn't hold back any longer. My entire body shook and then went limp as the orgasm took over. My mind went blank and I could see stars behind my eyes. I was still trying to catch my breath as I felt him start to untie me from the shelf, relief hitting my shoulders as my hands finally dropped below my head.

He pressed his lips to mine and I tasted myself on him. As we kissed, he guided me over to a table that was on the opposite side of the small closet and pushed some of the tools and random junk off the top of it. I had my arms wrapped around his neck and was kissing him as if my last breath depended on it. He spun me around and turned me away from him before pulling me against his body. He whispered in my ear again.

"Bend over and keep your hands on the table. Let me take you from behind like the good girl I know you can be." Under any other circumstances, being called a 'good girl' would have pissed me off. But hearing him call me that only made me want him more.

Doing as he said, I leaned over the table and shifted my feet back, spreading them further apart. My ass was higher than it normally was because of my heels and with my dress pushed above my waist, I was on full display for him.

"What do you think?" I asked, my voice coated in lust.

"I think I'm the luckiest man alive to be able to have something so gorgeous in front of me," he said as he pulled a condom out of the wallet he had just grabbed from the inside of his jacket. He slipped it on carefully before squaring his hips with mine. I jumped when he teased my center with the tip of his cock and we both exhaled deeply as he pushed inside of me. There's no better feeling than the relief you feel when your body finally gets what it's been craving. And mine had been craving him like this for hours.

"Mmm...you feel so good inside of me," I purred as he pushed and pulled against me.

"Nothing feels better than you do, hermosa[5]. *Nothing*," he growled.

With my hands on the table, I turned my head to look over my shoulder and watched as he fucked me from behind. He looked at me with so much determination and desire, I'd never felt sexier. I gasped as he pushed into me, deep and hard, and was turned on ever more by how deep he was inside of me. Hank was a blessed man and in turn, I was a very blessed woman.

"Te siento cada vez más apretada.[6] I can feel you getting tighter," he groaned as he continued to take me from behind. A shiver ripped through my spine as my pussy pulsed around him. He wasn't wrong, a second orgasm was building inside of me.

"And I can feel you getting harder."

"Ven por mí de nuevo, hermosa[7]. You will come for me again like a good girl, got it?" he demanded.

"Yes, soldier, whatever you say," I begged. My head dipped back as the sensations inside me started to build. He reached for my hair and pulled it gently, turning me on even more. With his other hand, he reached down and started to play with my clit which almost shattered me completely.

"Oh my god, if you aren't careful you're going to make me come," I begged. My body started to convulse at his touch.

---

5. beautiful
6. I feel you getting tighter.
7. Come for me again, beautiful.

"That's a good girl. Ven por mí ahora[8]. I want you to come for me." He played with my clit and was hitting my G-spot like it was nothing. My hips started to buck and match his rhythm as I felt him starting to come too.

"*Eres tan jodidamente sexy[9],*" he growled in my ear as we both went over the edge.

"Oh my god," I started to shout before quickly clasping my hand over my mouth, trying to muffle my cries. He shuttered and trembled behind me before finishing and slowly pulled out of me. We stood there, leaning over the table, for what felt like an hour before we both stood up completely.

He looked at me with admiration and affection before cupping my face in his hands again and kissing me lightly on the lips. "You know I meant what I said, right?"

"Actually, no, because I don't even know what you said. I don't speak Spanish, remember?" I teased as my brain pieced itself back together after the two orgasms I had just had.

"I *said,*" he dipped his head down and playfully bit my neck, sending shivers down my spine again, "You're the sexiest woman I know. You drive me crazy, Bailey, and I love how much that's true."

"You aren't too bad yourself." I winked before biting his ear.

We used some of the paper towels from the shelves to clean ourselves up.

He was kind enough to help me refasten the halter on my dress and even helped me fix my hair as best as we could before we exited the closet.

---

8. Come for me now.
9. You're so fucking sexy

Before he opened the door, he pulled me against his hip and looked at me fiercely.

"Thanks for coming with me and being on my arm tonight. I can't wait to watch all the guys drool over you the rest of the evening."

"Is that all you see me as? Just some hot piece of ass to show off?" I rolled my eyes and joked.

He pulled me in for a long, slow kiss that felt more intimate than what had just happened in the closet where we still stood.

"No, Bailey, that's not all I see you as. I see you as so much more than that. I see you as the most gorgeous woman I have ever laid eyes on. The strongest woman I have ever met. And the woman who I am totally and completely falling in love with," he said the last few words with so much ease and I could feel my heart start to quicken. Before I could speak, he pressed his lips to mine again and pulled me even closer to his chest.

"Now, let's go back out there and pretend like we didn't just totally fuck in this closet."

He opened the door and I didn't have any choice but to put on a poker face and make it through the rest of the night as if he hadn't turned me over a table and fucked my brains out.

Oh, and as if he didn't just tell me that he is falling in love with me.

33

HANK

The last few weeks of summer rolled past like the horse drawn carriages that roll down Calhoun Street each day. Bailey and I fell into a rhythm over the last month where we would see one another at the gym, text throughout the day, and then every few nights she would come and stay at my place. She hadn't said anything about my *'I'm falling in love with you'* comment that I'd let slip as we exited the janitor's closet at the benefit. Part of me wanted to ask her if she felt the same way but we were in a good place and I didn't want to jeopardize that. My phone buzzed on the top of my desk, pulling me out of my thoughts.

<u>Dungeons and Dickheads: 1 New Message</u>

> MALCOLM:
>
> There's an event at the bar today and there's going to be leftovers. You shitheads want some? I can bring them to campaign night.

KOLBI:

I'll never turn down free food.

CONRAD:

You better not be late again Malcolm.

MALCOLM:

Conrad, pull the stick out of your ass, I was late once and that was literally back in June. It's September. Let it go.

MALCOLM:

Everyone gets food except for Connie.

CONRAD:

Fuck you Malcolm 🖕

> I'm always in for food I don't have to pay for.

KOLBI:

Hank, you bringing Bailey tonight?

> If that's okay with everyone, she asked me this morning at the gym if she could come.

MALCOLM:

Fine with me. I never say no to having a beautiful woman around 😊

KOLBI:

Fine with me brother.

> Conrad?

I watched my screen, waiting for his reply to come in. When he hadn't answered my text after a few minutes, I texted him again.

> Conrad? Hello?

CONRAD:

Fine. If everyone else is fine with it I'm fine with it.

MALCOLM:

That response definitely makes it seem like you're fine with it.

CONRAD:

Fuck you, Malcolm. I said I was fine with it so I'm fine with it.

KOLBI:

Okay, you're fine with it brother. We're all fine if she comes, Hank.

I chewed on the inside of my lip, trying to dispel the irritation building in my gut. I couldn't understand why Conrad was so bent out of shape about her coming to campaign night. All she ever did was sit in the other room, read, and occasionally get herself something to drink. My fingers hovered over the keyboard on my phone before replying.

Okay then Bailey and I will both be there. On time.

I added on the last part to make a dig at Malcolm and hoped Conrad would see it as a peace offering. My phone buzzed once more.

MALCOLM:

Okay now Hank also doesn't get any food either. Kolbi, tonight we feast.

I PULLED up to the curb outside Bailey's building twenty minutes before we had to be at Kolbi's. Her living around the corner from him had proven convenient because on the campaign nights she didn't attend, I would stop by her place afterwards if she was still up to steal a kiss or two under the streetlights. While we could have walked, she was coming back to my place afterwards so I offered to pick her up.

When I kicked down the kickstand of my bike and lifted the helmet from my head, I looked up to see her running towards me. My core warmed as she got closer and I took in her signature smile. She was wearing a pair of light washed denim jeans that hugged her ass in a way that should be criminal and a bright yellow top that complimented her short golden hair. She had half of it pulled back and when she waved at her doorman, I noticed a pale pink ribbon tied in it. Once she was close enough to me, the scent of vanilla and honey flooded my nose.

"Hey there," she grinned, resting her hand on my leg as I still sat on my bike. I hadn't even had enough time to stand up to say hello to her before she had reached me. Her bottom lip was tucked over her teeth as smiled at me.

"Hey there, you look beautiful tonight." Her cheeks flushed the slightest bit and I pulled her in to kiss one.

"Thank you," she mused as she scrunched her nose at me.

"Do you have everything?"

"Yep!" She flashed me the small bag she was carrying that had been tucked behind her hip.

"What book are you reading now?" I raised my eyebrows at her as I asked the question.

"A spicy one about a soldier," she winked at me before tucking her purse into the saddlebag on my bike. I chuckled at her and stood up. Reaching into the other saddlebag on my bike, I pulled out her riding jacket that I always kept there. She had ridden with me a few times now and knew that I wouldn't take us anywhere until she had her jacket and her helmet on. I held up the jacket for her as she slipped both her arms inside. Spinning her around to face me, I reached for the zipper and pulled it all the way up until it reached under her chin. Then, I unlatched her helmet from the backseat and turned towards her again. She was waiting on me with a cheeky expression.

"What?" I questioned looking down at her.

"Nothing..." she paused for a beat, "I just appreciate how you take care of me." My heart squeezed at her words.

"I'll always take care of you, hermosa[1]. You're everything to me and I will always do anything I can to show you how much I mean that. I want you to know that you're safe with me."

"I know. I'm just very thankful for it. For you." Her words came out with a twang and I smiled to myself. Careful of her hair, I shimmied the helmet down on her head and took in her eyes whose color rivaled that of the deepest parts of the sea. I reached my finger in and tapped her nose before pulling her now protected head towards my lips so I could press them to the forehead part of her helmet. She giggled underneath it and I winked at her as I flipped the face shield down for her.

Once I had taken my seat, she placed herself behind me and wrapped her arms around my chest. I gave her a pat on her thigh, my signal to her that I was about to pull away, and revved the accelerator. We pulled away from the curb at last and headed off towards Kolbi's.

---

1. beautiful

———

HOURS HAD PASSED and the guys and I had finally made it past the Golem (a massive rock creature that was conjured up by our seemingly spiteful dungeon master). As we played, Bailey sat on the couch in the other room and read her book, only coming in when she was grabbing a drink or asking us if we needed anything. I could tell Kolbi and Malcolm liked her by the way they spoke to her, but Conrad was still distant. It took him time to warm up to new people so I chalked his behavior up to that.

Before leaving, she gave each of my friends a friendly hug and thanked them for allowing her to join us tonight. Kolbi gave her a peck on the cheek and told her she was always welcome. Malcolm held her close a second longer than what I was comfortable with and Conrad held his body stiff as a board as if she was a carrier for the plague. She then looped her hand into mine and we both waved to everyone before heading out the front door.

As we rode across the bridge on my bike, the night sky was dark and the moon reflected off of the water. She kept her arms wrapped tightly around my torso as we sped down the highway towards my apartment. I felt her turn her head and lean against my back. I grabbed her hand for a moment and held it in mine, relishing in the feelings doing so brought me. When we passed by another person on a motorcycle, we both gave them a low wave. After pulling into the parking lot of my complex, she slid herself off the seat and I followed closely behind her, standing from my bike and helping her remove her helmet. Once her jacket was tucked away and I pulled the cover over my bike, we headed towards my apartment.

Our hands were intertwined and she had her arm

looped around mine as we walked in silence. This was something I loved about her; she didn't need to say anything at all and you could still feel her presence around you.

"It sounded like a good night tonight," she started, looking up at me as we climbed the stairs to my place.

"Yeah it was. Kolbi is insane with what his brain comes up with," I laughed thinking about how Conrad and Malcolm had become fused together by a wizard after he wouldn't take their bribe.

"I always love listening to you guys play—" Her words were cut off by another voice. One that cut me to my core and made my heart stop all at the same time. One I hadn't heard since I left this city with nothing but a backpack and a fresh set of fatigues.

"Hey, Son."

34

BAILEY

I turned my head from Hank towards the voice I'd never heard before. Standing just outside of his apartment door was a man who looked to be in his mid-fifties and strikingly similar to Hank. His face was more mature than Hank's due to his age and he had a scar just over his left eye that couldn't be missed. His eyes were sunken and his skin was thick like leather. My eyes shot to Hank who wore a grim expression and he slowly moved to place himself between me and the man waiting on us, tucking his arm around me to push me further behind him.

"What the hell are you doing here?" Hank's voice came out low and serious.

"Now that's no way to greet your old man after all this time," the man jeered with a cocky smile and brought his arms away from himself as if he was opening up for a hug. My insides started to boil as I realized this was Hank's father, the man who beat him so badly growing up he had a back full of scars to prove it. His eyes flashed from Hank to me before he spoke again, "And who is this? You sure are beautiful, aren't you sweetheart." He took a step towards me but Hank blocked him with his body.

"Don't talk to her, don't even look at her," he warned, swatting his dad's arm away from me. "You need to leave, now."

"Now, Son, come on. I know it's been a long time but it doesn't have to be like this. You ran off as soon as you turned eighteen and then didn't even tell me you came home. How do you think that made me feel?" His dad's words came out in a fake, sympathetic tone that made my belly do a flip. Part of my brain was telling me I should be scared, but I wasn't. Hank was here and I knew he would protect me. Part of me wanted to protect him too.

"Ran off?" Hank barked. "More like escaped from Hell."

I stepped out from behind him and spoke. "I believe Hank told you to leave. I think it's best you do that, sir." The man's head fell backward as he laughed at me.

"The 'sir' is entirely unnecessary, it's Javier to you, *darlin'*," he mocked my Southern accent and I felt my face flush.

"And it's *Bailey* to you," I spat back. This man had no right to be cute with me.

"Ohhh, she's feisty. Just like your mother." Javier's eyes bore into me but it was like he wasn't looking at me at all. It was as if he was lost in a memory from the past. He returned his glare to Hank after a few seconds and composed himself. "Listen here boy, I just need a little bit of money and since you're my son, you're going to give it to me."

"I'm not giving you jack, especially not money. What do you need it for? A hooker? Maybe some booze to get drunk off of?" By the tone of his voice, I could tell Hank was getting angry. His fists were clenched at his sides and he was leaning towards his father threateningly.

"Hank," Javier started, giving him a menacing look, "it's embarrassing enough that I had to hunt you down like some animal and come up with some sob story to get the woman on the phone at the base to give me your new address. Now stop being difficult and just give me a couple hundred bucks and I'll be on my way." Rage grew inside of me every time he spoke. How could he talk to Hank like this?

Hank held me behind him with one arm to shield me as he pushed past Javier in order to unlock his door. We were all standing in the stairway between three other units and if the neighbors were home, they would definitely be able to hear us out here.

"Like I already said, I'm not giving you anything and you need to leave. And you can forget that I live here, you aren't welcome to come back any time soon." He had his key in the lock and pushed me towards the threshold when Javier grabbed his arm and turned him around.

"Listen here you good for nothing piece of shit. I raised you when your mother died and gave you a roof over your head. I made sure you got through school and I didn't tell you no when you came home and told me you were running off to play soldier. As if some worthless soul like you would be able to have any true sense of honor and respect. Instead of being a bastard, just give me some fucking money if you know what's good for you," Javier spat, nearly shouting at Hank.

I couldn't take it anymore, my rage towards this man exploded from inside of me. I took a step around Hank and squared my shoulders with Javier's.

"How *dare* you speak to him like that? Hank owes you nothing after how you treated him growing up. You think you have the right to come here and ask him for *anything*? You don't. You should be ashamed of yourself for expecting anything from your son who has permanent scars that your hands gave him. The only person in this situation who is a good for nothing piece of shit is *you*!" The words fell from my mouth with so much fury that it felt like I was breathing fire. Panting, I stared at Javier as his face twisted into a scowl. His eyes burned into me.

"You little..." he muttered as he raised his arm into the air. I braced myself for the impact of his hand across my face but it never came. Instead, Hank flashed from behind me, tackling his father to the ground and hitting him across the chin with a punch.

"How dare you try to hurt her! ¡Eres un hijo de puta![1]" He threw another punch, this time hitting his father in the gut. "I will never let you get near her again!" The two men wrestled on the ground and Javier struck Hank across the face with his fist. Using his age and strength to his advantage, Hank grabbed his father, throwing him to the ground and landing a third punch on him.

"Hank. Hank! Stop! He's not worth it, stop," I shouted, reaching for his arm as it lifted over his head for a fourth time. When my hand reached his wrist, his head whipped back to look at me and I could see the hurt in his eyes. "Stop, you're better than him. This isn't you." Tears welled in my eyes seeing so much hurt there.

He looked back to his father who had a bloody lip and a cut across his eye. Grabbing the collar of his shirt, Hank pulled Javier closer to his face and threatened, "If you *ever* come here or near her again, I won't hesitate to show you just how much of a mistake that would be." He shoved his father to the ground again and stood up. When he came to stand next to me I noticed he was bleeding above his eye.

---

1. You son of a bitch

"Now get the fuck out of here before I call the cops and report you for assault and harassment."

Javier stood up and brushed his hands off on his jeans and started to walk down the stairs. Before he descended, he turned back towards us one more time. "At least I know all those years of beatings made you stronger, Son. You have me to thank for that temper of yours. And your willingness to take a punch." He winked at Hank and snickered before limping down the stairs. We waited until he disappeared down the sidewalk before finally going inside.

Hank slammed the door and locked it behind him before reaching for me and pulling me into an embrace. As he held me, I could feel the thumping of his heart in his chest. "I'm so sorry you had to see that. I can't believe he—"

"Shhh," I soothed and shook my head at him, "It's okay. It's over now, he's gone. Thank you for protecting me. Maybe I shouldn't have said those things to him but I just couldn't stand there and let him berate you like that."

"I'm glad you did. Someone needed to put him in his place. You're fierce as hell and I love you for it. Thank you for standing up for me." He pulled me back into his arms, encapsulating me into his strong chest. He was breathing heavily and running his fingers through my hair.

"I love you too," I confessed into his chest. He pulled away and looked down at me, stunned.

"What did you say?"

"I said, I love you too," I repeated before pressing up on my toes and pulling him in for a kiss.

"I think I've loved you since the moment I saw you," he murmured. Our faces were hardly an inch apart and the way his lips pulled up into his signature goofy smile made my insides melt. He pulled me into a deep kiss that was more intentional than the one before. Our lips meshed together and our breath became one. When he finally pulled away from me, my eyes caught the now dried blood that had seeped from the cut above his eye.

"Come on, my love, let's get you cleaned up." I pulled him towards the bathroom and pushed his shoulders down, forcing him to take a seat on the toilet while I cleaned up the cut. As he sat, his eyes level with my chest, I used the first aid kit from under his sink to clean up and disinfect the wound. He brought his hands to my waist, held me in place, and closed his eyes while I cleaned him up.

"Bailey," he muttered as I pressed a bandage to his eyebrow.

"Yes?"

"I'm not like him." His eyes were low and he didn't meet my gaze.

I knelt down in front of him and brought my eyes to his, forcing him to look at me. "I know you aren't."

"I don't hurt the people I love when I'm angry," he nearly whispered it and I could feel the shame in his voice.

"I know you don't." I ran my hand through his dark curls as he looked up at me.

"I would never hurt you. I don't want you to be afraid of me." When his voice wobbled the slightest bit I felt a piece of my heart break. As I looked at him, I saw him for what he really was; a grown man who was once a young boy afraid of becoming his father. Thinking of little Hank, scared and alone at the hands of an abusive, angry man brought tears to my eyes. I pushed my way into his lap and he held me there as I nuzzled my nose into his neck.

"I've never felt anything other than safe and protected when I'm with you. You are not your father. You're a good man, I know it. I see it every day. You make me feel safe and loved every single time I'm with you."

"I love you, Bailey Brown. Eres mia para siempre[2]."

"I love you, too, Hank Martínez."

_____

2. You're my forever (You're mine forever)

35

HANK

My dad never came back around after our fight at my place. The next day when I went to work, I told Kolbi how he'd shown up and about our fight and he immediately sent someone over to place cameras outside my apartment. I told him he was overreacting and he told me to shut the hell up and let him do his job. When Kolbi set his mind to something, you couldn't talk him out of it. Now I have a semi-state of the art security system at an apartment where I'm pretty sure my downstairs neighbors are growing weed.

Work kept me busy as many of the wealthy elites of the city were having end-of-summer parties and benefits, raising money for their favorite charities and needing security to make sure things stayed kosher. With the uptick in music festivals and galas, there were a high number of celebrity clients who hired us to be their backup security while they visited the city.

Bailey and I fell into a new routine together as September rolled into October. I would head to her place after work and pick her up on my bike. Then, we would ride back to my place, cook dinner, spend the evening together and go to the gym the next morning. A few days a week we would lift together which I always loved because I got to make it very apparent to every man in the building that she was mine. There are few things I love more than getting to be her spotter and watch as her smooth, tight leggings stretched across her toned legs and ass. Once we were done, we would get cleaned up at the gym and I would drop her off at home before heading into the office for the day. She would tell me about the side gigs she picked up on the weekends and how she was saving whatever money she could to start her own event planning business one day. My girl had ambition. If anyone could do it, it would be her.

"Hank." Kolbi's deep voice cut through the almost silent office space and pulled me from my thoughts. "I need to see you, please." He had a serious look to him and the instincts I had honed while in the service told me something was wrong. I closed my laptop and stood from my desk before heading towards the two glass doors that led into his office.

He was sitting at his desk with his hands in his lap and rubbing the backs of them with his thumbs. Knowing the guy since he was nine years old, I could tell that he was uneasy.

"Why are you doing that?" I pressed, flicking my chin towards his hands. He looked down and immediately stopped when he noticed he was giving himself away.

"Sit down, brother," he sighed with a deep breath. I took a seat in one of the overstuffed chairs and stared back at my friend.

"Kolb...what's going on?"

"We found something," he started.

"Something?"

"From the night Bailey was attacked." I sat up straight as

if a metal rod had been implanted into my spine. Hearing her name and the word 'attacked' in the same sentence always made me sick to my stomach. It'd been nearly three months since I asked him to look into her attack and part of me had given up hope that we would find anything.

"Let me see it," I urged, standing up to move towards his computer.

"I don't know if you should, brother, it's not easy to watch. It wasn't easy for me to watch and I'm not bringing the girl home with me every night."

"Kolbi, please. I need to know if this is going to help her or not. Just let me see what you found." He studied me for a beat, his lips pressing together in a tight line. I wasn't sure what he'd found or the severity of it. Whatever it was, I was going to see it whether he liked it or not. I would tackle him from his chair and steal the computer off of his desk if I had to.

He typed on his laptop for a moment then turned the monitor towards me so I could see it. "It took some digging but one of our techs pulled this from a red light camera from the corner where the event hall she worked at sits. Don't worry, I didn't tell them who they were looking for, just that they needed to search the cameras in that area from that night and send me anything they found." His hand hovered over the play button and he looked at me, "You sure you want to see this?"

"I have to see this. This is my girl. I need to see if this is going to be something that will help her move on from this."

He sighed deeply again, "If you're sure."

He pressed play on a grainy video that looks like it was pulled from an old, early 2000's video camera. We watched as the timestamp rolled from 11:00 p.m., the seconds passing and the numbers changing as they did. After fifteen seconds or so, I could see a blonde woman exit the building holding two trash bags full of garbage and bounce down the front steps wearing a black dress and flats. Her hair was pulled back at the nape of her neck into a ponytail and when she turned the corner down the alleyway, my breath caught in my throat.

Bailey.

Not long after she disappeared into the shadows, a figure wearing all black followed her into the alleyway. They were walking with their hood up so you couldn't see their face but the figure had the same build and size of a man. The seconds clicked by and turned into minutes. Kolbi turned the playback speed up and I watched as almost twenty minutes passed. As the video sped by, my brain went to Bailey. What she went through during those twenty minutes. What she was still carrying with her now because of them. He slowed the video down just as the figure who had followed her into the alleyway walked out again, hiking his pants up as he looked both ways down the empty street. He turned and walked away as if he had done nothing wrong. My eyes stayed locked on the screen as a few more minutes went by. I looked at my friend, wondering why he wasn't stopping the video. Then, his eyes closed and he swallowed hard just as she came out of the alleyway, stumbling and looking around for anyone who might be there to help. I watched as she fell to her knees on the empty sidewalk, held her head in her hands for a few moments, then stood up again and walked down the street out of frame.

I felt sick. More than that, I felt angry and enraged. Seeing her attacker just walk away as if she was nothing made me want to put my fist through a wall. I started to pace the office in an attempt to control the burning rage I felt in my core. Kolbi sat at his desk and waited for me to speak first. My heart sank for my girl, mi hermosa[1]. As irrational as I knew it was, I was angry at myself for not being there to keep her safe. We didn't even know each other then but my need to protect her was so strong that I wish I could have gone back in time to save her. I had reached the opposite side of the office when something I'd seen from the video struck me.

"Go back to when that fucking bastard walked out of the alleyway," my head whipped back to Kolbi as I barked out the command.

"Rewinding now." I hurried back towards his desk and exhaled deeply as the video replayed Bailey stumbling out of the alleyway and falling to the ground. Seeing her like that broke my heart and made me want to scream all at the same time.

"Stop, right there." I pressed my index finger to the screen as he paused the video. It was grainy but with some cleaning up, the guy's face would be clear as day. We got him. "Why did the police not think to pull this video?" I asked, looking over at him.

"I spoke to some guys I know who work for Charleston PD about it and they said that if a rape victim doesn't report the crime soon after it happens, the likelihood of their case being investigated is low. You told me she waited a few days before she reported it, maybe that's why?" My blood boiled thinking about how her case could have been solved years ago if anyone would have just done a better job at looking. If they had even tried at all.

"That's complete bullshit," I hissed. My words were heated and I felt the anger starting to rise inside of me again.

---

1. my beautiful girl

"I agree, but that's how it goes." His voice was smooth as he spoke. "Listen, we have this now. We could take this to the police and she can press charges. That's what you wanted. Right?"

I was pacing his office again and turned to look at him once more. When I asked him to try and find anything from the night she was attacked, I wasn't sure what I'd do if he'd actually found something. Now that he had, I had to tell her what I had done and let her decide on what to do with it. I licked my lips and worried about what her reaction might be. Would she be grateful that we found her attacker or angry because I had betrayed her trust? I knew how much pain it brought her to tell me she had been raped. Would I be causing her more pain now that I discovered who had raped her?

My eyes met his, which were filled with cautious hope.

"It's not up to me to decide what happens next. It's up to my girl. And whatever she chooses to do, I'll stand behind it."

And I meant it.

Because I would stand behind her for the rest of my life, ready to protect her from whatever harm came her way. I just hoped that I wasn't the one who would be causing her harm by bringing her past back into her present.

36

BAILEY

I swiped the loose pieces of hair that had fallen into my face away and untied the apron around my waist. I'd been cooking for a few hours now, trying to make dinner for Hank and me. I'd invited him over for dinner and to watch a movie. He didn't know it yet, but we would be watching *13 Going on 30* again and I would be making him stand up and do the Thriller dance with Mattie, Jenna, and me when the scene played. Part of me wanted to ask him to dress up as Mattie and Jenna from *13 Going on 30* for Halloween and an evil part of me knew he would say yes.

Hank Martínez loved me fiercely and would do anything I asked him to, just like I would do for him.

After the night his father ambushed us at his place, we'd seen each other nearly every day. He would come here to pick me up after he got done working and then we would go and spend the night at his place. Ophelia had told me numerous times he was more than welcome to come stay at our place, but I didn't want to impose on her more than I already was. Hank was coming over tonight though because she was out of town again for work and would be away for the next few days.

She and I had shared a coffee this morning before she left and she asked me how things were going.

"So, did you tell him you love him yet?" she half joked as she sipped her coffee.

"Actually, yeah, I did," I confessed without pause. I wasn't afraid to tell people how much I loved Hank.

"Look at you, my sweet Bailey girl all grown up and falling in love with a hot, sexy soldier." She wiggled her eyebrows and shimmied her shoulders when she said the word 'sexy'.

"You know Ophie, you can fall in love too if you let your-self." I peered at my friend over the brim of my mug as I took a big gulp of coffee. She choked on her drink and started cackling.

"Bailey darling, don't make me laugh. Love is nothing but a myth for women like me." I studied my friend and tried to conceal the sadness I felt for her. I know she had her reasons for believing that love wasn't for her, but I wasn't letting go of the hope that one day she would find her match just like I had.

My head spun to find the clock that hung on the wall and noted that it was six fifteen and Hank should be here any minute. Everything for dinner was ready. Amanda had come over again to show me how to make a few more dishes Hank had told me about and I think I nailed them this time. Over the last few weeks, I had picked up several more side gigs planning private dinner parties and functions for some of the clients I'd worked with during my time at the event hall. Many of them complimented my hosting skills and ability to hire the perfect staff. Several asked me if I owned my own company. 'One day,' I would smile and tell them.

Just as soon as someone hired me for a full-time gig and I could save up for it.

When I heard the knock on the door, my heart fluttered a few beats faster and I nearly skipped to open it. As I opened the door, I was met with a fresh bouquet of flowers and a very handsome looking Hank. Having him come to me after work made my entire day. It made me feel like we were playing house, which I hoped that some day soon wouldn't just be playing. He wrapped an arm around my waist and pulled me in for a kiss as we stood in the door frame. Something about it felt off, like he didn't share his full self in it like he normally did. He handed me the flowers and followed me inside before I closed the door behind us and locked it.

"Mmm, something smells delicioso, hermosa[1]," he hummed as his eyes took in all the food laid out on the counter. His brown eyes grew wide when he saw what I had cooked for him and my heart swelled.

"I'm glad. I cooked some of your favorites tonight." I bounced up and down with pride watching him smell and eye the food.

He strode towards me again and wrapped his arms around me in an embrace. Looping my arms around his neck, he picked me up and squeezed me tight. My feet lifted off the ground and he spun me around the kitchen before setting me back down. Burying his nose into my neck, I felt him inhale deeply before kissing the spot behind my ear. As he pulled away from me, I caught a look of pain in his eyes. Between his somber expression and the way his kiss felt off when he first arrived, a nervous stirring started in my stomach.

---

1. delicious, beautiful

"Hank," I started as he held me where we stood, his eyes looking down into mine. "What's going on?"

He took a step back from me, startled, "What do you mean?"

"I can tell something's wrong, I see it in your eyes. What is it? Is it something with your dad? Did he come back?" He was holding my hands but had taken a few steps away from me. I didn't like how it felt; like he was standing right next to me somehow also hundreds of miles away.

"No, it's not my dad." His jaw clenched for a moment before he started again. "Come, let's sit and talk for a second."

I felt my heart sink lower in my chest and tried to not let my mind go to the worst possible place. *He can't be breaking up with me? Can he? I thought we were good. What did I do?* He held my hand in his as he led me into the living room. I followed him to the couch where he sat down and I took a seat next to him. He wore a grim expression on his face and was staring down at his hands. My heart was racing as I waited for him to speak.

"Hank..."

"I have to tell you something," he murmured, still not looking me in the eye. I had never seen him like this before, not even when he told me about his father for the first time.

"Hank," I whispered his name again and my voice hitched in my throat as I tried to hold back my emotions, "are you breaking up with me?" Tears welled up in my eyes as I said it because even just verbalizing it was too painful.

His eyes shot up and met mine, "What? Oh, hermosa, clara que no[2]. I love you. I love you so much it hurts. I think about you from the moment I wake up to the moment I

---

2. Oh, beautiful, of course not, no.

finally fall asleep and even then, I dream about you. You've made me the happiest I have ever been, happier than I ever thought I was deserving of. Please don't cry, I'm not leaving you. I just don't want to bring you any pain." He used his thumb to swipe the tear that had fallen down my cheek.

"Why would you bring me pain? If you aren't leaving, I don't know how you would cause me any pain. I've never been happier than I've been since meeting you. What do you mean you don't want to bring me any pain?"

He took a deep breath and swiped another tear away. He leaned in and kissed me on the cheek and as he did, I closed my eyes and committed the feeling of his soft lips on my skin to memory. I wanted to commit everything I did with him to memory.

"I know who attacked you."

I heard him say it but my brain couldn't fully process it. I sat next to him on the couch, completely stunned, as the five words sank all the way down into my bone marrow.

I know who attacked you.

"Wh–what?" I sputtered, blinking a couple of times as my brain caught up with what he had just said.

"I know who attacked you. Kolbi just gave me a name today. It took some time for him to find anything from that night, and a few more weeks for us to clean up the footage and track him down, but then today—"

"Wait, from *Kolbi*?" My eyebrows furrowed in the center of my face trying to comprehend everything he was telling me. "What do you mean, *from Kolbi*?"

"Earlier this summer I was thinking about how you told me you felt like you couldn't really move on from what happened to you because the man who hurt you was still out there. I wanted to try and help you, so you could move on from this and feel safe again, so I asked Kolbi to help me.

It took him a couple of months to find anything but eventually he did. Once we had something solid, it took a couple of weeks for us to clean up the footage and see if the guy's face was in any database, and it was. We have a name, Bailey. You have a name. You could take this guy down if you wanted." His eyes were filled with hope but my heart was filled with nothing but betrayal. I had trusted him with what had happened to me and he turned around and shared it with his friend.

"You told Kolbi about me..." I croaked, unable to hide my hurt. I'd trusted him with something so personal and even if he had the best intentions, he had shared my truth with someone else.

"Yes, but only because I wanted to help you." He gently shook his head at me, crestfallen.

"But I didn't ask for your help, did I?" I swallowed hard, trying to keep the tears at bay. "And I certainly didn't ask you to share my deepest secret with one of your buddies, did I?" I snapped at him before standing from the couch on uneasy legs. I was struggling to decide if I was angry with him for telling his friend my secret or touched that he wanted to try and help me. And my head hadn't even started to process the idea that the man who hurt me had been found.

"Bailey, please, don't be angry." He stood from the couch and reached for me as I started to walk towards my bedroom.

"Don't be angry?" I scoffed, spinning around to look at him again. "How am I not supposed to be angry when you shared something so personal about me with one of your friends? And you said you asked him about this months ago? That means that every time I've gone with you to campaign night, he's known about me all along. About what happened to me. How am I supposed to feel about that? Do the other guys know too?" I brought my hand to my heart and threw it out to the side as I spoke.

"No, they don't know. Only Kolbi and I know, I made him promise that he wouldn't say anything to them. Please, I know I broke your trust but you have to believe it was because I wanted to help. I love you." He tried to pull me into his chest but I pushed him away. My head was spinning and I could feel the tears threatening to come any second now and I wasn't going to cry in front of him.

"I don't know what to think, Hank. I'm sure you did this from a good place, but I don't know what to think right now." I wrapped my lips around my teeth and bit the inside of my cheek. "I think you should go."

"You want me to go?" His head hung to one side and his voice broke. He tried to pull me into him again, but I took a few steps away and wrapped my arms around myself, shielding myself from the shock of what he'd just told me.

"I need some time to think. You come here, drop this on me, and expect me to what? Jump in your lap and thank you?" I tried to take a few steadying breaths but my voice trembled anyway. "I just need some time to think. Please Hank, give me time." I stood in front of him digging my fingers into my sides and holding my breath, mere seconds away from completely breaking down. He set his shoulders back and pushed out a breath before closing the distance between us. When he pressed his lips to my forehead, I nearly collapsed in a mound of sobs and tears at his feet.

"For you, hermosa[3], I would give you the world. Eres mia para siempre[4]," he whispered before pulling away. I stood in

---

3. beautiful
4. You're my forever (You're mine forever)

my bedroom and listened as he slipped on his shoes, pulled open the door, and closed it behind him as he left.

Once I knew he was gone, I dropped to my knees in the empty condo and sobbed.

37

HANK

"**A**uffroy..."

"Auffroy?"

"Dude, AUFFROY!" Malcolm's fist met the side of my arm and pulled me out of my daze.

"What the hell, Malcolm? Why'd you hit me?" Annoyed and in pain, I hauled off and decked him back on his arm.

"Dude, you weren't fucking paying attention," he growled, flinching at me as if he was going to hit me again. "You haven't been paying attention all night."

I looked around the table to find three sets of eyes staring back at me with concern. They weren't wrong. We'd been playing for almost two hours but there was no way I'd be able to tell you what's happened since we sat down.

It had been five days since I had last seen her. After I left her place Friday night, I wanted nothing more than to go back, apologize, and check to see if she was okay. I hadn't even seen her at the gym the last few days either. When Monday rolled around and I still hadn't seen her, I asked the guy at the desk if she had been in. He checked the log books and told me she had been in the last few days, but in the afternoons, so I knew she was avoiding me.

'I just need some time.' Her words rang out in my head and I could still feel the pain in them. But how much time was that? Since leaving her, I felt like half of me was missing. Like I was walking around every day with a giant hole in my heart and until it was filled in, I wouldn't be able to fully function. Her reaction was exactly the one I was trying to avoid even if it was completely warranted. I had betrayed her trust and all I could hope for now is that she would be able to forgive me.

"Hank." Kolbi's deep voice pulled me out of my head and I looked towards him. "You okay?"

"Yeah. Sure, I guess." All three of my friends gave me a look that told me they knew better than that. My mind raced trying to collect my words, not wanting to share anything more about her than I already had. I pushed out a breath through pursed lips.

"Bailey and I are just..." I paused, considering my words, "going through things." Kolbi gave me a knowing look before dropping his gaze toward his hands and rubbing the backs of his hands with his thumbs. I could see the guilt on his face even though none of this was his fault. He did exactly what I asked him to do because he was trying to be a good friend.

"Hey man, I'm really sorry. I know how much you like her." Malcolm clapped his hand on my shoulder and gave me a sideways frown.

"What happened?" Conrad asked, always the one who needs to know all the facts.

"I was trying to help her with something and I think I caused her more harm instead," I noted, swallowing the massive lump that was forming in my throat. There was a pause around the table as my friends chewed on their thoughts. "I love her, you guys. With everything I am. I don't know what I'll do if she doesn't come back to me."

"You should apologize. I don't know what you did but I find that women always appreciate a man who can admit when he's wrong," Malcolm said confidently, crossing his arms across his chest and leaning back in his chair. He shook his head to toss his long hair out of his face.

"She asked for time," I explained, hearing her words run on repeat in my mind.

"Then you give her time. She'll come around, brother. She loves you, I see it when she's here with you. The way she looks at you, that's love." Kolbi gave me a reassuring look from across the table. When he nodded slightly towards me, I returned it, thanking him silently for not sharing our secret with the others.

"I hope so." I chewed on the inside of my lip and tried to shake off the sinking feeling I felt in the pit of my stomach.

"She'll come around man," Malcolm assured. "If she doesn't, you'll have us to keep you company."

"I'm not sleeping with you, though," Conrad said flatly from his seat and we all laughed. Leave it to my friends to get me to laugh while I feared that I was on the brink of losing the one thing I had truly loved for the first time in years.

———

I SWUNG my leg over my bike and pulled my helmet off my head as I walked up the stairs to my place. On my ride home from campaign night, all I could think about was her. She consumed my thoughts on the best days and haunted them on the worst. She was my everything and the thought of losing her felt like I would be losing myself. I was looking at my hands, trying to find the key to my place, when I heard her call out to me.

"Hey there, soldier." She bit her lip as my eyes found her standing just outside my door. My eyes widened as I looked at her and my heart started to race. I wasn't sure what she was doing here but I was happy to see her.

"Hey there, blondie." My voice teemed with hope and I slowed my pace, stopping just before I reached her.

"Can I come in?" Her eyes darted towards my door and she gave me a promising gaze.

"Ye–yeah. Please, come in." Sputtering, I unlocked the door and motioned for her to go in before me.

I followed behind her closely, picking up the familiar scent of vanilla and honey that followed her everywhere. It was one that I had come to long for by the end of my workday and breathed in selfishly once I was with her. Since we had been apart, it was just another thing that I felt missing. She walked into my small apartment and took a seat on the couch. When she sat down, tucking her legs under her butt as she got comfortable, it made me think of the first time she came over. How she had laid her head on my knee and asked me to play twenty questions. My heart ached thinking about how much I would miss those kinds of moments with her if she was here to tell me it was over.

"So," her voice came out anxious, "I've been thinking—"

"Bailey, wait," I cut her off and sat down next to her on the couch, pulling her hands into mine. Before she ripped my heart out I needed to remember how it felt to hold her like this again. My friends had told me I needed to apologize and I wanted to do that and more.

"I know what I did was wrong and I shouldn't have betrayed your trust. But I did it to try to help you, to try and help you move past what happened to you. Because I love you and I hate seeing you in pain. I don't want you to be scared or afraid anymore. I want you to be able to live your life freely and without fear that someone who hurt you is still out there."

"Hank—"

"I love you, Bailey Brown. More than anything or anyone I have ever loved before. I love you like I love my country and I fought for it for eleven years. I would fight for you for a hundred years and then a hundred years more. Please, let me fight for you for a hundred years."

"Hank." Her hand was on my cheek and tears welled in her eyes. She leaned forward on the couch until our foreheads touched. A tear fell from her face and landed on the back of her hand which I brought to my lips and kissed away. "I don't want you to fight for me, I want you to fight with me."

I pulled away to look her in the eyes and her gaze was full of hope. "You...what?"

"I want you to fight *with me*, not for me. This is a fight I need to fight for myself, and you've already done too much. But I know I won't be able to fight it alone, so I'm asking that you stand next to me in it. To be there while I take on the sick bastard who stole a piece of me and work to get that piece of myself back. What do you say?"

Unable to contain my excitement and pride, I lunged at her and tackled her on the couch. She started laughing as I wrapped my arms around her and breathed her in deeply. Holding her under me, I could feel the hole inside me start to fill again. Just having her close helped me to feel whole again.

"I'm so proud of you, mi hermosa[1]," I hummed into her ear as I started to sprinkle kisses against her neck. She hummed softly from under me and wrapped her arms around my back, digging her nails into my back as I gently nipped at her earlobe.

"Thank you for making me brave enough to do this. If it weren't for knowing you, I don't think I'd be able to do it." Her eyes shined up at me from where she lay and I brushed a stray piece of her golden hair out of her face.

"I did nothing, this is all you. And I can't wait to stand next to you and fight this fight *with* you." I moved my leg to hold myself up so I wasn't lying completely on top of her but as I moved, my dick gave away just how much I had missed her the last few days. When my hips pressed into her, she smiled as she discovered how badly I wanted her.

"Mmm, did you miss me?" she cooed into my ear, bucking her hips up towards mine as her lips pulled into a coy smile.

"More than you know," I hummed.

"Hey, Hank?"

"Yeah, Bailey?"

"Make me yours."

---

1. my beautiful girl

38

BAILEY

I rolled over and opened my eyes to find a pair of sleepy dark brown ones peering back at me. My lips pulled into a smile to match Hank's as we laid next to one another in his bed. His strong arm reached to pull the comforter over my exposed midsection after it had fallen free in the night. The way he carried me from the couch to his bedroom last night was something I was silently hoping he would want to do forever. Hoping he would want me like this, forever.

When I came over last night I hadn't planned on sleeping with him, only to talk to him about how I wanted to move forward with legal action. When I saw him though, my body reacted in a way that I couldn't deny or hold myself back from acting on. Looking at him now, lying across from me on his mattress, I wanted nothing more than to be able to wake up to this view every day.

"Good morning, hermosa[1]."

"Good morning." He leaned in and pressed his soft lips

---

1. beautiful

to my shoulder, sending a ripple of electricity down my spine. This man had a way of completely undoing me with the smallest gestures and I loved him for it.

"How'd you sleep?" His strong hand found my cheek and ran his thumb back and forth on it. Thinking about it, I realized I had slept better than I have in days. Ever since I asked him to leave my apartment last week, I hadn't slept through the night. My bed felt abnormally cold and empty without him next to me. But last night I had slept like a rock. Maybe it was the orgasms he pulled from me, maybe it was just his mere presence. Either way, I felt fully rested for the first time in almost a week.

"Pretty good," I cooed, scooching closer to him as he welcomed me into his arms. "How'd you sleep?"

"I slept like I knew I had my girl back," he spoke into my hair before kissing me on top of my head. The gesture sent another wave of electricity down my back and I squeezed my thighs together under the sheets. "So, have you thought about your next steps?"

"Well," I started, knowing he was talking about my plan to try and get justice against the man who attacked me. "I know I want to try and take some kind of legal action but I don't really know what my options are. I guess my first step is to try and find a lawyer." Thinking about it, I didn't really have a clue on where to start, but finding a lawyer seemed like the best first step to take.

"I'm sure Kolbi can connect you with someone. If you want, of course," he quickly added before looking down at me. "You don't have to have him in this anymore if you don't want but I know that—"

"Hank, breathe," I assured him. "If you think he has a way to help, I want him to. I would actually really appreciate it because I have no idea where to start with any of this. I just know that I want to fight this fight."

I'd spent the last five days thinking about what he told me he found and how he'd found it. While I was hurt that he shared my secret, I realized that it was for good reason. He'd only been trying to help me mend from old wounds and it wasn't right for me to try and use that against him. If he and Kolbi had found something that would be helpful, and he thought I had a fair chance at winning, I wanted to take it.

"I'm in this fight with you, all the way," he promised.

"I know you are, but right now I want you in other places," I hummed, rolling myself on top of him. His dick reacted to me instantly as I laid myself on top of him.

"Is that so?" he played, raising an eyebrow at me as his hands cupped my bare ass under the sheets. We had fallen asleep before replacing our clothing but the decision seemed to be working out in our favor.

"Mmhmm, it is so." I placed a tender kiss on the side of his neck before bringing his earlobe between my teeth and biting down gently. He sucked in a breath and squeezed my ass a little harder. I found both pain and pleasure in the sensation.

"Tell me where you want me," he begged as I pressed my exposed center down onto his dick. The friction sent a ripple through my body which was begging for more of him with every second.

"I want you here," I pressed, grabbing his hand and pulling it to my center. I could already tell how wet I was for him. My body started to shake in anticipation of having him for the second time in less than twelve hours.

"Here?" he growled as he pressed his finger against my clit. A low moan rumbled from the back of my throat as he started to flick his finger back and forth on the spot. He had strong hands that he had once used to fight for our country but you would never know by the way he used them on me. It was as if he was playing an instrument that was fine-tuned for his fingers and his fingers only.

"Yes," I managed to get out before he pushed one finger inside of me and brought his lips to my breast. The way his tongue flicked my nipple caused me to arch my back in pleasure. Goosebumps erupted across my skin and my heart started to race. Still sitting on top of him, he shifted me higher so he could reach me better. Now sitting higher on his torso, he used his lips to play with my nipples and his one hand to play with my pussy. The other hand held me in place as I felt his dick grow beneath me.

"Quiero cada centímetro de ti[2]," he groaned, pushing me off of him just as I felt the orgasm starting to grow in my core.

"Soldier," I huffed, a mix of frustration from him pulling away from me and humor towards him speaking Spanish when he knew I didn't understand him. "I'm really going to need to take Spanish lessons or something because I never know what you're saying. I only know what 'hermosa[3]' means because I looked it up." *Not that I care what you're saying because you sound hot as fuck as you say it.*

"You'll learn over time because I plan on speaking to you like this for a very long time," he panted as he pushed the sheets off of us and moved so he was on top of me now that I was on my back. "But for now, you just need to know that I said I want every inch of your body and I will have it. Right now."

---

2. I want every inch of you
3. beautiful

My head pressed into the pillow under it as he brought his mouth to my pussy. The way his lips moved across my center made me shout out in pleasure, almost unable to take it.

"Oh my god," I muttered, feeling the pleasure building from deep inside my belly.

"No, hermosa[4], I'm not God. But I will make you see him as many times as you'll let me."

His words sparked even more desire in me and within seconds I was taken over the edge. I cried out his name as he continued to flick and play with my clit, not letting up until he had pulled every last second of the orgasm out of me. Slowly, he crawled up my body as I tried to catch my breath.

"Eres mia para siempre[5]," he whispered into my ear.

"Yes, please," I panted, causing him to chuckle.

"Do you even know what I said?" He looked down at me with one eyebrow raised.

"No, but after what you just did to me I would say yes to anything."

"Anything?" My heart fluttered when his voice piqued just enough and he gave me a devilish grin. I would actually give this man anything he asked for if he looked at me like this every day.

"Anything," I repeated playfully, taking in his dark eyes and curls.

"Get on your knees," he commanded. He pushed himself up and pulled me up by my waist. He moved me so that I was up on all fours, holding myself up on my hands and knees facing away from him. I turned my head to look over my shoulder to find him squaring his hips with mine.

---

4. beautiful
5. You are my forever (You are mine forever)

"Are you okay with this?" he asked, catching my glance.

"Please Hank, make me feel good," I begged. I loved how much he respected me and always checked in before trying anything new. But I wanted him like this and in any way he wanted me. I watched him quickly reach into his bedside table, pull out a condom, and rip the foil open between his teeth before slipping it on.

From behind me, I felt him grab my hips and slowly guide himself inside of me. As he pushed his hard cock deep inside of me, I felt a new part of me come alive. Feeling him this way was something I never experienced before. He was in full control but so was I. From here, I could control how we moved just as much as he could and the power dynamic turned me on. He was sitting up on his knees behind me exploring every inch of my exposed skin with his hands. When he grazed my nipples with his fingers, I arched my back again and pushed my hips towards him even harder. He sank further inside of me, hitting my G-spot and causing another ripple of pleasure to course through my entire body. We found our rhythm like this, with him behind me and me on my knees, and before long, we were both panting and coming close to our finish. I pushed and pulled away from him faster now, needing more friction and more of him to take me over the edge. Sensing this need, he reached a hand towards my pussy and flicked my clit with his fingers. I yelped out in pleasure because it was almost too much at once.

"Vente para mi, hermosa, I want you to come for me," he commanded from behind me. Our bodies clashed into one another full of sweat and need.

"Fuck, Hank. You're so good," I begged, feeling my climax coming faster and faster with each flick of his finger.

"Come on, finish for me. Tell me how good I am. Beg for

me to play with your perfect pussy like this until you scream."

"Please, Hank. Fuck! You're so good. Don't stop." My hips started to buck but he was relentless. His fingers moved faster on my clit as he continued to fuck me from behind.

"Nunca, hermosa. Eres mí para siempre[6]," he growled as he continued to pound into me. Unable to hold my cries in any longer, I cried out his name for a second time and came completely undone underneath him. Sweat ran down my back as he went over the edge a few seconds later. Hearing the guttural moan come from him as he finished almost sent me over the edge again.

He pulled out of me slowly before falling down next to me on the bed and I lowered myself down to lie next to him. His eyes were closed as he worked to catch his breath and as he did, I traced the features of his face with my finger. When my finger reached his lips, he kissed it before grabbing my hand and kissing the inside of my palm.

"Te amaré por siempre, hermosa[7]," he mumbled, pulling me closer to his body.

"I don't know what you just said," I reminded him in a whisper.

"I *said*, I will love you forever, beautiful." Even though he had told me he loved me before, my heart never got tired of hearing it. I don't think it ever will.

"Te amaré por siempre[8]," I attempted, trying not to feel silly for speaking Spanish back to him.

"Very good, blondie, very good."

---

6. Never, beautiful. You're my forever (You're mine forever)
7. I will love you forever, beautiful
8. I will love you forever

39

HANK

The next several weeks were long and painful as Bailey worked to get the proper counsel to take her attacker to court. With Kolbi's help, she had gotten in contact with one of the best defense attorneys in the city. I met some fierce people during my time in the military, but no one was as intimidating as Remi Keeton. She wore pointy leather shoes and a pantsuit that cost more than my monthly rent, but it was clear she wanted the best for my girl. Of course, she and Bailey hit it off and became fast friends and due to Remi's connection to Kolbi, she represented Bailey pro bono.

Because of the involvement Kolbi's company had in finding the tape that showed her attacker going into and out of the alleyway, both he and the tech who scanned the footage were called to the stand to testify. Once Bailey had given him the okay, he turned the footage over to the police and the investigation of her attack was reopened. It didn't take them long to find the man who hurt her and from there, it was all court proceedings.

There were a lot of horrible things I witnessed while in

combat, but nothing compared to how gut wrenching it was to hear my girl sit on the stand and tell her story. When it was her day to speak in court, she asked me and my friends to come and support her. She and the guys had become close due to her constant appearance at campaign night and when she asked them to come, they all agreed without hesitation. Even Conrad, who was slowly warming up to her, though still a little standoffish. We all knew that it wasn't because of Bailey, and if push comes to shove, he would do anything for her just like the rest of us.

Plus, I think he's afraid of her just the smallest bit, which I found hilarious. They had formed this unique, older brother/annoying little sister bond and my girl took way too much joy in making him uncomfortable any chance she could. It was all in good fun and watching her hold her own and find her place with my chosen family made my heart swell.

I never valued my friends more than I did as I watched them listen to her story one night before our weekly game play and then again as she sat on the stand. They all showed up for her, and me by default, and doing so meant the world to me. She looked at me as she spoke on the stand and described in detail what she went through that night. A few times, she was brave enough to look the sick bastard in the eye and remind him of just how strong she is.

That's my girl. That's my Bailey. Mi hermosa[1].

Remi had assured us this was a slam dunk with the amount of evidence we had against him, but my heart was still pounding in my chest as I sat next to her in the gallery waiting to hear the ruling be read. Her trial had taken just over three weeks and I was ready for it to be over for all of

---

1. My beautiful girl

us. Bailey, Ophelia, my friends and I all sat next to one another as we waited to hear the final verdict.

"Have you reached a verdict?" The judge spoke with conviction towards the foreperson who was standing, holding a small piece of paper.

"We have, your Honor."

"What say you?"

"We the jury find the defendant guilty of the charge of first-degree rape and assault."

Bailey burst into tears next to me and Ophelia hugged her tightly. My friends and I exchanged handshakes before standing as the judge dismissed us. She moved closer to me and I pulled her into a protective embrace. It was over. It was all over. My girl was free and she never had to worry about him hurting her or anyone else ever again. Our group moved out into the hallway of the court and exchanged hopeful glances. I shook Remi's hand multiple times, thanking her for helping Bailey out.

"We couldn't have done this without you," I said gratefully.

"Nonsense, Bailey had it in her the entire time. All I did was present the facts and speak all the legal jargon people find boring." Remi winked at us and smiled, "Congratulations, Bailey. Kolbi, I'll see you around." Remi waved at the group before walking down the hallway with her briefcase in hand.

"I vote," Malcolm started, unbuttoning his suit jacket and giving us all a playful smile, "we head to the bar and have a round of drinks on me to celebrate."

I looked down at Bailey who was now wrapped under my arm and leaning her head on my shoulder. For the first time since meeting her, she looked truly relaxed. She smiled up at me before looking at the group. "One drink won't hurt."

My friends and Ophelia all cheered and started down the hallway towards the front door that led out of the court house. We followed slowly behind them, my arm wrapped around her shoulder, until she stopped me in the center of the hall. People bustled around us as the court was packed with different trials and hearings.

"What's wrong?" I asked, pulling away from her.

"I just...I just wanted to say thank you. For doing what you did. For helping me through this. For fighting this fight with me." She beamed up at me. I reached for one of her hands and swiped my thumb across the back of it.

"Of course, hermosa[2], I would do anything for you." I brought her hand to my lips and kissed the back of it. Her cheeks turned a faint shade of pink as I did.

"I love you, Hank Martínez."

"I love you, too, Bailey Brown."

"Would you two lovebirds get over each other and come on?" Conrad shouted from down the hall. We both looked towards him and laughed before heading down the hallway again.

"Come on, you owe me a drink," she said with a wink. She pulled me down the hallway and I gladly followed behind her.

Just like I always would.

---

2. beautiful

After drinks with the group, Hank and I headed back to his place for the night. We had been sitting at the bar with everyone when I leaned over and whispered into his ear.

"You know how thankful I am for you helping me get past this, right?" I said loud enough for him to hear me over the music that was blaring through the speakers.

"You've already told me as such. You don't have to thank me though, I would do anything for you." He looked at me with so much reverence and love that I wanted to pull him into me and never let him go.

"Can we get out of here soon so I can show you how thankful I am?" I asked, giving him a coy smile. While it had been nice to go out and be with friends and not feel as if something was looming over my shoulder for once, I really just wanted to be with Hank.

The last several weeks had been hard for me, hard for us. But he stood by me unwavering, just like he promised he would. He fought my fight *with* me instead of *for* me and I wanted to show him just how thankful I was for it. His eyes widened as my request sunk in and he quickly said goodbye to his friends. Ophelia gave me a small wave and an evil grin as I left her at the bar with the guys. We rode back to his place on his bike but only after he strapped me into my helmet and zipped up my riding jacket for me. I had become accustomed to this ritual and never fought him on it. Besides, I liked watching him take care of me in this way. Once we got to his place, he frantically threw the cover over his bike and pulled me up the staircase to his door. I laughed the entire way because I found his hurriedness endearing.

"Hank, Hank!" I laughed as he pulled me inside his apartment and pressed me up against the door. "You're acting like this is the first time I've asked to come home with you."

"It is the first time you've asked to come home with me. This version of you, the freest version of you," he stated, stealing my breath from me. I hadn't thought about it before he said it, but he was right. Every time I had stayed with him before I had felt like there was a dark cloud hanging over my head and preventing me from being fully me. Now though, I didn't sense the dark cloud looming.

I felt...*free.*

I grinned widely at him before he pressed his lips to mine. He kissed me with so much force and passion that it awoke a new part of me that I'd never felt before. The part of me that wanted him raw and unbridled, with nothing between us. Now that I knew I was safe and free from my past, I wanted to give every part of who I was to him. My hands found the hem of his shirt and pulled it up and over his head. As he threw it to the floor of his kitchen, he picked me up with both hands and held me around his torso. I wrapped my legs around his center like a koala as he walked us both towards his bedroom. My hands swooped across his back, felt the deeply embedded scars that were a permanent reminder of his past.

"You know," I said through heated breaths, "I feel like you have helped mend me. Like I was broken before meeting you and now every time I'm with you, you're mending me a little more."

He pulled away from me and gave me a goofy smile before speaking, "You know that's a spell in Dungeons and Dragons, right?"

"What is?" I asked as we stood in his bedroom now. He held me as if I weighed nothing as I waited for him to answer my question.

"Mending. It's a spell in the game you can use to restore something that's been broken, to help return it to its most perfect form." I looked at him in pure shock. Only he would bring up his game while I was trying to get in his pants.

"Oh my god, you know what I just realized?"

"What's that?" he quipped, lying me down on the bed finally.

"You're a big, fat, stinkin' *nerd*," I teased before laughing deep from my belly.

"A nerd? Did you just call me a nerd, blondie?" He started to tickle me and kiss my neck. I tried to wiggle away from him but he had me enclosed, surrounded by his strong arms and muscular body.

"I sure did. You're a big ol' nerd," I doubled down on my claim before pushing him away from me so I could look at him. "But a nerd that I love. And I wouldn't trade you for anything."

"Eres mia para siempre[1]," he whispered in my ear as he

---

1. You're my forever (You're mine forever)

lowered himself on top of me. The weight of his body brought me a sense of peace and arousal all at once and I wanted him now more than I ever had before.

"Hey, Hank?"

"Yes, Bailey?"

"Make me yours."

41

BAILEY

I skipped out of the front door of my building to find him sitting on his bike waiting for me. This had become our ritual every Wednesday for campaign night. He would pick me up, I would come down and jump on his bike, and we would go to hangout with his friends together. I always brought a book to read with me and looked forward to my weekly game night with the boys. At first, I could tell that my attendance wasn't welcome, but over time, everyone seemed to come around.

I was wearing a pair of light washed jeans and a yellow sweater that I bought with my sign-on bonus from Kolbi. He recently brought me on as a full-time event planner for his company because he was hoping to expand into new markets after the start of the year. I gladly accepted the role and was honest with him that I planned to use my income to fund my own business one day. He told me he expected nothing less and would be proud to partner with me once I had it launched. I didn't tell the others this, but Kolbi was my favorite.

The temperatures had dropped as December began and

I was glad I had added another layer under my sweater. As I approached Hank, he stood from his bike and extended his arm towards me.

"There she is, mi hermosa[1]," he hummed, pulling me in and planting a kiss on my cheek. I smiled at him as I tucked my purse into the saddlebag of his bike.

"Hey there, soldier." I slipped my arms into my riding jacket and waited for him to zip me up and snap the button under my chin. Then, I gently pulled my helmet over my face and tilted my chin up so he could affix the buckle.

"Hey," he started, looking at me with a smile through the open visor on my helmet. "I just want you to know you're the most beautiful girl in the world and I love you."

"I love you too." I smiled back. He slipped a finger into my helmet and touched my nose before tilting my head down to kiss the top of my helmet. This had become something he did before every ride together and I loved it. He carefully pulled the visor down and took his seat on his bike. Once he had his helmet on, I slipped in behind him and we took off for game night.

As I hugged my body to his, the air whipping around us as we maneuvered through the city, I realized just how safe I felt. The one undeniable thing about Hank is he always made me feel safe, no matter where we were. From the first time I saw him to the first time I spoke to him, he brought me a sense of peace and safety I hadn't felt before meeting him.

He had helped mend me by just being himself and by letting me be me.

And for that, I would love him forever.

---

1. my beautiful girl

42

HANK

"Alright Tolith, don't fuck this up man," Malcolm barked at Conrad causing Kolbi to laugh.

We had been playing for several hours now and our campaign was getting heated. Kolbi spun a story that had us cornered by a monster and all Conrad needed to do was roll the right number to cast an enchantment and we would finally be able to beat him. If he fucked this up, it would be on me to salvage the fight. Conrad took the die into his hands, shook them, and tossed them across the board.

"God dammit, Tolith, you had one job," Malcolm exclaimed, slapping his face with his hand. He looked at me now with intensity. "Alright, Auffroy, it's all on you buddy. Don't fuck this up like Tolith did and you will become my favorite friend."

"Hey! I'm not the one who got us into this situation, need I remind you of that, *Denis De Brey*?" Conrad scoffed at Malcolm as I released a big belly laugh. He was right, the whole reason we were stuck in this battle in the first place was because of Malcolm and his big mouth.

"Alright boys, take a breath. Auffroy's got this," I assured them as I tossed the dice across the board. Both Malcolm and Conrad cheered as the die landed on the number we needed to win the battle. Kolbi started to spin the next part of our story and Malcolm and Conrad slapped me on the back.

"Nicely done, Auffroy." Bailey had just walked into the dining room from the kitchen with her water and leaned over my shoulder. When her hand landed on my back, a warm heat started to grow in my core. I glanced up at her and smiled before she planted a soft kiss on my forehead.

"Not to be rude, but no philandering while in the middle of a battle please," Conrad snipped from his seat. I rolled my eyes at him and flipped him the bird before tilting my head up towards her, silently asking for a kiss. She gave me what I wanted before standing up again.

"What's the matter Conrad, you feeling left out? You want a kiss too?" she teased him, approaching him while making kissing noises. The guys erupted in laughter when Conrad's face twisted up in pure disgust and pushed her away.

"No, thank you. I'm pretty sure Hanky boy would break my kneecaps if I laid anything but a finger on you."

"You would be correct," I confirmed, sulking playfully from across the table.

"You know what's weird?" Malcolm commented, pulling a drink from his beer. "No one's rolled a nat twenty yet."

"Well there's only a five percent chance you can roll one, so I'm not super surprised," Conrad added.

"You would fuckin' know the percentage," Malcolm sneered, rolling his eyes. Kolbi chuckled softly from his seat, shaking his head at the two of them.

"What's a '*nat twenty*'?" Bailey asked, still standing behind Conrad's chair.

"It's a perfect roll. When you roll a nat twenty, or a natural twenty, it creates the best possible outcome for the characters and the situation they're in." Kolbi moved his hands out in front of him as he spoke and I watched as she took in the information.

"Interesting. Well, enjoy your game boys. I'm going back to my book now," she said with a smile before heading back to the living room.

As she walked out of the room, she turned and gave me a wink. I watched her longingly and knew that she was meant for me. She had helped me mend from my old scars just like I had helped her mend from hers. We were each other's missing piece and together, we completed one another. She was my real life nat twenty.

My blondie.

My Bailey.

Mi hermosa.[1]

---

1. My beautiful girl.

EPILOGUE

HANK | THREE MONTHS LATER: MARCH

Who knew that nine months could feel like forever and nine seconds all at the same time? Not me, that's who. But I was ready for my forever with Bailey to start now and I could only hope that she wanted the same thing too.

I had asked all of my friends to help me today and even got Ophelia in on the surprise. Without her, this entire thing would have fallen apart. She kept Bailey distracted for the day while my friends and I set everything up. I had been planning this for months and was ready for the wait to finally be over. For her to be mine, forever, if she wanted to be.

I was standing in the newly furnished living room of my downtown apartment waiting for her to be delivered to my door by Ophelia. As the plan went, Ophelia was going to take her out to get her nails done, buy her a new outfit for her birthday, and bring her here without telling her anything. I knew I wanted to do this around her birthday because the best present I could give her was this.

A fresh start. A new place. And a ring.

"Ophie, where the hell are we?" I heard her say from the hallway. My heart started to race and I pulled the jacket of my dress blues down to make sure it was straight. I had pulled them out of my closet this morning and took pride in wearing them for this occasion. Men were only supposed to wear their dress blues for important or formal events. I couldn't think of a more important event than asking my girl to marry me.

"Just hush up and come on. Hurry up! Why are you walking so slow?" I heard Ophelia bark and tried not to laugh. You would think those two were sisters by the way they argued.

"Uhm, I'm trying not to rush into whatever strange place my best friend is taking me. Ophie, are you even sure we're allowed to be here? We don't know anyone in this building. How'd you get the passcode anyway?" *My girl always did like twenty questions.* "Ophie, what are you doing? You can't just knock on a random door. Hello? Are you listening to me?"

Ophelia knocked twice on the door just as we planned before swinging it open. Once she did, she stepped out of the way so Bailey could see me standing inside. She stole my breath away wearing an off white dress and flats. Her golden blonde locks were curled and hanging down her back like satin ribbons. Her face screwed up into a confused expression and I moved to her to bring her inside. Her eyes traveled the length of my body as she took in my dress uniform before locking her eyes on mine.

"Soldier? What are you...why are you dressed in your blues? What's going on?" Her words were hurried and her eyes darted from me to Ophelia who still stood in the hallway, smiling at us. "Ophie, what's wrong? Why are you crying?"

"Oh! It's nothing, sorry, don't mind me. I'll just be over

here." Ophelia moved down the hallway and out of sight, wiping the tears from her eyes as she did.

"Hank." Her voice wobbled as she looked back towards me. "What's going on? Where are we?" I took her hands in mine and ran my thumbs across the backs of them and tried to steady my breath before speaking.

"I wanted to bring you here to give you something," I started, pulling out a chain that held two small metal tags on it from my pocket. She held out her hand as I placed the chain inside of it, and inspected them closely. Her eyes flicked back to mine before I spoke again.

"You know what this means right, when a soldier gives his girl his tags?" She shook her head slowly as her mouth formed an O. "When a soldier gives a girl his tags, he's asking her to be his. And I'd like for you to keep those forever." I placed my hand over hers that held my tags and closed our fingers around them. Tears started to well up in her eyes as what I just asked her sank in.

"Are you asking me—" Before she could finish her question, I dropped down on one knee in front of her and pulled the ring box from the inside of my jacket. She fell to her knees with me, tears streaming down her face, and squeezed my hand tightly.

"Bailey Brown, will you make me the luckiest man and be my wife?" My voice broke as I said the word 'wife', the thought of her as my wife nearly causing my heart to burst. The thought of taking pictures with her in white like I had seen the couple doing last summer was almost too much.

"Yes, oh my god, yes!" she agreed before pulling me into an embrace. We hugged and kissed right in the middle of the living room for a few moments before I helped her to her feet again. Once standing, I slipped the ring on to her finger and pulled her in for a kiss.

"Welcome home, hermosa[1]," I whispered in her ear as I held her close to my chest.

"What?" she exclaimed, pulling away from me and looking around.

"This place, it's ours. I'd like for you to move in with me, here, if you want." I gave her a hopeful smile and I watched her face light up even more.

"Of course I want," she squealed before jumping into my arms.

At that moment, Ophelia and the guys walked in from the hallway. Another girl I felt like I recognized from somewhere came in holding Kolbi's hand. Before I could ask any questions, the sounds of Bailey and Ophelia's squeals filled the room as they jumped around ooing and ahhing at Bailey's new ring. My friends all congratulated me before Kolbi introduced me to the girl.

"Hank, this is Magnolia," his deep voice cut through the ear-splitting squeals with ease. I extended a hand towards her and she took it to shake.

"Nice to meet you, Magnolia," I stated, giving my friend a sideways glance. He only smiled at me. *Why does her name sound so familiar?* And then it hit me. *No fucking way.*

"And you too, Hank. Congratulations on your engagement." She was tiny compared to Kolbi and had long, dark hair. Her fair complexion was a steep contrast to the deep brown color of his skin. I looked at my friend and gave him another sideways glance that said, *'you're not serious right now'*. But he only smiled at me.

"Thank you. Thank you for being here." I gave her a friendly smile before looking towards Malcolm and Conrad to see if they understood who our friend had brought with

---

1. beautiful

him tonight. They both just shrugged at me. Bailey grabbed my arm and pulled me into another hug as our guests moved into the kitchen to pour some champagne.

"I'm so excited to be your wife, Hank Martínez. And I'm so excited to move into this place with you. I can't believe you did this."

"I'm so excited to make you my wife, Bailey Brown. You sure you wanna do this thing? I've been told I'm kind of a nerd," I chuckled softly before kissing her on the nose which resulted in her scrunching her face up at me.

"Oh I'm sure. I'm sure now and I'm sure forever," she started before pressing her lips to mine once more. "Make me yours, Hank."

THE END

ACKNOWLEDGMENTS

I remember sitting down to write this story. I was midway through early readers consuming my first book, Feels Like Coming Home, when Hank and Bailey's story popped into my brain. Sparked by the image of a random guy at the gym in combat boots and the idea of a girl being saved by a stranger when she was being uncomfortably hit on. These were two separate ideas I had jotted down in my "Book to Write" list on my phone, and when I put them together, Hank and Bailey's story started to write itself.

So many amazing people helped with the creation and release of this book and I would be completely selfish to not acknowledge them now. First and always, to Jess, who is always the first person I send my wild ideas to and is always the first to have eyes on my words. Your partnership and friendship mean the world to me and I will never get tired of you telling me to use some goddamn contractions. Next, I would like to thank my incredible beta readers who helped make this book even better than it was before you read it. Elizabeth, Maroua, Janice, Amanda, Kimberly, Skye, Wren, KK, Bayler, Katherine, Emily, and Jenah, thank you times a million for giving me your feedback and reading the roughest cut of this story without judgment. To my sensitivity readers, Marlene and Katherine, I am in debt to you both for your willingness to teach me everything I didn't know and support me in making sure I represented Hank and his culture appropriately. Writing diversly is a very scary thing, but you both made me brave enough to do it. To the humans who made this book beautiful, Kristen and Melissa. Thank you for making the inside and outside of Mending Me beautiful in all the ways it deserves to be.

I'd also like to thank all the amazing friends, both online and in real life, who have supported me as I wrote this book. Writing a book is a very intensive process and it takes a really special human to support a writer as they live in the creative cave for months on end crafting their story. To my husband and my biggest supporter, thanks for always bringing dinner up to my office because you knew if I got up it would ruin the flow and for giving me the idea for this friend group in the first place. To Elle, for finding the best photos of Hank for me as inspiration and totally pissing off the Pinterest search bar. To my mom, who always sends me posts on Instagram about Read with Jenna just so I can *maybe* make it on the Today Show one day. When the call comes in, you get to be my plus one.

And finally to you, beautiful reader. For giving my writing a chance for the first (or second) time. Mending Me is only my second book and I know that you have so many incredible books you could have chosen from, but you chose this one and I'm so grateful for it. I hope you continue to give me more chances and more opportunities to help you fall in love with more couples in the future.

XO,
Rebecca Wrights

ABOUT THE AUTHOR

Rebecca Wrights is a romance author writing stories about swoon-worthy men and the people they adore. She is all about creating stories and characters that her readers can connect and relate to, while also falling madly in love with them. Small-town romances and steamy love scenes can be expected in each of her stories.

Be sure to follow along with her writing journey on Instagram, @RebeccaWrightsAuthor.

Love Hank and Bailey's story? Want more from The Nat. 20 gang? Stay tuned for the next installment in this interconnected, standalone series coming Winter 2024.

WANT MORE OF HANK & BAILEY?

Scan the QR below to get access to an exclusive BONUS
scene between Hank and Bailey.

*Please note this bonus scene takes place after the final chaper but
before the epilogue of Mending Me.*

XO,
     Rebecca Wrights

Printed in Great Britain
by Amazon